*Cat*astrophic
Connections

Joyce Ann Brown

This story is a work of fiction. Some Kansas City place names are real, but the names, characters, incidents and places of action in the story are the product of the author's imagination. Any resemblance to real events or persons, living or dead, is entirely coincidental.

Cover art by Susan Myers

ISBN: 150065101X
ISBN-13: 9781500651015

DEDICATION

To animal shelters everywhere.

CONTENTS

Joyce Ann Brown

ACKNOWLEDGMENTS

I am grateful to many friends and family members who read my struggling beginning drafts and gave me feedback and encouragement. My husband, Richard Brown, has been my soundboard and my greatest supporter. He took on the grocery shopping and the omelet making so I could write. Janet Wildeboor, Sandy Schaffer, Katherine Souza, and certain book club and writing group members (you know who you are) kept me going. Joyce Greer and Leeanna Wilder told me wild stories which became the initial ideas for this book. Patricia Smith did some early proofreading, and my sister, Sharon Caponetto, provided special help by reading my final drafts and providing her unbiased and essential editing skills. She guided me with kindness and honesty. Policeman Sam Burroughs and attorney Michael Dailey helped with technical questions. I couldn't have completed this project without support and suggestions from teachers and mentors I have worked with, including Sally Jadlow, Juliet Kincaid, and Sunny Frazier.

Joyce Ann Brown

In the Nighttime

To the individual working in near darkness, the place felt like a basement at midnight, illuminated only by a dim light bulb at the top of the stairway. No. Better. It felt like a mortuary in the middle of the night, the perfectionist mortician preparing a corpse for a starring role at its own funeral. An undertaker is an artist, after all, who must exult in the unveiling of his handiwork—or her creative artwork—as gawkers pass by the open casket.

The lone figure's grin appeared as grotesque as the thoughts in its wearer's head, illuminated as it was by the dim glow from the flickering computer screen. The only other light in the room came from distant street lamps through the two small office windows. During workday hours this large room, which housed the construction company's accounting and human resources departments, suffered from harsh fluorescent lighting and the constant noise of clicking keyboards, telephone conversations, and inner-office communication. Not now. Now—stillness, dark shadows, the circumspect use of a muted flashlight, necessary upon arrival for finding the correct workspace.

Overtime work, even late into the evening hours, was not unusual here when a big project came toward a close. All essential employees knew the door codes. But at two o'clock in the morning, no one else was likely to be around the building to observe this covert operation. To make sure, the lone worker had parked on a residential street three blocks away among autos belonging to apartment dwellers. The car wouldn't be associated with anyone headed for Renfro Construction Company. Being discovered would require an explanation, and the prepared story might appear a little thin.

This task wouldn't take long. The transaction had been set up earlier on a computer in a different room. All that remained to be done was to make sure the last of the payments to Master Flooring duplicated to a bogus Masters Flooring account located in a Virgin Islands bank. It had to be routed before the company's annual audit began the next day.

A few final gloved keystrokes, a couple final minutes of frequenting this gloomy place during the wee hours, and all those pesky money problems would be solved. The collaborator would be set. The lady would be impressed. A few million dollars would bring not only security, but also respect.

Oh, there might be some old so-called friends sacrificed along the way. All for the greater good, of course. Besides, people who left, who lacked loyalty, who were more concerned about their own interests—those people deserved whatever happened to them. It was a dirty shame most of them would never know the details of the careful planning or of the brilliant execution of this scheme. Foolproof. The money had disappeared; the getaway was assured. By the time connections were uncovered, if ever, there would be too many miles to work across and too many scapegoats to investigate.

One last check, at a different desktop. One couldn't be too careful. Yes! The transaction would be recorded at the Kansas City bank early next morning and received in the Virgin Islands a little later in the day. Some people claimed accounting work and bookkeeping were slow and boring occupations. It might be true when dealing with someone else's money, when working for one company and doing the same work over and over. But this clandestine bookkeeping activity sent a thrill straight through the body. Now— now, all the uncertainties, all the disappointments, and all the humdrum days were about to end.

Banging and bumping sounds reverberated through the empty building. The edgy computer user logged out and shut down while peering back and forth into the darkness and listening for noises— sounds which could be heard beyond the individual's own thumping heartbeat. The wind. Damn. It had blown open the dumpster out back. That was all it was.

The computer screen faded like a shimmering dream interrupted by a harsh alarm clock. Its final pinpricks of gray light illuminated a deep frown, a focused squint, and a clenched jaw.

Chapter 1—Caterwauling Cat

"Cats are cats the world over! These intelligent, peace-loving, four-footed friends—who are without prejudice, without hate, without greed—may someday teach us something.
- James Mackintosh Qwilleran"
- Lilian Jackson Braun, *The Cat Who Saw Stars*

The low resonance of three low funereal organ notes reverberated throughout Beth's body. She shuddered, stopped with a gasp, and clutched her knees in the middle of the Trolley Track Trail where she power-walked several days a week. Beth shook her head of floppy curls to fend off her feeling of foreboding and straightened up when she heard, or rather felt, the unnerving tones again.

Then she rolled her eyes. Arnie had been switching her mobile phone ring tones again. This one was spooky. As she caught her breath and dug her cell phone out of the pocket of her windbreaker, she made a mental note to devise an evil plan to get him back. She held the phone to her ear.

"H—puff—hello?"

"Is this Mrs. Stockwell?" the caller said in a high-pitched and shaky voice.

"Yes, this is Beth Stockwell."

"This is Eva Standish. I live in the condo next door to your tenant Adrianna Knells. I got your number from the Condo Association."

"How can I help you, Eva?" Beth said. She bent over again to massage her left calf.

"You know about Adrianna's cat?" Eva asked.

"Sure."

"Well, it has been yowling for the last two days, maybe longer. Do you know where Adrianna is? I tried calling her but got no answer and no return call. Can you do something? The Condo folks told me to ask you to handle it first before they step in and require her to get rid of the cat. I'm not normally a complainer, but I can hardly hear my television set, let alone sleep, with that noise."

Beth looked skyward as if asking for help from beyond, although none was forthcoming, and resumed her walk on the trail at a pace more leisurely than before. The eerie phone tone was appropriate. A call from Eva definitely qualified as a creepy thing.

"Well, I'm sorry about the disturbance," Beth said. "I'll be right over to find out what's ailing the kitty. He's usually so quiet and good." She mentally crossed the fingers of both hands—since that last part could have been a little white lie. "Thank you for calling me about this. I wouldn't want Adrianna to lose the pet that she loves so much."

"I hope you make it soon. My nerves can't take this much longer."

"It'll only take me a few minutes to get there, dear. Thanks again for calling."

Beth remembered other run-ins she had with Eva Standish, the tiny seventy-five-year-old with the white fly-away hair who lived next door to the rental units Beth and her husband, Arnie, owned on the sixth floor of the funky West-Gate Condos, sided with salmon-colored panels, in the Brookside subdivision of Kansas City. The Puce Goose, as locals called it, restricted its residents to people twenty-one and older but contained mostly senior citizens. Eva, a long-time resident of the condo building, wore a scowling expression that made her look like a grumpy leprechaun guarding a pot of gold every time Beth saw her.

Was Eva Standish a complainer? Sheesh. When Beth was renovating the condo unit Adrianna now rented, hadn't Eva Standish complained about the smell of paint and the noise of the power tools? When a nice computer guy lived there, didn't Eva grumble about the young man coming in late at night? Adrianna said Eva left her notes comprised of crazy predictions about how soon she would marry her boyfriend, when she might have a terrible bicycle accident, or even how a pretty girl like her might be kidnapped by some evil man she wouldn't suspect—notes Adrianna laughed about and threw away. Now Eva complained about the pet. Well, the best bet was to find out at once what was going on with the unpredictable Psycho Cat.

Erratic as a funnel cloud better described the feline. Adrianna Knells, Beth's tenant and also her step-niece, could set the whole family rolling on the floor at family gatherings with her stories about Sylvester, dubbed Psycho Cat early on. She told how he could be sweet and lovable to visitors one minute and then attack with his claws bared the next, sleep without moving for hours and then charge around the apartment knocking over lamps and vases for half an hour, jump into a bathtub full of water while his unsuspecting owner was in it, and undertake any variety of other crazy antics. Maybe the yowling was merely a result of one of the cat's moods.

Only a few blocks north of Brookside on her midtown walking trail, Beth turned and caught the toe of her running shoe on a crack. She almost fell, but only almost. She headed toward the condo building. On the way, she called Adrianna's cell phone but got no answer. After sending a text message that she was going to check on the cat, she followed the trail past the cafés and shops of Brookside. In ten minutes, Beth stood under the awning at the entrance to the ten-story building, becoming dizzy with the sweet aroma of the blooming red azaleas and violet lilacs which bordered each side. Before she could find her front door key, Chuck, the hunky security guard, opened the door for her, greeted her with familiarity, and recorded her visit.

"Hey, Chuck," said Beth. "I've got to take care of something up in my rental, but when I come back down I want to find out how your family is doing."

"No problem."

Beth wanted to linger long enough to have a little chat with Chuck as usual. This time, however, she felt obligated to get up there and find out about the cat. Without thinking, she took the stairs to the sixth floor—another way she jammed exercise into her daily routines. However, she sprinted up the stairs at such a rapid pace she stumbled and fell rounding the corner on the third landing.

"Ow! What a klutz." she said out loud. Why did she do this to herself—rush up here so fast she could have killed herself because of the convoluted whim of Adrianna's neighbor? She knew why. She always went out of her way to avoid conflict, to appease people. Beth continued up the steps at a slower pace, favoring her skinned knee.

The yowling became audible as soon as she stepped into the sixth floor hallway. She unlocked the condo door with her landlady key, peeked inside, and came to a dead stop. Her step-niece's usually clean neat apartment now smelled like a dirty litter box. Papers, pictures, and pillows littered the floor. Psycho Cat went bonkers when she entered, exploded toward her, hissed when she reached down to pet him, and then tried to climb her leg. She put her arms around the seventeen pound, yellow, tiger-striped kitty and hefted him to her shoulder in an attempt to pacify him. Beth's soothing had little effect, and he continued his plaintive meow.

When she put him down, Psycho Cat darted toward his food and water bowls in the kitchen. They were both quite empty. Beth filled the water bowl and then found the expensive cat food Adrianna preferred and poured a bunch of it into a hand-painted blue ceramic cat dish. Psycho Cat chowed down, lapped up some water, and finished by licking his chops and then his paws in prissy cat fashion. The litter box in the bathroom was foul, and it took a while to find clean-up supplies. After she scooped the box, added clean litter, and sprayed the condo with some air freshener, the atmosphere improved, as did Psycho Cat's manner. In fact, he rubbed around her legs and purred so loud she thought Eva Standish might start complaining again.

Finally, after giving the kitty what she hoped was a reassuring pat, Beth determined to give the condo a thorough inspection. As the landlady of several properties, she normally respected her tenants' privacy. If she, or she and her self-taught handy-man hubby, Arnie, had to go into one of the rental units to do some repair work or put a new air filter in the furnace, she would glance around and admire or disdain the decorating and housekeeping. The tidiness, especially, caught her eye because she knew how hard it was to clean a filthy apartment in order to rent it again after a tenant moved out.

In the case of this condo, however, Beth had been here several times for friendly visits, because Adrianna was her sister Meg's step-daughter. Since childhood, Adrianna had known her as Aunt Beth and her children as cousins. Adrianna kept her one-bedroom apartment very clean and as well decorated as a 27-year-old single could afford.

Now why would she suddenly leave her cat alone so long that he would wreck the place? When she went on a vacation or a business trip, she always put her step-mom in charge of the kitty. Adrianna's step-mother, Beth's sister Meg Knells, had raised Adrianna and was more of a real mom than Adrianna's birth mother, who hadn't raised her daughter since Adrianna was about three years old.

It was 10:30 in the morning. Meg would be at school where she taught social studies to middle school students. Since Beth had received no reply to her text message to Adrianna, she called Meg's cell phone, knowing Meg checked her messages around noon when she had time. "Meg, call me on my cell phone, please. Nothing to worry about, but I need to ask you about Adrianna's cat." That wasn't much information, but she guessed it would be enough to get a return call.

Meanwhile, what would Beth do about Psycho Cat? She picked him up. He nuzzled her ear and started purring again. There was no doubt the kitty had been left alone for several days. Beth realized she would feel bad setting the appreciative kitty down, and she couldn't walk out and leave him there alone. Maybe she should carry him the short distance to her house. That might also avert another call from the irritated condo neighbor, Eva Standish. Beth could hand the cat over to her sister or maybe to Adrianna later this afternoon.

Eva Standish opened her door a crack while Beth was shuffling her load of cat and cat paraphernalia in order to lock up. Beth turned her head toward the opening and glimpsed Eva raise a shaggy eyebrow before she yanked the door closed with her shrunken apple hand.

Chapter 2—Missing Step-Niece

"Cats are fond of mooning."
- Lilian Jackson Braun

All the way back on the trail to home, Psycho Cat squirmed and howled.

Good grief, I'm glad I found the cat carrier for this big cat.

If Beth had carried him in her arms along with the little zip-lock bags of litter and cat food she brought along too, there's no telling what would have happened. She might have been found later lying on the ground, her chest and head tattooed with paw prints. Beth giggled to herself while she clipped along at a good pace in the sunshine and approached the tennis courts on the outskirts of the shopping center.

No, you don't owe me an award. I'm naturally resourceful. It's just my nature to rescue...

Her grandiose inner-speak came to a sudden halt when an unidentified flying object dropped like a meteorite directly on top of the cat carrier and knocked it out of her hand. A half second of complete silence followed, and then there came a hair-raising wildcat scream, amplified by the container. Two elderly gentlemen, one of whom had hit the tennis ball over the fence, stared at Beth and her carrier with suspicion. She returned the look and then knelt to examine the damage.

"It's only a kitty cat—really," she said. Beth righted the box and turned the front toward the men. "Your ball hit his carrier and scared him." Psycho Cat had crunched his body deep into the back of the box where he was hard to distinguish. Both men came to the fence and squinted. Their expressions changed to mere skepticism.

The elder of the two, a man with scrawny legs on which the sagging remains of muscle definition suggested the probability of their owner at one time being able to chase tennis balls all over the court, pointed at the offending sphere. "Uh, would you mind throwing our ball back over the fence, please?"

Beth did as she was asked, in only two attempts, with no naughty comments about how the men should keep their balls on the court. She made it almost all the rest of the way past the little brick buildings of the Brookside shopping district and to her two-story Tudor with nothing more tragic than several stares and a few pitying smiles from joggers and bikers on the Trolley Track Trail.

Then, when she was about to cross the street to her house, a rabbit ran across the trail right in front of her, and hot on its tail came a big black cat. Psycho Cat meowed and shook the cat box so hard it caused Beth to drop everything. The door of the carrier flew open, and Psycho Cat catapulted out.

"No, Sylvester," Beth yelled. She lunged for the cat and landed on the trail in a head first slide. Anyone watching would think she was practicing to join the Kansas City Royals baseball team.

Beth sat up and wiped pea gravel off her hands while visions of chasing the cat through the neighborhood danced through her head. However, Psycho Cat ran only a short distance towards the cat and its prey when he stopped, sat still with his tail thumping, and hissed. The rabbit disappeared into the bushes, and the black cat turned to take stock of the huge, tiger-striped cat. An almost certain feline confrontation threatened. However, it took Beth only a few careful steps to reach Psycho Cat. With one more hiss and a disdainful look toward the more experienced bunny chaser, he allowed her to return him to the carrier without a fuss. Beth avoided the steady green-eyed stare of the black cat.

Hmm, was this the start of a beautiful friendship, or the beginning of a series of unfortunate events?

Beth picked up the rest of the cat gear and tramped across the street and into the house. Around noon, she picked up her ringing phone which showed "Meg" on the caller ID. "Hi Meg, about time you called back. You know I could have died by now if this had been an emergency." She and her sister had always been saucy with each other.

By then, Psycho Cat had curled up on the window seat in a sunny window and was sleeping, oh so sweet and innocent-looking, as if he had not spent the past few days tearing apart an apartment. It had taken awhile to get the kitty settled, but Beth was glad she could now tell her sister Psycho Cat was fine.

Sometimes Beth still felt as she had most of her life, as if she couldn't live up to Meg's expectations. Beth was fourteen when their father died, and after that their mother turned distant and unreachable. Meg became protective and also directive toward her sister, three years her junior. Beth reacted by becoming rebellious during her teens. Now they were best of friends, but still their kidding became sometimes half-serious.

"I'm sorry I didn't return your call sooner." Meg was practically shouting and sounded a little harried, not in the mood for a sass contest. "I'm at a state social studies conference in Wichita. My friend and I presented our plan for the unit on Asia we developed in our K.U. class after the school district helped pay for our trip to China last summer. She and I spent the last forty-five minutes answering questions from teachers who want to incorporate our unit plan into their curriculum. It's so amazing! But, hey, what's this about Psycho Cat?"

Beth answered in a voice duplicating Meg's, loud enough so Meg might hear her over the boisterous noise level audible in the background. "Oh, I didn't know you were out of town. Do you know where Adrianna went or how I can get in touch with her? I left her a message, but she hasn't replied. I was called over to the condo today by Eva Standish, Adrianna's next-door neighbor, and it looked as if Psycho Cat had been alone for three or four days. I brought him home with me so he wouldn't continue to disturb the folks in the condos. He's okay here, but I want Adrianna to know where he is."

Meg raised her voice a pitch. "You're kidding. Adrianna didn't tell me she was going anywhere. She always tells me, and she always asks me to take care of her cat. Let me call Paul and find out if he knows anything. I'll get away from this crowd and call you back after I get in touch with him. It might be after our presentation this afternoon before I can get back to you, though. Is that alright?"

"It's fine. Call when you can."

Paul Knells, Adrianna's father, worked arduously in the electrical business he had started fifteen years before and was normally so tired at the end of each day that he dropped in front of the TV while his wife Meg checked school papers. Beth and Arnie had started using the nickname "Poppa Paul" early in Paul's relationship with Meg because he brought his baby daughter Adrianna along with him so often. Since then, the couples had practically raised their families together.

Only minutes after Beth put down the phone, Arnie appeared. He worked for an insurance firm in an office very close to their house, and he occasionally changed into sneakers and walked home to eat lunch, as he did today. Immediately after he entered the front door, Arnie's eyebrows shot up and he gave his wife a "what now?" look. Beth explained why Adrianna's cat was making himself at home in their living room.

"I got hold of Meg," she said, "who's out of town and doesn't know where Adrianna went. Adrianna hasn't answered the message I left for her. Meg is going to call Paul to find out if he knows what's going on but won't be able to let me know what she finds out until this evening."

While Beth told Arnie more about the condo fiasco, she disturbed the sleeping cat only slightly by caressing his silky fur. Psycho Cat opened his eyes a crack and then closed them tightly and wrapped one paw around his face.

"I could go ahead and call Paul at work to find out about this," she said, "but he's so busy. Anyway, he doesn't always pay good attention to his *girls* and their plans." Beth lapsed into the cutie talk she reserved for small animals, small people, and sometimes for bantering with her husband. "Especially concerning poor li'l ol' Psycho Cat."

"Oh yeah…that poooorrrrr cat…he gets more attention from you three women than Paul and I do." Arnie grinned at Beth and then looked at the cat. "Paul undoubtedly knows where Adrianna went. He probably just hasn't had time to tend to the cat. Meg will call later today. I agree you shouldn't bother Paul."

After lunch Arnie stooped to scratch the cat behind the ears before he kissed Beth and headed back to work. "Don't worry your head about this ol' Psycho Cat, Sweetie. I've no doubt you'll manage to give him a good home until Adrianna comes to get him. She'll be apologizing all over the place for causing you trouble."

Beth spent a large part of the April afternoon working in her backyard vegetable garden where beans, potatoes, salad greens, and a whole variety of herbs sprouted. The Red Bud trees were in bloom, and the grass sparkled emerald thanks to the early spring rains. She stood to stretch and admire the yellow daffodils, pink tulips, and tiny violet crocuses which graced her flower beds and reminded her of a Monet painting. Her cell phone was in her pocket, and she wasn't thinking much about Adrianna and her cat--that is, until Meg finally called her back around 4:15 p.m.

Chapter 3—Concluding, No News is Good News

"To rush into explanations is always a sign of weakness."
— Agatha Christie, The Seven Dials Mystery

"Beth," Meg said, "it took me awhile to get hold of Paul at work. He was preoccupied—isn't that a surprise? Anyway, he refocused long enough to remember he had checked the answer machine over the weekend and found a message from Adrianna. She didn't know I was out of town. She asked that I take care of her cat for a little while. According to Paul, she didn't say how long it would be or where she went. Paul erased the call, but then he got busy and forgot to check on Psycho Cat."

"I'm not surprised," Beth said. She cradled her phone on her shoulder and continued pulling weeds.

Meg sighed. "Me either. Anyway, he said he really didn't think the message was very important. Adrianna sometimes goes on a little weekend trip to a concert in St. Louis or on a bike trip down the Katy Trail through central Missouri. Usually, when she goes, she asks me to check in on Psycho Cat and is home by Sunday night. The voice mail was sent Saturday morning, and now it's already Wednesday. I'm so sorry you had to take the heat from Adrianna's condo neighbor because of this, and I feel bad the kitty was left alone for so long."

"Well, don't worry. Psycho Cat is doing fine, and when Adrianna calls back I'll tell her to pick him up at my house."

"I left a message on her cell phone, too," Meg said. "It's very strange she hasn't called to check on her cat. It seems as if she would have tried my cell if she couldn't catch me at home, because she knows how poor we are at checking the message machine, and we don't text. I guess I worry too much, but something could have happened to her. I checked our home machine remotely, and there were no new messages from her."

"No news is good news, Meg," Beth said, although the seed of worry started to grow a little in her mind, too. "If an accident happened, a nurse at a hospital, the police, or her travel companion would have called. Adrianna merely got busy having fun and forgot to call. She takes after her dad in that respect."

"You're right. She'll call one of us back and I'll feel silly for getting all worked up. I told Paul to send her an e-mail message to get in touch. I'll find a computer here at the hotel or at the conference that I can use, too. Whichever one of us hears from her first will call the other. Okay?"

"Knock 'em dead at your conference, Meg. Meanwhile, I'm fine with keeping Psycho Cat here."

Beth waited all evening to hear back from Adrianna, and she was sure Meg was doing the same. She discussed with Arnie what kind of work needed to be done on one of their rental units, one which was being vacated at the beginning of July. The current tenants had lived there for four years before the husband graduated from dental school and the wife had a baby—lovely family.

Beth grew attached to many of her tenants. She wasn't sure if that tendency was an asset or a weakness of her personality; when the people moved on it became a loss but usually a good memory. As for the renovation, she told Arnie she would probably tile the backsplash in the kitchen to update the look, the bathroom lavatory needed to be replaced, and all of the walls had to be repainted. The conversation concerning the work took Beth's mind off of Adrianna for a short time.

When she went to the kitchen for a cup of herbal tea, she found Psycho Cat on the counter top.

"Off!" Beth yelled.

Psycho Cat jumped on top of the refrigerator and glared at her. Beth laughed and got a stool to get up high enough to lift him down. He batted at her, tried to nip her, scooted to the back, and lay there until Beth's calls brought Arnie to the kitchen.

"That must be his safe spot at home," Arnie said. "He really isn't hurting anything up there."

"Well, I don't want him on the kitchen counter where I prepare food, and he'll land on the countertop before he jumps to the floor."

"Okay, I'll get him down, but I can't promise he'll stay down."

Before Arnie could reach him, the cat jumped off the refrigerator, onto the counter, to the floor, and under the corner table. It took Arnie, Beth, and a little nudge with a broom to swipe him out. He streaked into the hallway.

After being shooed away from the kitchen and taking his own sweet time to skulk around the house a bit, Psycho Cat found his way into the living room, where the couple relaxed in front of the television, and jumped onto Arnie's lap. Beth watched the cat knead Arnie's legs and stomach with his paws and then curl around for a little snooze. She shook her head.

Then she snorted. "You are a bit of an ingrate, Kitty. After all, I'm the one who rescued you. I cleaned up after you. I almost killed myself saving you from a fight with a huge black monster cat. And now you prefer Arnie's lap?"

"We guys stick together. Don't we, Sylvester?" Arnie said with a wicked sideways grin in Beth's direction.

Beth knew Psycho Cat had been with Adrianna since he was a kitten. What men had he even known before, Arnie and Paul occasionally? Well, there was that ex-boyfriend, Max, who was at Adrianna's condo quite a bit, Beth assumed, before he moved away. Hmmm, maybe male animals preferred male companionship.

She found, though, when feeding time was near, the kitty jumped on the back of her chair and nuzzled her hair. He learned fast who controlled the food bowl around here and seemed to know instinctively how to get back into her good graces.

Beth couldn't concentrate on the evening TV shows. Her step-niece Adrianna, Psycho Cat, her sister Meg, her brother-in-law Paul, and even Adrianna's cranky neighbor Eva Standish—all of their comments kept swirling around in her head. Arnie was probably right—she was being a worrywart. Finally, around 9:30, her sister Meg called.

"Have you heard from Adrianna?" Meg asked.

"No, I haven't. Have you?" Beth said.

"No, and now I'm really worried. I called Paul again to see if maybe he had another call from her or had an e-mail message, but he didn't. I even called Adrianna's mother in case she might know where Adrianna went."

"What'd she say?"

"As usual, Meredith sounded only half awake, which might mean she was stoned or drunk. I think I made her understand what I was asking, though, and she said, 'You think I know where Adrianna is? Why would I know? There's no reason I would know.' She can be really weird. I even wonder if she's telling the truth."

Beth smirked to herself. She knew Adrianna's mother, Meredith, was probably the only person Meg really couldn't handle. The confident and sarcastic tone she used to talk about her husband's ex-wife to Beth ran counter to the awkwardness Meg exhibited when she was around Meredith. Beth thought it was because Meg had never come to terms with what Paul had seen in the woman when he married her, and, because he refused to talk about that early relationship, she couldn't quite put Paul's marriage to Meredith into a neat little compartment in her mind.

Meg said, "That's all Meredith would say. Do you think I should leave the conference early and come back home?"

Beth gave herself a sharp mental slap for her momentary self-serving gloat over her sister's discomfort. "No, don't do that. You have more presentations, don't you?"

"One more, tomorrow morning at 10:00."

"You stay there and finish. I'll call or drop by Adrianna's office tomorrow morning and see if I can find out anything. She probably asked for vacation time, and maybe she lost her cell phone or broke it or…you know. There are lots of explanations."

"Thanks, Beth. You're the best. Oh, and Adrianna has a good friend at work, a bookkeeper. Abby is her name. Maybe she knows where Adrianna went. I wish I had Abby's phone number or could remember her last name, but you can ask for her at the office."

"I'll do that, for sure. Get some rest, and I'll call you tomorrow," Beth said. For some reason, though, she wasn't as confident about the situation as she tried to convince Meg.

"I think I'll go by Adrianna's condo tomorrow morning to see if there are any schedules or notes which will give me some information about where Adrianna may have gone," she told Arnie as they got ready for bed. "I know Adrianna would call Meg or me back if she had gotten the messages. It doesn't feel right."

Arnie gave her a cuddly hug in his strong arms. "Okay, if it'll make you feel better my cute little Blondie. Don't get too worked up about this, though. It'll all be resolved as soon as Adrianna returns."

Beth loved it that Arnie, her tall fit husband who still had all of his dark hair, still called her his 'cute little Blondie'—even though she had all that silver mixed in with the blond of her curly locks now.

There was a time in their marriage when the children were young; Beth tried so hard to meet all deadlines and expectations that she became tired and irritable. She fantasized about making rags out of Bert and Ernie, frying Big Bird up for dinner, and spending the rest of her time reading smutty romance novels. Much of her petulance was directed toward her husband, because he was handy. Arnie withdrew. It was a rocky road back, but their marriage and friendship had survived the ride.

After she removed her makeup, Beth studied the lines crows had etched beside her eyes. She traced the creases from her mouth to her nose. Smile lines. Those wrinkles showed the world she was—let's see—wise and experienced. She smiled. Ah, better. Then the day's misgivings came back, and she frowned. She wished she shared Arnie's optimism about Adrianna.

Chapter 4—Checking for Clues

"There is nothing more deceptive than an obvious fact."

- Sherlock Holmes Quote, The Bascombe Valley Mystery

The next morning, after Arnie left for work, Beth got a call from one of her tenants. The young man told her he was having trouble with the air conditioner in his duplex. In the warming spring weather, most people had turned on their air for the first time this year, and it wasn't any wonder this forty-year-old unit didn't work well. The young tenant's A/C was the last one needing replacement in the rental units Beth and Arnie owned.

Beth called their heating and cooling company to find out when she could get service. The receptionist was unsure when a service person would be available; so Beth left her number. She expected quick service, because the owner of the small HVAC firm was a friend whom she and Arnie had met through her brother-in-law, Paul. Heating and cooling specialists, plumbers, and electricians tend to know and recommend each other if they do good work. Those connections served her rental business well since she needed one or another of them several times a year.

After she fed the cat and finished her coffee, Beth put on her walking shoes and set out for her morning walk on the Trolley Track Trail. She intended to stop by Adrianna's condo apartment to see if she could find a clue to her niece's whereabouts. It was a beautiful sunny morning but still early enough for her to wear a knit cardigan. She shed the wrap and tied the sleeves around her waist after about five minutes of walking at her normal power-walk speed.

The cardigan loosened and dropped off after a few minutes. A jogger picked it up and called to her. Beth startled, turned suddenly, and caught one foot with the other. Down she went. With a hand on her bruised fanny, she hobbled back several paces to retrieve her garment. *Good thing my parents didn't name me Grace.* Being a klutz was a condition she had learned to accept, but it still annoyed her.

With her cardigan sleeves tied around her middle in a double knot, Beth arrived at the condo building a short time later and used her owner's key to enter the back door.

Once inside, she spent a few minutes visiting with big Chuck, the most capable door man ever. Over time, he had shared his story with Beth. He had been a University of Kansas football player right after high school but felt it his duty to follow his father's example and join the Marines when a serious build-up wave of servicemen were being sent to Iraq. He told her about war wounds, a marriage, and a child, all of which kept him from returning to college. None of those life events had left him bitter. Quite the contrary.

"I'm a fast healer," he bragged and then winked. "If you want to see the scars, I can take off my shirt and pull down the pants a little."

"You know, I really like you with your clothes on," Beth said with a blush. "Save the pretty scars for your wife."

It didn't take much convincing to get Chuck to show the pictures of his family he kept at the desk. "This little guy is already throwing balls with me. I'm going to raise him up to be the best he can be. My job here is temporary. I'll figure out soon what I need to do to get a good career started. It might be I'll go back to school, but we've started talking about having another baby before we get too old, and school would be expensive. Anyway, when I leave here, I know you're going to miss me."

"I will, for sure, but when you retire from your great career, you can come back. I'll probably still be toddling in here as a great grandma landlady."

Now, although Chuck shuffled ten-hour day and evening shifts as security doorman at the West-Gate Condos with family life and a commitment to stay in shape, his happy demeanor captivated residents and visitors alike. Because she couldn't help enjoying the eye candy, Beth took another look at Chuck's muscular brown biceps bulging below his short-sleeved uniform shirt, wished him a good day, and made her way through the lobby toward the stairway. The upholstery and oriental rugs looked new, and fresh flowers graced the tables. Older draperies and floor tile projected an elegant, rather than an outdated, feel. A few residents sat on the comfortable seats, while they gossiped or waited for visitors.

Once inside Adrianna's apartment, Beth had trouble deciding where to look or for what to look. With daydreams running through her head of being the family heroine who finds the answer to Adrianna's whereabouts, she began by checking the top of Adrianna's desk in the bedroom. She noticed there was no computer, and neither was there anything that gave a clue to Adrianna's whereabouts. None of the papers on her desk looked relevant. Beth decided young people didn't keep books of addresses and telephone numbers anymore; those were kept in the computer and on their smart phones.

No notes were to be found anywhere in the living room or kitchen, either. Beth stopped to look at the photos pinned on the refrigerator door with magnets. A picture of Adrianna with her father, Paul, and stepmother, Meg, caught her eye. Adrianna resembled Paul, in that she was slender and athletic looking. She had her mother's full lips and high cheek bones, but she had the brown eyes and dark hair of her father's youth, her locks long and smooth with reddish highlights. There was a small picture of Adrianna's mother, at a much younger age and with not quite as many tattoos as now, and several pictures of Adrianna with a young man. He was several inches taller than she, had sun-highlighted blond hair, and in most of the photos wore a toothy grin on his tanned face.

Beth remembered having met Max briefly on a couple of occasions. She thought they broke up last fall.

She scrutinized a picture of Adrianna with Max and another couple and made a mental note to ask Meg about it when she returned. On second thought, she decided to borrow the picture so she could show it to Meg. It was the only picture there of Adrianna with a friend other than Max; maybe there was a clue here to help them know who to contact in order to find Adrianna. She locked the apartment door and turned toward the stairway. On the way she spotted Eva Standish down the hall stooping to place a folded paper under a door. So Adrianna wasn't the only one who received Eva's quirky ministrations.

Beth smiled to herself and made her way to the parking garage where she spotted Adrianna's car still in its designated place. Her step-niece must have left with someone or taken another form of transportation to wherever she went.

As Beth walked home, her cell phone rang. Still the three organ notes. "Ugh," Beth said aloud. Maybe she'd change Arnie's tone to a cymbal crash, see how he liked that.

"Yes?" she answered, with uncharacteristic curtness.

"Hello? This is Stan Granger. Is this Beth Stockwell?"

"Oh, yes. I'm sorry, Stan. I've got to change the ring tone on my cell phone. It causes me to be too gruff, especially when I'm in my deep thoughts mode."

"Well, maybe I can relieve your mind a little. I can meet you at your duplex to check the air conditioning system at 11:00," said Stan.

"Thanks, Stan. That'll help solve one problem today. I'll see you at 11:00." Beth closed her phone with a satisfied snap but then furrowed her brow when, immediately, she started thinking about the next errand she'd promised to do today—visit Adrianna's office. To enter a construction company office, ask to speak to an employee she didn't know, probe for answers—these were tasks outside of her comfort zone. Beth had to submerge her all-too-ready rationalizations for procrastination. She shoved the phone into her pocket and hurried home.

Chapter 5—Visiting the Construction Company Offices

"I know there's a proverb which that says 'To err is human,' but a human error is nothing to what a computer can do if it tries."
— Agatha Christie, Hallowe'en Party

Beth drove to the building which housed the offices of Renfro Construction, the firm where Adrianna worked. She related better to people face to face, felt she needed to look the people in the eye to determine if anyone there knew where Adrianna went. In theory, it would be easy, assuming she could find Adrianna's friend, Abby, whom Meg had mentioned. She figured she'd have enough time to check this all out at the construction company before she needed to meet Stan at 11:00.

"My name is Beth Stockwell. Do you know how I can get in touch with Adrianna Knells?" Beth asked the young blond receptionist with the pierced eyebrow. The name plate on the front desk revealed the receptionist's name, Allison.

"She's outta the office this week," Allison said, showing a dimple. "Can someone else help you?"

"Do you know where she is or how I can contact her? I'm her aunt, and I need to find her."

"I don' know. I've been told to refer her business to one of the other project coordinators 'til she comes back. When those project managers get time off, they don't wanna be bothered by business."

"This isn't business. It's, uh, a personal matter, and it's really important. May I speak to one of your employees named Abby, or Abigail? She's one of Adrianna's friends, and she may know where I can find Adrianna."

"Le's see," Allison said, peering at her computer, "that must be Abigail West. She works in the accounting department. I don't usually send people back there—"

"It's very important. I'll only take a minute of her time," Beth said with a sad, hopeful-looking smile.

"Okay," Allison said, looking relieved to be won over, "I'll ring her desk to let her know you're comin'. It's down that hall to the left."

Beth walked down the hall feeling out of her element, asking questions of unknown people, acting like a detective. Then she remembered she was doing this for Meg, who would do it for her if one of her kids was missing. Of course, one of Beth's kids lived in San Diego, one had settled in Chicago, and the youngest had recently landed a good job and moved to Milwaukee. They were almost always missing. But at least they returned calls when she left messages.

Those thoughts melted as she entered the door to the small accounting department and was greeted by a young woman who looked somewhat familiar. She had a small curvy build, a round face with highlighted brown hair twisted on the back of her head, and a faint sprinkling of freckles under her light make-up. The young woman appeared to be a teenager at first glance, although she was probably Adrianna's age. She looked at Beth with a wide dark gaze and gave her a courteous smile which did not extend to her eyes.

"I'm Abby West," she said. "Our receptionist phoned and told me that you're Adrianna Knells' aunt?"

"Yes, Beth Stockwell." Beth extended her hand. "I'm sorry to bother you during your work day. It looks like you are all very busy."

Beth surveyed the room. Two desks were stacked with papers which looked like orders, bills, and receipts, similar to her desk at home but on a much larger scale. A youngish, blond, red-lipped woman wearing a low-cut shirt made of some flimsy fabric looked up from her work and watched them with unabashed curiosity.

"Adrianna's stepmother Meg Knells is my sister," Beth said. "Meg is out of town and told me you're Adrianna's friend and might be able to help us. Have you met Adrianna's stepmother?"

"I guess maybe once." Abby cast her eyes sideways in an evasive manner. "What kind of help do you need?"

"We need to know where Adrianna is or how to get in touch with her. She left a brief message which said she was going out of town, but we haven't been able to contact her either by e-mail or by phone, not even by texting. Maybe we're overreacting, but Meg is worried something may be wrong—something may have happened to Adrianna."

"Well, she didn't tell me where she was going. I heard she asked for vacation time at the last minute on Friday, and she hasn't checked in since then as far as I know." Abby paused for a second or two. "We used to hang out together sometimes, but she doesn't confide in me anymore. Her job is way over on the other side of the building, with the big shots. You know how that works. She's a project manager now." Her eyes became even darker.

"Sure.... Well, when you did hang out with her, did she talk about anyone or anything that might make her leave all of a sudden as she did Friday?"

"Gee, I really can't remember," Abby said. She hesitated again, a sullen expression on her face. "Maybe her real mother needed help. Adrianna always worried about her."

"That's a thought. And—has Adrianna had any recent boyfriends?" Beth did not in any way want to react to Abby's sneering tone. "Aunts aren't always kept in the loop about boyfriends." She added a sincere smile.

"None since Max Zeller that I know of. Like I said, I don't have any idea where she might be. She didn't tell me anything before she left—I kinda need to get back to work, you know?"

Beth glanced around at the people in the office. The feeling someone watched them made her cut her eyes with a nervous twitch toward a small adjoining glassed-in office off the large main area. She could barely see the head of a man, mostly hidden by a computer screen, inside the partially closed blinds of the office. His head was topped with a crop of dark reddish hair; half glasses for reading sat on his nose; and he peered over the top of them. The face, registering disapproval, disappeared back behind the computer monitor after several seconds. Beth thought she caught something else in that look—distrust, or maybe a threat? Or was this detective business getting her imagination all fired up?

"Well, thanks for talking to me, anyway, Abby. I don't want to get you in trouble with your boss. If you hear from Adrianna, will you ask her to call her dad and stepmother?"

"Sure. And my boss...well, he's not...I mean...we're really busy this week; that's why he watches us."

Before Beth could muster a comment, Abby's boss opened his door, walked toward them with a small commander-in-chief smile on his face, and asked if he could be of help. Abby introduced him as Mr. Peter O'Neill, excused herself, and went back to her desk. When Beth briefly explained why she had been talking to Abby, Mr. O'Neill assured her in a most charming manner that he had enjoyed working with Adrianna, but since she no longer worked in his department, no one there was likely to know her whereabouts.

"Well, I thought Abby might know, because she and Adrianna were good friends."

"They were friends. I remember that." Mr. O'Neill glanced back at Abby and lost his smile for a split second. The smile returned, and he laid one hand across his chest. "I always counted Adrianna as a friend, too, as well as one of my staff members. Anything I learn about where she went for her vacation I'll let you know, if you give me a number to call. This is a small company. Maybe when I meet with other department heads, one of them will have some information about her plans."

Beth rummaged through her purse for one of her business cards. "Thank you for your interest. I'd appreciate a call if you find out, I mean, if you learn anything."

"No problem. It was nice to meet you. Can you find your way out?"

"I can."

In the hallway, Beth glanced back through the office window, and she noticed Abby watch Mr. O'Neill walk back to his office. When he turned at his door to survey the outer office, Abby's eyes immediately focused back on her computer screen. Her expression was blank.

Beth thought about Abby West and her boss while she drove to the duplex to meet Stan Granger, the air conditioner repairman. Curious reactions. Were they both envious of Adrianna's advancement? Was Abby afraid of her boss? Mr. O'Neill would be good looking if his smile reached his eyes, and he might be fun to work for if he could extend the same charm to his employees that he showed her. Maybe Abby and Adrianna had a falling out while Adrianna was still employed in the accounting department, and it affected the work environment. That would explain the underlying curt tone that she sensed from Abby and, at first, from her boss. At any rate, they had been no help in finding Adrianna, had they?

That thought led to another. She realized why Abby looked familiar—she was the girl in the picture Beth had taken from the front of Adrianna's fridge.

Chapter 6—Investigating Detective

"The impossible could not have happened; therefore the impossible must be possible in spite of appearances."
— Agatha Christie, Murder on the Orient Express

That afternoon, Beth ate her salad and checked her e-mail to find out if Stan Granger had sent his estimate for the new AC unit he'd told her she needed. She felt restless. However much she checked her maintenance budget, tried to catch up on bills, and tried every which way to keep busy, Beth had trouble keeping her mind on business. She couldn't help conjecturing about the next step to take to find Adrianna. Arnie had a lunch meeting at work; so she couldn't brainstorm with him. She fed Psycho Cat and chuckled when he ran circles around the feeding bowl and climbed her leg.

After she stuffed the cat food into the pantry, she heard her cell phone. The irritating noise brought to mind the Edgar Allan Poe stories she loved to read, "The Tell-Tale Heart" and the "Pit and the Pendulum." In both, a disconcerting sound kept recurring. Before she could bring herself to answer the phone, it took a physical shaking of her head and a snort at herself to ward off the involuntary foreboding.

"Hello?"

"Beth Stockwell?" the caller said in a high-pitched voice.

Beth recognized that voice, Adrianna's next-door neighbor, Eva Standish. Beth's antennae went up, and she sighed. "Yes, Eva?"

"This is too much," Eva said. "Now the police are coming around asking about Adrianna Knells. One of them spent a long time here asking questions. Well, of course, I wouldn't say anything bad about your niece, but I did have to tell them that I hear her music sometimes when my television is off and that she used to have a boyfriend who visited at all hours of the evening and friends who showed up and made noise in the hall sometimes. I always thought well of that girl, you know, but now… My nerves are on edge."

"The police?" Beth said. "Did they say why they were asking questions about Adrianna?"

"No they didn't. They told me it was a routine investigation and they needed to ask her a few questions. That's all they would say. I thought probably you filed a police report because she went away and left her cat. That's why I called you. I really can't deal with detectives visiting me and asking all sorts of questions. You understand my nervous condition, don't you?"

"Yes—yes, Eva, dear, I'm sure they won't bother you again, since you answered all of their questions already. What kind of questions did they ask?"

"They asked when I saw Adrianna last, how long she's been gone, if I had noticed anything unusual happening next door lately—things like that. I told them that the last time I saw Adrianna was last Friday afternoon when she came home from work—I saw her in the hallway—and that nothing unusual has been happening—except the cat started making noise. You know about that already. I told them I had to call you concerning the cat because I couldn't take it any longer. They said they understood. They left here a few minutes ago."

"Eva, you are so observant. Can you remember anything else? Did you hear anything besides the cat from Adrianna's condo after Friday evening?"

"Umm, come to think of it, I may have heard Adrianna up and around very early Saturday morning, before I even got up. I forgot about that when I was talking to the police. I didn't really think much about it at the time because Adrianna often goes bike riding with a group on Saturday morning. I did happen to notice, though, that her bike is still in her storage bin. Her car is here, too. Um…well…is Adrianna okay?"

Beth reassured Eva again and hung up. She looked at the clock. It was almost 3:30. Meg would be in the car on her way home from Wichita, probably. Beth wondered if Adrianna's dad had called the police with a missing person report. She didn't think Meg would have done that; so she decided to try to contact Paul first.

"Paul," Beth said when he finally answered his mobile phone with his somewhat gruff *Paul Knells here.* "This is Beth. Did you call the police department to report Adrianna missing?"

"No, of course not!" Paul said. Beth could picture Paul's dear balding head pop up from whatever business paper he was perusing and his eyes become alert. "Adrianna left a message about going out of town last weekend. She's merely on a trip or something. Why did you ask if I'd called the police?"

"Well, the police apparently went to Adrianna's apartment to look for her and have been questioning her neighbor. I don't know why they were there, but I thought maybe you knew."

"I have no idea. This is bizarre. They must want to ask her about someone else, someone she knows."

"Did Adrianna tell you where she went this week, or do you have an idea?" Beth asked.

"Uh, no. I sent her an e-mail message about you finding her cat and explained that I goofed up and didn't get over there to feed him. I hope she'll answer that pretty soon. She's probably trying to stay away from e-mail and phone messages this week. That's what I do when I'm on vacation."

Beth's brow puckered. In her recent experience, young people seemed to be handcuffed to their electronic devices and to check them every few minutes. She told Paul she was going to his house to meet Meg.

"I think we should call the police department to try to find out why they are asking questions about Adrianna," she said. "Meg sounded pretty upset about this, not as laid back about it as you are."

"Okay, you calm Meg," Paul said, "and I'll be there as soon as I can. I'll reschedule a couple of things for tomorrow and go on home. We'll find out what the police want and make a concerted effort to get in touch with Adrianna this evening. Then we'll all feel better. I'll send another message to her again right now. Appreciate your concern, Beth. With any luck, this'll be resolved soon."

Chapter 7—Continuing Conundrum

"It is the quietest and meekest people who are often capable of the most sudden and unexpected violences for the reason that when their control does snap, it goes entirely. (Hercule Poirot)"
— Agatha Christie, *Hercule Poirot's Christmas*

As soon as she finished her conversation with Paul, Beth called Meg to find out when she'd be home.

"I'm turning off I-35. I made it from Wichita to here in less than three hours. My eyes are stinging, my insides are shaky, and I have to go to the bathroom really bad. Have you found out anything?" Meg said.

"I've got some important news. I'll meet you at your house." Meg started to ask what was up, but Beth cut her off and promised to tell her as soon as she got home. Beth grabbed her purse and car keys and headed toward her sister's house. It was fifteen minutes away in a suburb across the state line in Kansas. On the way, she called Arnie to tell him about the day's events, but he didn't answer; so she left a short message. She'd fill him in later. It didn't seem right to string her family along like this, but she didn't know how to explain over the phone. She couldn't explain it to herself yet.

Beth stopped at the coffee shop. She bought two fresh roasted coffees and a pastry to share. Meg was a larger person than Beth, and she liked to eat. Maybe the treats would soften the potential emotional impact of Beth's news. It was worth a shot.

Beth arrived at Meg's house a few minutes later, and her sister answered the door, shoulder length brown hair in disarray, looking as if she had been running her hands through it, her clothes a little wrinkled from the long trip. Her normally bright smiling face assumed a concerned look as soon as she saw Beth's grim expression.

"What's wrong? Have you found out something dreadful about Adrianna?" Meg asked.

"Now, sit down and relax, Sis," Beth said. "I brought you some coffee and a little piece of coffee cake for your afternoon snack. If you'll sit here at the breakfast bar with me, I'll tell you what I know."

Like a compliant school girl, Meg sat, sipped the rich coffee, and sampled the cake. With her routine good manners, she thanked her sister for her thoughtfulness, but after the first taste the snack was forgotten, and she begged to hear all. Beth took a breath and then told Meg how she found out from Eva Standish that the police had been asking about Adrianna at the condo building.

Meg's hands flew to her chest. "But why? Why would police be asking about Adrianna?" Her eyes widened. "They didn't find...?"

Before Beth could answer that she didn't know, they heard the garage door open and a car drive in. Meg ran to meet Paul. Beth shifted from foot to foot in the front room. She turned to gaze through the picture window and watched a dark blue Ford sedan pull up to the curb. A stocky, large-faced, middle-aged man wearing a sports coat and chinos got out and headed toward the house. Beth answered the door. Meg and Paul walked in with their arms around each other.

"Good afternoon, I'm Detective Carl Rinquire," the visitor said, looking from Beth to the couple behind her. "I'm here to see Mr. and Mrs. Knells." He spoke in a low-pitched voice, suited to his size.

"We're Paul and Meg Knells," Paul said, "and this is Meg's sister, Beth Stockwell."

"Ah, yes, Mrs. Stockwell." The detective consulted his notes. "You're the owner of the condo in Brookside rented by Adrianna Knells. I need to talk to you, too, about Miss Knells."

Beth could feel her heart beat faster inside her chest.

"What's this about?" Paul asked.

"Has something happened to Adrianna? Where is she?" Meg spoke in little more than a whisper, looking as if she might faint.

"We hoped that you could help us find the answers to those questions. I need to find her and talk to her."

"Talk about what?" Paul said.

"Information concerning the company where she is employed. I can't discuss the details."

The detective interrogated them with the same kinds of questions he had asked Adrianna's neighbor, Eva Standish. Meg fluttered hen-like to the kitchen for her address book and returned to give the detective the names and numbers of a few of Adrianna's friends from high school and college who still lived in the area. She told him Adrianna's job consumed much of her time these days, but there were a couple of friends from work she talked about, especially one named Abby.

Paul volunteered Adrianna's cell phone number and her e-mail address. He explained that he, his wife, and Beth had left messages for her and had not received answers. Beth nodded. Meg wrung her hands.

"And Mrs. Stockwell," Rinquire said. "Can you tell me precisely how you discovered your niece is missing?"

"Um, well, Psycho Cat clued us all in to start with," Beth said. The detective raised an eyebrow. "I mean...I'll start at the beginning."

Striving to think of every detail, Beth told him about the call from Eva Standish, the cat, what she had learned about Adrianna's making noise on Saturday morning, and about the bicycle still in storage. Carl Rinquire didn't seem surprised. He must have conducted a thorough investigation of Adrianna's possessions and of the neighbors, the doorman, and the garage attendant at the condo building.

Beth was relieved to notice how Detective Rinquire's manner softened after he talked to them and observed their reactions. He wasn't nearly so brusque when he handed one of his cards to each of them and prepared to leave.

"Call me if you hear anything from Adrianna," he said. "It's in her best interest to talk to the Kansas City police as soon as possible."

They all nodded. "And will you please let us know if you find out where she is?" Meg asked in a trembling voice.

"Of course, Ma'am," Detective Rinquire said. He continued writing in his notebook as he walked toward his car.

The family stood and watched him until he drove away. Then Meg collapsed on the couch in tears. She sobbed, her hands over her face, and didn't try to talk. Paul sat with his arm around her and looked sober.

Beth paced back and forth, thinking. She mumbled her thoughts out loud as she moved around. "It's something about her work. Why would they need to question Adrianna, and what has that got to do with her being gone? That is, unless she's in a position to know something that's forced her to disappear—in which case she could be in danger. Or maybe she's being accused of something and needs to be here to defend herself. Maybe this is the reason Abby and her boss acted funny. At any rate, we need to find Adrianna and warn her, and I won't even think that it may be too late. I need to go to Renfro Construction again and see if I can find out more."

"Beth, leave the detecting to the detectives," Paul said. "That fellow Rinquire seems to know what he's doing."

But Meg sat up straight and looked at her husband. She spoke through her tears. "Paul, I really need to go back to school tomorrow after having been gone for most of the week; so I will be tied up most of the day. And I know you are jam-packed at work. We won't have enough time to scramble around for information tomorrow."

Paul shook his head and opened his mouth to respond, but Meg turned to Beth.

"Beth, I don't know what you can do. I don't want you to do anything the police will have issue with. But I agree with you. We need to find out why Adrianna is missing, where she is, and why the police are looking for her. We'll appreciate any news you can give us.

I'll keep my cell phone in my pocket, and you call me as soon as you learn anything. Okay?"

"Don't get yourself in trouble. That's all I'm saying, Beth," Paul said, "I'm going to send another e-mail message and another phone message and let Adrianna know what's going on—in case she's getting her messages and not answering for some reason. And…I guess I'd better call Adrianna's mom. Meredith needs to be informed about Adrianna's absence and the police questioning. Possibly she knows something about where Adrianna went. I'll call Herb Reynolds, the president of Renfro, too. We've been introduced to him. Maybe he will tell me what's going on. Then you won't have to go back to the office."

***

That evening, during dinner, after Beth had filled Arnie in on the day's happenings, she received a call from Meg. "Paul got hold of Adrianna's boss, Herb Reynolds, but he wouldn't tell Paul anything. He insisted he had been told not to discuss the case.

"There's good news, though. We finally heard from Adrianna. Paul already told Detective Rinquire about this," Meg said, "but let me read the message Paul found in his e-mail in-box this evening. It says,

'I finally found a place to access the Internet and check my e-mail. Sorry about the mix-up with Psycho Cat. Didn't know Meg would be gone all week. Please thank Aunt Beth for rescuing him. Be gone a little longer. Tell you everything when I return. Love and kisses, Adrianna.'

"She's being so vague. I don't understand. Paul sent a reply for her to phone us immediately, but so far we haven't heard anything."

"Get some rest, Meg. We'll get this sorted out. Did you and Paul eat dinner?"

"Neither one of us can eat a thing. But we're going to try to sleep. Call me with whatever you find out tomorrow. Okay Beth?"

"You know I will, Meg. And since tomorrow is Friday, you and Paul come for dinner at my house. We'll all put our heads together. Maybe you'll have heard again from Adrianna by then and everything will have been resolved. In that case, we'll celebrate."

Chapter 8—Interrogating the Bookkeeper

"There is nothing like first-hand evidence."

- Sherlock Holmes Quote, *A Study in Scarlet*

As soon as she thought the Renfro office would be open on Friday morning, Beth presented herself to Allison, the front desk receptionist, the perky young lady now adorned with a scarlet-colored streak on one side of her champagne blond hair. Allison stared at her for a few seconds with an open mouth.

"You're Adrianna Knell's aunt, aren't you? I can't believe you're here."

"I am her aunt, and why can't you believe I'm here?" Beth said, knitting her brow.

"Well, you know, after she stole all of that money. Embezzled, I mean. I found out that's what they call it. I wouldn' want to show my face if I was one of her relatives."

Beth did a double-take inside but remained calm on the outside. "I was here yesterday morning, and no one said anything about a theft."

"I don't think anyone knew until around noon yesterday. The police were here by 12:30. Then everyone in the company found out. I'm not suppose' to talk about this, but I assumed you'd know everything anyway, since you're part of her family. Have they found her yet?"

"No, not yet. I was hoping to talk again to Adrianna's friend Abby West. I want to run some ideas by her about Adrianna's whereabouts."

"I can' let you go back to the accounting department! The police said no one is to go back there except our bosses and them. And Pete said—Mr. O'Neill, I mean..." Beth thought it strange that Allison's face flushed slightly when she said Pete. "Mr. O'Neill is Abby's boss, and he said that no one can be snooping around in there. Abby's not the one who reported the fake accounts where the money was sent, anyway. It was Trish, that auditing accountant, who discovered the crime." Allison sat back and looked self-satisfied, as if she were speaking police jargon with authority.

"Of course, it makes sense an auditor would find the evidence." Beth strove for the right words to elicit information. "Was the audit already scheduled for this week?"

"Sure, everyone was scramblin' around to get their accounts logged and in order last week because they all were gettin' ready for the audit."

The young woman drew a breath, and her eyes grew perceptibly wider as she gazed over Beth's right shoulder. "Here—here comes the one who, you know, whose office is affected by... You'd best get."

When Beth turned to locate the object of Allison's sudden distraction, she recognized the accounting department boss, Peter O'Neill, looking dapper in a black turtleneck and herringbone pants, sporting a TV news anchor haircut. He was walking past the reception area on the other side of the glass partition. At Beth's movement, he turned his head to see them looking at him, stopped, reversed his stride, and came to the doorway. His eyes flickered over Allison for an instant, and he raised his hand the slightest bit, as if to quiet her.

"Good morning," he said to Beth with a polite smile. "Are you looking for Adrianna Knells again today?" He asked the question in a deep, quiet, almost soothing voice.

"Yes!" Beth's answer sounded more severe than she meant it to sound; perhaps needy would be a better description. "Do you know where she is? Can you tell me why she's being blamed...?"

"No," Pete O'Neill interrupted her. "I can't discuss this matter of theft with you. Police orders." He came into the room and touched Beth lightly on the arm, as one would calm a child. "However, I know there must be some mistake about Adrianna being implicated. Please don't worry about it. The police will have it cleared up in no time, and you'll have a good story to tell Adrianna when she returns."

Beth bounced her head, to acknowledge his comments. She couldn't think of a response. O'Neill turned his benevolent smile on the receptionist for a second and then left.

"Isn't he nice?" Allison sighed.

"Very personable," Beth said, turning back to the desk and eying the receptionist with a furrowed brow. "But I still would like to talk to Abby."

Allison adjusted the besotted look on her face and scrolled to a new page on her computer. "Well, look here. This says that Abby West isn' here today--called in sick; so you couldn' see her even if I could let you."

"This is really important," Beth begged. "Abby and I might be able to find Adrianna and bring her back, but I have to talk to Abby about my idea. Could I get her address from you?"

"Well, I don' think..."

"Please. I won't tell her or anyone that I got it from you. I'll say that I looked it up in the phone book."

"I guess...if it's that easy...I might as well...Okay, I'll show it to you on the screen and you write it while I look out for anybody comin' this way."

Beth dropped her pen to the floor as she took it out of her purse. "Darn." She stooped to pick it up and had to reach under the desk to drag it out. Before she stood up, she looked up in her normal embarrassed survey to see if anyone noticed her clumsiness and saw Peter O'Neill walk back past the front office. He must not have seen her, because he gave Allison a beneficent smile and an A-Okay sign and then continued down the hall. When Beth stood up, Allison's wide smile faded and her complexion looked pinker than before. Beth found her notebook and copied Abby's address from the computer screen before anyone could stop her.

***

Twenty minutes later, Beth knocked on the door of an apartment on the second floor of an older three-story brick building in Midtown. The Westport neighborhood, north of Brookside, boasted some of the oldest buildings in Kansas City, many of them built of red brick. Most of the buildings had been renovated, restored, or at least well-maintained. The area was very popular with young people because of its trendy shopping, restaurants, bars, and music venues. Parents knew of crimes and rowdy behavior in Westport and discouraged their kids from living there, but the twenty-somethings were always elated when they could find an affordable apartment in the vicinity.

A young man answered the door. A thin five foot ten, he had narrow shoulders, olive skin, a Roman nose, dark brown hair, and dark eyes. He sported a two-day growth of beard and needed a haircut (at least according to Beth's standards of grooming.) His baggy jeans and stretched-out Tee-shirt caused Beth to think he might be out of work rather than simply taking a day off. The young man looked vaguely familiar, as Abby had when Beth first saw her. Beth gave him her name and asked for Abby.

"She's home sick today and can't talk to anyone," the young man said, blocking the door.

Through the small space between this bouncer and the door frame Beth could clearly see Beth sitting on the sofa facing the T.V. in an untidy room, a cola beside her on the end table—no tissue box, no red nose, no blanket or pillow. The room, though messy with mail, magazines, shoes, jackets, cups, and pop cans strewn about, contained expensive furnishings. Leather seating, an entertainment center, occasional tables, a solid oak dining set, and fancy custom-made window scarves, with colors matching the wool area carpets, adorned the room.

With false bravado, Beth barged into the room past the young man and, smiling broadly, called out to the girl, "Hi, Abby, remember me? I'm Adrianna's aunt. I have an idea, which I want to discuss with you, about how to find her. I know about the embezzlement."

Abby quickly closed a laptop computer which was sitting on her lap. Beth, coming from behind the young lady's perch, had already noticed a travel-booking web site that was open on the screen.

"It's okay. I talked to her before," Abby said from the couch. Joey gave her a frown and a slight nod. Abby motioned to a straight-back chair that sat on the other side of the end table.

Beth sat. "Are you ill, dear?" she asked. She glanced around the room. The apartment was clearly occupied by both young people. There were slippers and shoes and various articles of clothing belonging to both sexes on the floor and on furniture. Joey walked off to the kitchen, which was open to the living room, and started filling the dishwasher. He remained within earshot.

"I'm mostly just, uh, you know, upset," Abby said. "Yesterday I learned that Renfro Construction had a gob of money stolen. Six million dollars! I should have discovered the missing money because I've been the main bookkeeper for nearly a year. On top of that, I found out all of the money came from Adrianna's clients' accounts. The police were all over the office talking mostly to Trish, the accountant who found the fake fund accounts, but also to the rest of us. They wanted to look at all of our files. It was exhausting."

"I can't believe Adrianna would do a thing like that," Beth said. "Is it possible that Trish misdirected the funds and blamed it on Adrianna because she isn't there?"

"The police thought of that, but Trish is a contracting accountant who works part time for the firm that does our audits. She does the audits at several companies and is at Renfro only once a year for a short time. Trish has been at Renfro this past week, but funds have been accumulating in the fake accounts for a few months, and now the money has been withdrawn from them. The accounts are closed. Anyway, I'm not supposed to talk about this--the detective said."

"I know," Beth said, in what she contrived to be a soothing manner. "It's because we both care about Adrianna, and I'm concerned for her safety, whether she's guilty or not guilty. If she is guilty, I wonder if someone else is involved, someone who may have threatened her or enticed her in some way. Do you know of anyone who may have had such an influence on Adrianna this past year?"

"Ummmm, well, maybe her mom...like I told you before, she was always talking about how sorry she was for her real mother."

"Okay, a possibility!" Beth frowned. "How about her ex-boyfriend, Max?"

"Yeah, very possible," Abby said. She looked toward the open kitchen. Joey was standing and listening. They exchanged a glance. "But Max is gone."

Beth caught the exchange but couldn't interpret it. She continued, "Do you know how to contact Max or where he is precisely?"

"No, all I know is that he went off to work, somewhere exotic I think, and Adrianna broke it off with him. Do you suppose he might be involved and that Adrianna might be with him?"

"That was one theory I had, but I was hoping you had more information about how to find him. Joey, do you have any contact information for Max?" Beth turned toward Joey.

The young man scowled. "No! I mean, why would I? Listen, Abby is trying to rest from this entire trauma. She doesn't need any more questions. She already told the police everything she knows. Do you mind leaving her to get over it so she can go back to work on Monday feeling better?" He attempted a smile, with his lips only, and walked toward the door.

Beth wanted to ask more questions but felt compelled to give it up for now. She thanked the two young people and left.

Had she learned anything important? Why was Abby so upset that she needed to take a day off work? Was she protecting Adrianna? Was she protecting herself, or was she really distressed she hadn't found the fraud earlier and now might be under job scrutiny? In that case, she should have stayed at work today and been very diligent.

With so many details to keep straight, Beth decided she should take notes. When she got to her car, she got out a little notebook that she kept in her purse for reminders and such and started a section with a glum title: 'Clues for Finding Adrianna.' She made a list of the people she had talked to about Adrianna's disappearance. Beside each name she made a small note about what they had told her and the questions she still had. She even listed her husband, Arnie. He was a good listener and maybe could help her wrap her mind around some of the questions that were bugging her. As she drove home, Beth thought about Beth and Joey and Max and then started thinking about Adrianna's real mother, Meredith Knells. Maybe she should talk to Meredith about this. This was exhausting!

In her nervous state, hated thoughts kept popping into her mind. "If Adrianna is innocent, why did she disappear like this? If Adrianna is guilty of embezzlement, what will that do to Meg and Paul? How could she, Beth-the-Ordinary, even hope to help in a case like this? When she was in college, Beth had planned to major in sociology and become a social worker. Would more education have helped her now?" She squelched the negative thoughts. Adrianna was innocent and must be found.

Right now, Beth wanted to go home and cook a good dinner for her distraught sister and brother-in-law. They had to work all day and probably couldn't think about anything else but Adrianna, let alone eat a good lunch.

Beth's mother's favorite book was *Little Women* by Louisa May Alcott. She and Meg had been named for two of the main characters in that book. In an uncanny way the two sisters' personalities somewhat reflected those of their namesakes. The eldest Little Woman, Meg, tended to the conventional and good, while shy Beth fought flaws in her own temperament. Now the present-day Beth could hardly believe her worthy sister, the person who had been her guide after their father passed, was being put through this torment.

She left cell phone messages for both her sister, Meg, and brother-in-law, Paul. Beth told them she had been to Renfro Construction, had talked to Abby, had a little more information, and would tell them all about it tonight at dinner. To Meg's message she added that she needed Meredith's phone number. She didn't have the heart to tell them about the embezzlement accusation through phone messages. Arnie wouldn't be home for lunch again today; so Beth spent the day cooking, getting her thoughts in order, and taking care of Psycho Cat—with everything else to worry about, she hadn't even thought of taking the cat to Meg and Paul's house. She didn't mind keeping him until Adrianna came home.

Chapter 9—Dining and Details

"No one ever owns a cat...you share a common habitation on a basis of equal rights and mutual respects...although somehow the cat always comes out ahead of the deal."
— Lilian Jackson Braun

"**N**ooooo! Psycho Cat, down! Shoo!" Beth flew into the kitchen when she saw Adrianna's cat standing on the kitchen counter with his whiskers in the apple pie. In one leap and two seconds, Psycho Cat avoided Beth's swat and was off the counter and down the stairs to the basement to hide out until the coast was clear.

No wonder Adrianna had given Sylvester the nickname Psycho Cat almost immediately after she adopted him. Beth remembered more of Adrianna's stories about the silly cat—the ones about him hiding in silence in closets, under furniture, or on top of a bookcase and then jumping out and scaring her. He could be a handful, but Psycho Cat was Adrianna's ex officio baby boy. It was not feasible that she had run away for good and left her kitty.

Beth surveyed the damage and reached for a spatula to work on the pie. Fumbling, she dropped it on the floor. "Balderdash!" she shouted, picked up the elusive instrument, and threw it down the stairs toward the cat's destination in frustration. Well, there was no time to bake another pie, and it looked and smelled so yummy, its juices oozing out of the crumb top, that she didn't want to throw it out. Maybe she'd cut out the half with the cat damage and use the other half. It could work.

The appealing results of Beth's home cooking sat on the counter and stove top. Her Boatman's Stew scented the air with thyme, the mandarin orange salad tantalized with tangy vinaigrette dressing, her own home-baked rolls with their yeasty aroma invited yellow butter, and the damaged fresh apple pie infused the kitchen with a sweet cinnamon scent. The meal was calculated to tempt anyone's appetite, maybe even those who were so full of anxiety that they hadn't eaten or slept for the last couple of days.

Beth set the dining room table. Arnie would be home in a few minutes, and Meg and Paul were supposed to be here by 6:00. Maybe if they put some ideas together over a good meal, Meg and Paul would eat, and they could come up with some inspiration about where Adrianna might have gone and why. That her lovely step-niece was guilty of theft was plain preposterous, Beth told herself again.

***

"Paul called the people at Renfro today and learned Adrianna is out for a three week leave." Meg told Beth and Arnie at dinner, with a hint of a catch in her voice. "She has four weeks of vacation a year, but she already used part of it to go to her grandfather's funeral in January."

"It's not like her to fail to tell us when she plans to be gone for so long." Paul said, as if Adrianna were a teenager who stayed the night with a friend without permission. "In fact, this is the lengthiest vacation she's ever taken."

Choosing her words carefully and trying not to be alarmist, Beth filled them in on what she had learned from the receptionist at Renfro Construction. The others were horrified that Adrianna was the prime suspect in the embezzlement, but they had expected something dreadful because of the questions they were asked by the detective. There was a pause as it entered all of their minds that Adrianna's absence certainly helped validate the suspicions.

Paul looked at his plate for a minute, pushed his chair back, and stood up. He looked furious enough to kick something, but he controlled himself after several seconds and sat down. "I don't believe for a minute that Adrianna is guilty," he said. "If she knows something, though, she may have left without telling us in order to protect us."

"I found a picture on Adrianna's fridge that I want you to look at." Beth held up the photo that she had put on the sideboard for this purpose. "Here are Adrianna and her old boyfriend, Max. Here is Abby West, whom I met at Renfro, but do you know anything about the other young man? I think I might have met him today, also."

Paul paced the room, but Meg eyed Beth with a quizzical tilt of her head. "I haven't visited her at her apartment for a while; she usually comes to our house. It's crazy that Adrianna displayed a picture with Max in it. The two broke up at the end of last summer when Max left to work at a bar in the Virgin Islands. I think the other young man is Max's buddy and possibly Abby's boyfriend. His name is Joey something. The four of them stopped by our house one night on the way to a movie. Why? Do you think it's important?"

"I met this Joey today. It looked as though he and Abby live together. They didn't mention Joey being a good friend of Max's, and they didn't seem to know where to find Max."

Arnie and Paul glanced at each other. "Beth, you need to leave the detective work to the police." Arnie cautioned in a mild manner.

"The police will find Adrianna. We don't want them spending their time accusing us of interfering or maybe think we're withholding information about where she is," Paul said.

Meg seemed to be trembling. "But they want to find her to arrest her for embezzlement!"

Beth looked down at the photo in her hand. "You're right, Arnie. Sorry Paul. Detective Rinquire will find her and get this all sorted out. Any information I get will go directly to him."

She looked at her sister's stricken face and realized she couldn't bear to let go of the search until they found Adrianna.

I need to talk to Meg or maybe Adrianna's mom, Meredith, and find out if one of them knows how to contact Max. As yet I haven't discovered anything Detective Rinquire wouldn't know, but I can still hope to find Adrianna before he or some dangerous person finds her.

After dinner Beth and Meg prepared dessert plates and coffee while Arnie and Paul went to sit in the living room. "Meg," Beth said in a low voice, "Do you have Max's address or phone number or perhaps his e-mail address?"

"No, I don't," Meg said with a surprised look. "Why? Do you think he has something to do with this? Adrianna was very adamant about breaking it off completely when Max insisted he should experience that Virgin Islands adventure while he was young and had no responsibilities. I'm sure she thought that was the end of them. I felt bad for her and kept assuring her that she'd find someone better."

"I remember that. But now we find out that she still keeps pictures of him on her refrigerator along with photos of her family and other friends. There were several pictures of Max and Adrianna together. I hate to ask this, but is there any possibility that Adrianna would have stolen the money to help Max?"

"Absolutely not!" Meg raised her voice and looked at her sister with an indignant look on her face. Then she said, "I'm sorry. I admit that I had a fleeting doubt for a moment, too." She lowered her voice. "We have to remember the Adrianna we know. She has always been honest and aboveboard. Since Adrianna was old enough to understand, she wanted to prove she was a good girl and very unlike her mother. I remember one time when she was about twelve. She accidentally walked out of a store with a piece of costume jewelry she had intended to buy with her own money. When she found the bracelet in her pocket she made me take her back to pay for it even though we were already home. I told her we'd pay the next time we went, but she wouldn't hear of it." Meg folded a napkin over and over on the table and looked into the distance with misty eyes.

"She's also very protective of her mother, isn't she?" Beth said, probing in a different direction.

"She really is."

"So protective that she would take money to help get Meredith turned around?"

"Oh, I don't think Adrianna would embezzle money for any reason. I honestly don't," Meg said. "She might have sent her mom some money from her paycheck, but she wouldn't steal."

Tears threatened to spill out. Meg looked as if although she hated having doubts about her step-daughter, ideas such as these were forcing those little uncertainties in again. She jiggled her head, as if to shake them away. "I'm absolutely certain that Adrianna wouldn't steal."

"Have you seen Meredith since Adrianna has been missing?" Beth asked.

"No. Paul called her yesterday to tell her the police wanted to talk to Adrianna. He said Meredith didn't have much of a reaction, at least none that Paul considered worthy of a mother. She told him the police had talked to her, too."

"Since tomorrow is Saturday, let's go pay Meredith a visit. You told me Adrianna visited her fairly often. Maybe we can get some insight. Do you know anyone else who might have some information?"

Meg considered. "Yes, I was thinking about this idea already, and it would be easier with you to help. Adrianna's boss, the president of Renfro, is an acquaintance of mine. I had all three of his kids in my social studies classes. They're all grown up now. The youngest is in her last year of college. When Adrianna first went to work at Renfro Construction in the accounting department, Herb Reynolds, the president of the company, recognized her last name and asked if she was related to me. Since then, Paul and I have been to the Reynolds' house for a few dinners and staff parties. He told Paul he couldn't discuss the embezzlement, but Herb might talk to us if we visit in person. I know he likes and respects Adrianna. He promoted her to project manager after she had worked at the company for a couple of years and had proven herself. It's too late tonight, but I can call him first thing tomorrow morning. Will you go with me?"

"Well, sure I will. He may not be able to talk to us," Beth said. "I'm sure the police have warned him, but if you'll make the arrangements we'll visit both Herb Reynolds and Adrianna's mother tomorrow and find out if they can or will tell us anything. Let me know what time they'll see us, and I'll pick you up."

"Paul will be off to work early tomorrow morning. I'll call you as soon as I find out when Herb and Meredith are available," Meg said.

Not one more trip-up or fumbling drop afflicted Beth that evening, and she gave Mr. Sylvester Psycho Cat the free run of the house for the night when she finally went to bed.

Chapter 10—Walking and Talking

"It is a capital mistake to theorize before one has data. Insensibly one begins to twist facts to suit theories, instead of theories to suit facts."

- Sherlock Holmes Quote, *A Scandal in Bohemia*

Beth and Arnie nearly always walked the Trolley Track Trail together on Saturdays, and this Saturday was no exception; they were out early. The spring air was damp and chilly. Dark clouds filled the sky. Arnie wore loose-fitting shorts and his favorite short-sleeved royal blue sweat-wicking shirt, but Beth, who tended to feel the cold more acutely, wore sweats.

Part of the trail ran along a median which lay between a major conduit and a side street lined with typical Brookside two-story stone, brick, and frame Tudor-style houses built in the 1920's or 30's, all maintained with nicely painted exteriors and well-kept lawns. Beth normally made it her practice to notice which aspects of each house made it eye-catching and appealing so she could apply those concepts to her rental properties. The most attractive homes were those which sported a background color, a secondary color, and one or two accent colors. Observing the color of houses did not enter her mind today, though, as Beth trekked with Arnie through the Brookside shopping area, past back yards, and along the edge of open park areas until they reached the northern end of the Trail at the Country Club Plaza and then retraced their steps.

Beth shivered, not only because of the nip in the air, but also from her chilly contemplations. Close to home, Arnie slowed to a crawl and took her hand.

"Alright, something's eating you. What is it?" he said.

"You're not going to like it."

"Well, spit it out. Like it or not, I want to know what's up. Maybe I can help."

Beth told him about her plan to visit Herb Reynolds and Meredith Knells with Meg. Arnie stopped and pulled Beth to a stop with him.

"I understand you're upset over Adrianna's trouble," he said, "but you can't go and interrogate the owner of the company from which she's accused of embezzling. That's police work. You won't find out anything they haven't already asked. I can't believe he'll even agree to talk to you and Meg."

"I'm not yet sure he will talk to us, but Meg's going to call him and let me know. All he can do is say no. On the other hand, I'm sure the police aren't going to tell us anything. Maybe we can learn something from him which will help us know where Adrianna might have gone and why.

"As for talking to Meredith," she said, "I don't have any expectations, but Meg has told me Adrianna attempts to be close to her mother. Maybe she told her mother something which will help."

"I don't want you getting into trouble or into a dangerous situation trying to do detective work."

"We're not doing anything illegal or dangerous. Besides, the goal of the police is to find the company's money and bring the culprit to justice, and they believe Adrianna is the thief. Meg's and my goal is to help Adrianna. We know she has to be innocent and maybe is in trouble."

Arnie halted on their front walk and took Beth by the shoulders. "You're a doggone good property manager, a great gardener and cook, and you have many other fine qualities we'll concentrate on later." Arnie traced his finger along Beth's collar bone until Beth giggled and grabbed his hand. "But I still think you'd better leave the investigative work to the detectives. After this trip with Meg, will you please wait for the police to do their work?"

The sky was dark and turning angrier-looking by the minute. A cold wind blew the two onto their front porch, and a bolt of lightning with a clap of thunder stopped the conversation before they reached the front door, giving Beth an unforeseen but welcome opportunity to avoid answering Arnie's question. Spring thunderstorms were not uncommon in Kansas City, but this one threatened to be a dilly. As they pushed the door closed, Beth's cell phone rang. Arnie raised his eyebrows and grinned. Beth shrugged at the tone she kept forgetting to change and shook her index finger at him accusingly.

"Hello," she said.

"Beth, should we put off this trip? The weather forecast is for rain and possibly hail today," said Meg.

"It's supposed to be worse tomorrow. I think we need to find out as much as we can as fast as we can," Beth said.

"Okay, you're right. I'll be ready. Adrianna's boss, Herb Reynolds, is expecting us at about 9:00 this morning. He has an appointment later and wants us to come early. I already called Adrianna's mom to tell her to expect us late this morning. She wasn't even up yet and probably won't be until 11:00 or so."

Arnie stood with arms crossed and mouth tight while he listened to Beth's end of the conversation, but he said nothing about it. Instead, he closed his eyes for a moment, gave his head a quick shake, kissed his wife on the cheek, and told her she could use the shower first.

Chapter 11—Coming Straight from the Boss's Mouth

"It is a curious thought, but it is only when you see people looking
ridiculous that you realize just how much you love them."
— Agatha Christie, *An Autobiography*

A light sprinkle turned the spring tree blossoms into sparkling water
nymphs by the time Meg ran from her front door to Beth's car in the
driveway. Serious-faced Meg was wearing a knee-length belted khaki-
colored rain coat, long dark pants, and sensible black shoes, her hair
pulled to the back of her neck. All she needed was a Sherlock
Holmes deerstalker hat to make her look like a classic detective.
Regardless of the situation, Beth couldn't help smiling to herself.

"Tell me more about Adrianna's boss, Herb Reynolds." Beth said
as soon as Meg settled herself in the passenger seat.

Meg dabbed the rain from her eyes and blew her nose with a
tissue. "Like I told you before, he seems like a nice guy. He's always
been very gracious to me and so good to Adrianna. There's one thing
Paul told me that I didn't know, though. I don't think I ever told you
how Renfro Construction got its name. The company was started by
Herb Reynolds, who is now the President, and Alex Frommer, who
retired a little over a year ago. It seems as if Herb and his old partner,
Mr. Frommer, are in the midst of some financial disputes. Paul
learned about it from some people at his Rotary Club. Alex Frommer
claims that Herb Reynolds and Renfro still owe him some of the
money promised in his retirement settlement. That's all hearsay, of
course, but when a lawsuit is being considered, the grapevine usually
knows."

"Whoa, so Herb Reynolds has money problems besides the embezzlement. And he's a real go-getter—would never let his company go under..."

***

Although it still threatened to be a stormy weekend, the present cloudburst had passed over when Beth pulled up in front of Herb and Connie Reynolds' impressive suburban home. Herb Reynolds opened the door to the subtle blue-gray foyer which appeared as large as Beth's breakfast room. From there, one could see the landing at the top of a wide curving staircase. A sitting room and a large dining room occupied one side of the entry; a den and a door leading to a master suite were located on the other side. Through a hallway to the back of the house, Herb led them into the great room which opened on a sun room and a large kitchen with a breakfast nook. "Great Room" was an accurate title for the living area. It had a huge stone fireplace which separated it from the sun room on one wall and a gigantic flat screen T.V. built into another wall. A semicircular leather sectional sat in the middle of the floor and allowed loungers to enjoy the fireplace and the T.V. at the same time. Beth gazed around the room and spotted small speakers that suggested Surround Sound.

Herb seemed assured of himself and intent on making them feel as comfortable as possible, under the circumstances. His wife did not appear. "I have some coffee made," Herb said. "Will you join me with a cup?"

Both sisters assented, and while he was in the kitchen Meg whispered there were four more bedrooms and three more bathrooms upstairs and a huge living area with a pool table and an even bigger T.V. in the finished basement.

Herb set the coffee tray containing sugar, cream, and a small plate of various cookies on the oversized coffee table. "There's a story about your sister that I bet she's never told you," he said.

He was a slightly rotund, albeit muscular, man in his early fifties, and he had a successful and polished look about him despite his Saturday jeans and sweatshirt. Herb Reynolds had started out at the ground level of the construction business and had helped build his medium-sized construction firm at an early age. He passed a cup of coffee on a saucer to each woman and asked them to help themselves to the tray of goodies.

"When my younger son was in Meg's social studies class in seventh grade, we got a call from her telling us that Chad hadn't turned in any homework assignments since the beginning of the year. It was the middle of September, about a month after school started. She said he was doing okay on tests but still had a failing grade because of all of the missing assignments. Well, Chad had always been a pretty good student; so when my wife and I learned about his missing work, we were stumped. Anyway, when we approached Chad about it, he told us the reason—a reason that made perfect sense to him. It seems that I had tried to motivate him before the school year began by telling him his older brother had been in Mrs. Knell's class and had done well because she was a great teacher. I said Mrs. Knells deserved to see only Chad's very best work in social studies. Well, apparently he didn't think any of the assignments that he had completed so far had been his very best work; so he didn't turn them in. After we talked to him and clarified that we really meant for him to try hard and didn't mean the work had to be perfect—that it wasn't a competition with his brother—he handed in all of his assignments and made good grades in that class. Because of my unfortunate remarks, Chad might have failed the class. You see, Meg could have just let it go until midterm, but she was proactive with all of her students."

Beth smiled at Meg. She knew Meg was respected by the students and parents and by the other teachers, too. She sipped her coffee and nodded. "Meg has always been a good teacher. She taught me lots while we were growing up. Unfortunately, I was less than a model student and didn't appreciate her lessons at the time."

"You usually did the opposite of what I suggested," Meg said. "I started using reverse psychology. I guess you can thank me for your present fine character."

Beth nodded briefly at the compliment, but she felt eager to get to the subject at hand.

"Mr. Reynolds," she said.

"Herb, please."

"Herb, it appears that you like Meg and she tells me that you have been a promoter of Adrianna's, as well. Can you tell us what makes everyone so sure that Adrianna embezzled money from the company?"

Herb Reynolds paused for a few seconds, seeming to consider. Beth wondered if he would tell them he couldn't talk about the case. Instead, he looked serious and cleared his throat. "Yes, well, I debated how much to tell you about this. But I want you to know as much as you can so you'll understand why the police and the company suspect Adrianna."

Meg spoke up. "We appreciate that, Herb. We can't fathom how anyone can suspect Adrianna of dishonesty."

"Okay. Here's what they've found. We're a small enough company that, although we have a small accounting department which doubles as the human resources department and we hire our own bookkeepers, we also have an accounting firm which does an audit once a year to make sure all of the accounts are in order, our profit margin is in line, and so on. For several years the firm has sent the same auditor, a gal named Trish Wilcox. This year she found that the company had paid out over six million dollars more to subcontractors than was projected by our bids. After more research she learned that that very amount had been deposited into two bank accounts, which had apparently been opened by Adrianna Knells. The bank accounts were under fake company names similar to the names of the companies we use to do our construction work.

"Maybe I'd better not tell you the exact names, but, let's say we used ABC Roofing to do our roofing work. Adrianna, so it seems, opened an account for a fake company, ABC Roof. Then she wrote billing orders for the accounting department to pay both ABC

Roofing and ABC Roof. The company was, in effect, paying double for the work done by ABC Roofing. Anyway, now those fake accounts are closed, and the money is gone." Herb looked at his lap. "And so is Adrianna."

"If the account was under ABC Roof," said Meg, "how do they know Adrianna opened the account?"

"It was opened with her social."

"Someone could have stolen her social security number," Beth said.

"I would like to have her proven innocent as much as you would," Herb said, "but why did she disappear the week of the audit, and why can't anyone find her? The police discovered that her mother started spending money not long ago without getting a raise at work. Where did that come from? All of these questions point at Adrianna and not at anyone else."

"Mr. Reynolds…," Beth said. "I mean Herb. Did you have to approve the three-week vacation Adrianna asked for at the last minute?"

"Yes, of course I did. Adrianna had finished up a big project that week, and we have other project managers who could bid any new projects that came up. It made sense to me then that this would be a good time for Adrianna to take off. I didn't question why she wanted all of that vacation time at once. She's always been a hard worker."

As they left the house, Meg asked Herb Reynolds to give her best to his wife. Herb looked surprised and taken aback for an instant. "I will when I see her," he said, "She's, uh, temporarily out of town visiting a-a friend in St. Louis."

"What do you think Herb meant when he said that is wife is 'temporarily' out of town?" Beth asked when they got to the car.

"It sounds as if they're having marital problems," Meg said. "I didn't know anything about that. I haven't seen them since their staff winter holiday party. They seemed cozy as bedbugs at that time. Had their arms around each other and were laughing together."

Chapter 12—Meeting with *Mom*

"The truth, however ugly in itself, is always curious and beautiful to seekers after it."

- Agatha Christie, *The Murder of Roger Ackroyd*

No rain was falling 45 minutes later when Beth pulled into the parking lot of the sprawling, new, modern apartment complex north of the Missouri River, where Adrianna's mother Meredith Knells lived. However, the gusting wind made the tree branches slant in an impossible angle toward the northeast, and cumulonimbus clouds turned the southwest horizon the darkest of grays. A huge storm was publishing its promise to punish the area later that day.

Beth parked the car in front of the fourplex with the correct address and admired the stone and brick building and its lush, landscaped setting. "When did Meredith move here?"

Meg thought for a minute. "I guess she moved about a month ago. Wherever she got the money, it's not going to last long with the rent she must be paying."

The steps to the front door were slick, and Beth, gawking at the lovely stained glass window above the impressive entrance, tripped and almost skidded down them. She caught herself, with only a wet pant leg and slimy hands to tend to.

"I hope you get over that gawkiness before you are ninety," Meg said. "One of these days you're going to fall and break a hip."

"Thanks for your concern. Good thing I have cat-like reflexes right now. I'll start paying better attention to where I'm going when I'm ninety, okay?"

With a bearing almost as hospitable as a pit bull at a dog fighting arena, Meredith Knells opened her door without a word and then skulked over to her coffee and ashtray at a small table without offering a thing to her guests, not even a chair. The kitchen sink and counter top were filled with dirty dishes, and Beth caught a glimpse of a syringe half hidden by a soup bowl full of what looked like cold coagulating canned beef stew.

Meredith's red hair, an inch of gray showing at the roots, straggled down around the shoulders of her once-pink housecoat and emphasized her crinkled parchment face, on which appeared large red-lined eyes at half-mast, and once full lips which now looked like dried apple slices. Adrianna's mom was around 55 or 60, about the same age as Meg, but looked 15 years older. She had multiple piercings in her ears but no earrings. Tattoos covered much of her neck, peeked out above the scruffy slippers on her feet, and snaked their way from her fingers, across her hands, and into the sleeves of the housecoat. It was an exercise in imagination to picture what other body parts the tattoos decorated—not a mind journey Beth cared to take.

"May we sit?" Beth asked.

Meredith held up the limp hand that wasn't holding the coffee cup and, with no expression, motioned toward two chairs at the table. The only other furniture in the open space of the kitchen/dining/living room consisted of a dirty sofa with thread-bare throws, a scratched coffee table, and a large brand-new TV.

Meg sat on the edge of one of the kitchenette chairs with her hands clasped in her lap, her lips tight. Beth had witnessed her sister being a commander, a comedienne, and a confidante to whole classrooms full of seventh graders. Meg Knells never missed a beat when she responded to smart-alecky backtalk from kids. When in the same room with Meredith, though... The word meek came to mind.

After waiting for a few moments and eyeing Meg, who showed no signs of taking the lead, Beth got to the point. "Meredith, do you know where Adrianna is?"

"No. I already told you and Paul and the police. I don't know where she is," Meredith said in her limp, raspy smoker's voice as she glared at Meg.

"What did you tell the police?"

"I told them that I don't know anything about any of this, especially about stolen money. But I sure as hell don't think Adrianna stole it."

"We don't either, Meredith. We do have a theory, though, about where Adrianna might have gone."

Meg turned her head to look at her sister with a surprised look but didn't interrupt.

"I'm sure you remember Max Zeller—Adrianna's ex-boyfriend? Did Adrianna talk about him to you after he moved away?" Beth watched Meredith's face. The normal sour look softened, and the sides of her mouth turned up the slightest bit.

"Adrianna still loves Max. She expects him to come back sometime this summer."

"Do you have Max's address or phone number or any way of contacting him? I think Adrianna might have gone to the Virgin Islands to visit Max, but we can't get a hold of her. We want to find Adrianna before the police locate her and drag her back here in handcuffs."

Meredith looked down at her hands. She mumbled, "I can't tell you."

From shocked attention to Beth's sudden theorizing, in an instant Meg turned into strict teacher disciplinarian mode. "Meredith, for God's sake, if you know something, you've got to tell us! Adrianna has protected you all of her life. Now you need to protect her! Do you know how to get in touch with her or with Max?"

Meredith squinted and looked at Meg, her face contorted. "Course I know where Max is. Adrianna told me everything. You and Paul, all high and mighty, didn't approve of Max just because he doesn't have a college degree and wants to get some adventure before he settles down. Well, you can't stop Adrianna from choosing the man she loves, and why should she tell *you* that she's visiting him?"

Meg looked shocked and opened her mouth to say something but closed it without saying a word.

"Great, Meredith!" Beth said at once. "Then you can give us his address or phone number or e-mail address."

"Uh, no I can't." Meredith looked down again. "I promised not to tell."

"You mean you promised Adrianna? Well, this is a reason to break your promise. Adrianna needs our help."

"No, not Adrianna. I was given some—uh—insen—*insensitive* not to tell."

"Incentive," Meg said.

"Yeah, a threat. If I tell you, it'll put me and Adrianna in danger. I'm trying to protect her, too. I didn't tell the police about Max, and I can't tell you how to find him, either."

"The police will find him, you know, with or without your help," Meg said. "Then they'll probably find Adrianna, too. When they do, do you think they'll listen to her and understand her motives? No, they'll think she's been hiding out and will not be kind to her. Is that what you want?"

"No, but the guy said..."

"What guy?" Beth and Meg shouted at the same time.

Meredith picked at her fingernails as she spoke. "Well, there was this guy named Tom Collins who came into the bar where I work—a few weeks ago."

"Tom Collins?" Meg said.

"I kidded him about his name, but he said that he always got that when he went to a bar. He was a real gentleman. He bought me a couple of drinks while I was still working. You know. I put the glass under the counter and sipped on it when I wasn't busy. Then he waited until I got off work and bought me a few more. He even walked me home. I lived near the bar then. But when we got to my apartment he told me that he needed to know Max's address and phone number in the Virgin Islands. He said that he wanted the information to help Adrianna.

"So maybe I wasn't thinking too great by that time, but I gave him the name of the bar and grill where Max went to work and his apartment address and cell phone number. I got all of that from Adrianna right after Max moved down there. Adrianna wanted me to know—I think I promised I'd send him a birthday card. Uh, I mighta forgotten to. Um, anyway, after I gave all that info to Tom Collins, he took out a big wad of money and handed it to me, said that Adrianna wanted me to have it and that there would be more if I kept my mouth shut. He said that if I told anyone else about what I know, Adrianna would be in danger. He squeezed my shoulder and held me by my chin and made me look right at him. 'Danger,' he said, 'do you understand?' Well, I was sober enough to understand a threat when I heard one and to see that he meant business. So I promised to keep quiet."

"This Tom Collins—what did he look like?" Beth asked.

"He was medium height, medium build, maybe a little beer belly, but nice strong shoulders, darkish hair and a mustache, a nice big smile, and he was wearing jeans and a sweater. I think he was pretty young, like in his thirties or forties or...I don't know, everyone younger than 55 is starting to look young to me."

"Could it have been Max's friend, Joey?"

"Damn, I don't know. I never met Joey."

"Any other identifying marks, like a scar or a tattoo?"

"Uh, in the bar he pulled his sweater sleeves up, and I could see only part of a tattoo that must have been near his elbow. I don't know what it was, but the bottom of it looked like part of a design of some kind, not a face or animal and not a word."

"Has Tom Collins contacted you since?"

"I got a call after the police questioned me. He asked me if I told them anything, and I swore that I didn't. He said he'd know I had if the police showed up at Max's address in the Virgin Islands. Then he reminded me, strongly reminded, that Adrianna would be in plenty of danger, too, if I snitched."

Beth saw Meg lose her nervousness around Meredith in her concern for Adrianna. "Think about this, Meredith. This guy probably gave a fake name. No mother in this century would have called her son Tom Collins."

"Well, yeah, maybe."

"And he might have even had a fake mustache, or grew it as a disguise. There's nothing else you've told us about him which would distinguish him from a million other men. He could have kidnapped Adrianna or threatened her just as he's threatened you."

Beth put her thoughts into words. It always helped her think things through. "Adrianna's car is still at the condo building. She left Psycho Cat in her apartment. She hasn't answered her phone messages, and she only answered one e-mail with a very brief note which told us nothing except that she's alive—thank goodness. If she didn't run away from a crime, then doesn't it sound as if she was coerced into going? Maybe Max threatened her or her family if she didn't bring him the money. Maybe the guy who gave you the money found Max and held him hostage until Adrianna would bring the money. I don't know the answers right now, but I do know that we need to find Adrianna, and it'd be best if we could find her and bring her back to turn herself in before the police bring her back in handcuffs."

"You don't think Adrianna stole the money, do you?" Meredith said with an accusatory glance toward Meg.

Meg put her elbows on the table and her head in her hands. "I know she wouldn't do anything dishonest unless someone very important to her is in danger, or unless she was forced to do it. We need complete honesty here." She sat up straight and gave Meredith a piercing look. Meredith didn't seem to notice.

"Okay. Adrianna is honest. We all agree. But the police and everyone at her office seem to think the evidence against her is overwhelming." Beth stood with both hands on the tabletop and also looked at Meredith, who sat with her hands clasped around her coffee cup, eyes down, her face more haggard than ever.

Beth emitted a deep sigh before she spoke again. "If you give us the information we need to find Max, we will tell no one it was you who supplied it, and we won't tell the police until after we make sure Adrianna is safe. After all, Max has other friends and family who must know where he is. But we'll be able to locate Max and find out if Adrianna is with him much faster if you give us the information."

Meredith was not easily convinced. It took further descriptions of the possible ugly repercussions of letting Adrianna be brought in by the police, and the reiteration of the promise that her name would not be mentioned, until Meredith gave in. She located the contact data she had about Max in her grimy address book and handed it over to Beth. Against her better judgment, Beth assured her once again they would tell no one where they got the information and if they did locate Max, they'd make sure no one knew Meredith had assisted them.

"We're not going to send the police to Max," Beth said, "We'll call Max, and I hope we can talk to Adrianna first. So no one is going to hurt you for telling us."

Chapter 13—Forming a Plan of Action

"Courage is the resolution to face the unforeseen."
— Agatha Christie, *Death Comes as the End*

Beth headed straight into a wild thunderstorm as she drove away from Meredith's apartment with a silent Meg in the passenger seat. Beth, too, remained quiet, thinking her own thoughts, mentally pummeling herself for promising anything to morose Meredith. The two were jerked out of their contemplative moods by a burst of lightning and a loud peal of thunder which made the car shake. Meg began sobbing.

"Are you okay?" Beth slowed the car and took one of Meg's hands while the windshield wipers moaned with their rhythmical sweep which attempted to wipe away the tears with the rain water.

"I'm so upset. Adrianna confided in her mother and did not trust Paul and me. And now she's in so much trouble. If only we'd known; if only Meredith would have told us or the police immediately when she and Adrianna were threatened. Now I don't know what to expect or even what to think. And I hate myself for even considering that Adrianna may have actually stolen the money."

"Well, I don't believe she would have done it unless she was forced, and neither do you. There was someone else behind it, probably this so-called Tom Collins. That's what we need to find out. Let's grab a bite and talk about it, and then we can call Detective Rinquire at the police station. I promised Arnie I'd tell the police anything new I learned. Meredith may need protection, too. I'll tell the detective everything which doesn't break my promise to her. And maybe, just maybe, we can find out some more about what the police have discovered."

"Okay. Come eat lunch at my house. I have some deli ham and turkey in the fridge, and I can check my messages on the home phone and on my e-mail. I guess I'm still hoping Adrianna will get in touch and I can call and talk to her."

"Sounds good." Beth pointed the car toward Meg's house in Kansas.

***

Frowning and grimacing as if in pain, Meg came from her den back into the kitchen where Beth was fixing sandwiches. "I have no messages from Adrianna, but there is one from Detective Rinquire, who wants me to call back. I'm beside myself. I don't know if I want to hear that they've found her and have her in custody or that they still don't have a clue. And I can't even consider she might be hurt. What do you think I should tell him if he asks whether we have any news?"

Beth had been pondering what to do with the information they got from Meredith, and her heart leaped at the realization her usually confident sister had asked her opinion. She set the butter knife on the counter and turned to face Meg. "Before you call him back I want to run something past you. I'm kind of stumbling about here—well, guess I'm always stumbling about." She shrugged and made a face.

"The thing is—I've been formulating a plan. We keep saying we need to find Adrianna before the police do. But that's not going to happen if she's in the U.S. Virgin Islands somewhere and we're here. What if I look for a last minute flight to the Virgin Islands so I can try to locate her? If we call Max and he's involved, it will tip him off that we suspect she's there. Then, I don't know what will happen. Even if Max is being used, if Meredith is telling the truth, her mystery man must have a spy or spies in the Virgin Islands. They'll think Meredith talked if the police show up there looking for Adrianna, and they might harm her or her mother or Max, or all of them. If you and

Paul go, the police will follow you. They won't be trailing me. I'm merely her step-aunt and landlady."

"But wouldn't you be placing yourself in danger in case someone is watching for people who are looking for Max or Adrianna?"

Beth thought for a minute. "What if I pose as an acquaintance of Max's who's on vacation, knows he's working down there, and just wants to say hi?"

"Arnie's not going to be happy about this, and neither is Paul."

"Maybe I can convince Arnie to go with me. If not, he'll object to me going but will come around."

"Oh, Beth, I don't know if you should do this. The bad guy could hurt you, too. And what will I tell Detective Rinquire?"

"Tell him we think Herb Reynolds is having some financial difficulties. And be sure to tell him Abigail West, one of the company bookkeepers, took off work the day after the embezzlement and was looking at travel sites on her computer. He might already know all of this, but tell him also we have some suspicion Adrianna's mother is in danger. Be sure to tell him Adrianna may have gone to visit her boyfriend. We need to tell him that, but we'll let the police talk to Meredith to find out more, if she'll tell them, so as not to break the promise I made."

Meg frowned. "We just don't want to put Adrianna in danger."

"Well, I've been thinking about that, too. If Adrianna did take the money, the man who needed Max's contact information must have somehow used Max to persuade Adrianna to do it. The danger to her in that case is that she becomes the scapegoat, the only one the law can pin it on. If Adrianna didn't take the money, which we believe, then they still need to keep her safe so they can send her back to take the rap. Either way, I think they need her; any physical threat to Adrianna is probably a ploy to help ensure Meredith's cooperation."

Meg considered, "Meredith seemed too frightened to tell the police anything. The police may not even know about Max Zeller. I mean, maybe we should forget the promise, tell the police what we found out about someone wanting Max's address, and let them take care of it. I agree we still need to find Adrianna, but I don't want you to get yourself into a dangerous situation."

"Don't worry," Beth said. "I have a healthy respect for safety, and I know how to call for help when it's needed." She sat eating her lunch for a few minutes while she pondered her idea about trying to track down her step-niece. Could she do that? Did she have the courage or the ability to go to an unfamiliar place, track down a virtual stranger, and possibly encounter a nasty criminal or criminals?

She thought about herself, about past experiences. It was true that she didn't enjoy being assertive because of the fear that she might offend someone, but when confronted with a challenge, she had always been able to meet it head-on. She was in awe of Meg's legacy. Her sister had helped her through her teenage years, had taught tons of students with love and intelligence, and had raised a step-daughter who may not have had much of a chance without her. Could Beth summon the nerve to find Adrianna? If so, she might be able to make a difference in the world, too.

Beth wiped her mouth on her napkin and said to Meg, "Oh, and don't forget to tell Detective Rinquire that Abigail West has a boyfriend named Joey who is a friend, or at least a close acquaintance, of Adrianna's ex-boyfriend."

"Okay. This is to keep the detective looking at other suspects, right?"

"Exactly. I mean, this Joey looked as if he could use the money. He could be the instigator, or at least a player in the embezzlement scheme."

As Meg spoke to Detective Rinquire on the phone, Beth heard her side of the conversation. At one point Meg declared, "A Pick-up Order in the Virgin Islands? What does that mean?"

When Meg hung up, after shakily finishing her conversation, she turned to Beth. "He said they checked at the airport and found out Adrianna was on a flight to St. Thomas in the Virgin Islands last Saturday morning. Now they have a BOLO on her down there, which means the local police and the FBI in the Virgin Islands are looking for her already!"

That afternoon, after taking the time to write all the new facts in her notebook, Beth filled Arnie in on the details. "I'm going to see what kind of deal I can find to fly to The Virgin Islands tomorrow. Do you want to go with me?"

"What? Beth, are you crazy? You need to let the police do their job. A BOLO, I believe, means 'be on the lookout for.' It merely indicates they're looking for her as a person of interest; it doesn't mean they're going to put her in prison and throw away the key."

Outside the house the wind shrieked through the trees and rattled the drainpipes, and the rain which had been coming in small patches all day turned into a sudden deluge. Any debate about Beth's mental state was interrupted as Beth and Arnie ran around closing windows which had been open to the spring warmth. The air pouring in with the rain was icy, and at one point they could hear the roar of the sleet on the windows above the whir of the wind. The overcast sky became dark as night, compelling them to turn on lamps. Beth looked into the storm with her clear hazel eyes. The thought popped into her mind that this might be a prediction of the coming storm for Adrianna, for herself, or for both of them. In spite of that thought, Beth turned toward the lighted rooms and went to her computer in the small office off of the living room to start her search.

"You're right, Arnie, sweetie," she said. "This is a bit insane, but I'm sure Adrianna either doesn't know any of this embezzlement business is going on or is under the misconception that she's helping someone. You remember what I told you—Meredith said Adrianna thinks her Dad and Meg don't approve of Max. Suppose she isn't monitoring her e-mails and cell phone calls while she's in the Virgin Islands to avoid telling them she's with Max. If I can find Max, then, hopefully, I'll find Adrianna. And if I have trouble or find anything suspicious, I will immediately contact the Virgin Islands' police or the F.B.I. and let them know."

Arnie shook his head and went into the kitchen to get candles ready in case of a power outage. After a short time, he came back. "See what kind of travel deal you can find," he said with forced enthusiasm. "If you're determined to go, I'm going with you."

Beth spent an hour searching the travel sites she knew and finally shouted out, "I found a great deal through one of the online sites! We can get a three night stay at a hotel in St. Thomas plus a flight for about the same amount we might spend visiting our kids. Or, there's another deal where we could spend a little more and stay on the beach. I think the bar where Max is working is near the beach."

"Go for the beach. I need to call the office right now to leave a message that I won't be in for a few days." Arnie went back to the kitchen to use the phone.

Chapter 14—Raging Storm

"When you don't know what to do with yourself, do something for someone else."
— Lilian Jackson Braun, *The Cat Who Went Bananas*

"I can't find my navy shorts. They've got to be in here somewhere."

"Well, keep looking. You'll find them. I found my swim trunks at the very bottom of my shorts drawer. In case we have time to swim, the beach at the resort you found looks like something we shouldn't pass up."

"Oh, yeah, here's my bathing suit. I'll stick that in. Ew, all these summer clothes smell a little musty from being packed up all winter, and we don't have time to wash."

Beth threw the swim apparel into her case and plopped down heavily on the edge of the bed in the gloomy room. The artificial light couldn't compete with the storm clouds which had turned the late Saturday afternoon sky to night or the pound of rain on the windows which chilled the atmosphere.

"I sure hope we get to enjoy the resort," she said. "We should be able to find Max pretty quickly. I have all his contact information. We'll find Adrianna with him first thing, and she'll be fine and won't know a thing about the theft and will come back home and clear things up and—"

Arnie folded a shirt and refolded it. "Beth, you realize..."

"I know. I know. Things might not work out." Beth slipped off the edge of the bed and pulled the bedspread half off trying to catch

73

herself. She glanced at Arnie to find out if he'd seen her, but he was busy with his own packing struggles. She tidied the coverlet. "I'd better get busy. There's so much to do, and we need to get to bed really early to get up at 4:00 in the morning in order to make the early flight. I've got to find those good shorts."

"It won't matter how early we go to bed," Arnie said. "I'd guess we won't be sleeping very well tonight."

"We can nap on the planes, I guess," Beth said. "Argh. I remember now. The navy shorts were ripped on the Benson's lawn furniture. I put them in the rag bag and planned to buy a new pair this spring."

That evening, while Beth was online putting their mail delivery on hold for the duration of the trip, she heard a plaintive meow. Psycho Cat had been hiding under an ottoman during the worst of the storm, but now he put his front paws on Beth's leg and demanded attention. "Oh, you dear kitty, I haven't forgotten you. I'm sure Meg will look after you while we're gone. Come on up." Beth patted her lap. The cat jumped up, kneaded her legs with his paws, curled around, and lay down while she continued her task.

"You can help me pack," Beth said. She picked up the cat, laid him over her shoulder, and lugged him upstairs where he jumped on the bed and watched while she finished tucking some toiletries she'd remembered into her suitcase.

The wind picked up again, the lights flickered, and Beth's cell phone tone sounded. She kept forgetting to change it. Those mournful organ notes didn't help lighten the mood when branches were scraping against the windows, sst, sst, and her heart was beating in her throat. Beth draped a sweater over the goose bumps on her shoulders and answered the phone. It was Meg, who wanted to know whether Arnie was going to the Virgin Islands.

"He is," Beth said, "and we have vowed to scour the islands for Adrianna until we find her and whisk her back home to establish her innocence. We've never been to St. Thomas or any of the Virgin Islands, but I found maps and all sorts of information online. With those and Max's contact information, we'll try our best to get her back here in no time."

Meg said she and Paul wished they could be going, too, but Paul agreed with Beth—it made more sense for them to stay home and monitor the police findings.

"Paul says you and Arnie should take all precautions and should let us know as soon as you find out anything. Oh, I hope you find Adrianna the first day and get to take a little vacation the rest of the time!"

"We're going with that attitude."

There was a clap of thunder and a loud meow. Psycho Cat ran under a bedside table and hunkered down. As soon as the noise was gone, the cat started to lick a paw in a casual way as if that was what he had in mind all along.

"I heard that," Meg said on the other end of the line. "What a storm! It and the waiting are turning me into a trembling idiot. I forgot to tell you I'll come get Psycho Cat and bring him home with me. That'll give you one less duty tonight."

"Thanks, Meg. I was hoping you would take him."

"Of course I will. Taking care of her cat is something I can do for Adrianna until I can see her again and know she's safe."

While gathering the cat's bowls, food, and cat litter for Meg, Beth remembered they needed to find out for sure if their cell phone plan would allow them to call from the Virgin Islands. It wouldn't do to have to hunt for a phone if they needed to call the police or phone home to Meg and Paul. She put Arnie on that project. He looked it up and saw that most of St. Thomas, the island where Max apparently lived and worked, was covered by their mobile plan.

When Meg arrived, Beth was all ready to hand Psycho Cat over, but they looked in all of the napping places the cat had used since he'd been there and couldn't find him. Soon all three adults were roaming the house and calling his name, as if that would bring a cat out of hiding. They were about ready to go outdoors, thinking that somehow Psycho Cat had escaped when Meg entered.

Instead, Arnie stopped in the kitchen doorway. "Listen," he whispered.

Sure enough, there were smothered sounds of a clawless paw against wood and a tiny mew from somewhere in the kitchen. Arnie followed the thin noise to the cabinet door above the refrigerator. When he pulled it open, Psycho Cat stepped out with dignity, sat atop the fridge, and looked down at them with disdain.

"Ohmygosh!" Meg said. "How did he get in there?"

Arnie regarded the unconcerned cat. "You know, I got some candles out of there when the lights started flickering earlier. I must have left the door partly open. I've noticed Psycho Cat loves to jump to the highest place and look down on us mere mortals. And he loves to curl up in little nooks and crannies."

Arnie examined the door. "This door is fairly heavy and has a little magnet that keeps it closed. I guess our Mr. Psycho got in but couldn't manage to get back out. He must be really good at getting his paw into a small space and nudging a door open." Arnie lifted the cat off the appliance, and the big kitty nuzzled his ear. He put Psycho Cat into Meg's arms and gave him a little caress.

Psycho Cat didn't act especially happy about going with Meg and showed it by struggling so hard to get down that Meg couldn't hold on. The cat ran under an ottoman where Arnie had to pull him out and offer to carry him to the car. Beth admitted that they had spoiled the kitty. Psycho Cat meowed and squirmed all the way to the car, as if possessed of the same wicked spirit as the menacing storm, while Arnie struggled to hold on to him in the strong wind and to avoid the deepest mud puddles.

Finally, after Arnie dropped the cat into the back seat and Beth piled all of his paraphernalia into the car, Psycho Cat jumped onto the floorboard and hunkered down as if preparing to fend off the enemy. Before getting behind the wheel, Meg gave Beth a hug.

"Be careful, Beth. Please find Adrianna! Use this to help with expenses." She pressed a cash card into Beth's hand. Beth tried to refuse, but Meg got into the car before she could give it back. "Paul and I want a report every step of the way, please." Meg drove away.

That night the storm hit the city hard. Kansas City has a history of spring thunder storms, ice storms, and tornadoes. This one threatened to be a combination of all three. The weather reporters appeared on TV all evening with constant updates on the storm's pathway and severity. High winds and hail pounded the city, but apparently no tornadoes were sighted. Every time there was a boom of thunder, Beth and Arnie jumped. The lightning lit up the yard with its jagged torches, and they could see the wind forcing the trees to bend low as if bowing to the thunder gods.

When they finally got into bed, Beth, as she anticipated, was unable to sleep. At one point her doubts hit her. Her pulse raced, her hands sweated, and she felt almost nauseous, as if she were having a heart attack. She didn't consider herself especially courageous. What was she doing? Why had she talked Arnie into this? Maybe the dreadful weather was washing away her resolve. She wasn't sure they'd find Max, let alone Adrianna, and the worst thing was they didn't even know for sure that she was innocent. This last thought made Beth feel guilty for even thinking it. The emotion reminded her that she didn't want to be a quitter; she wanted to do this, not only for her sister and her family, but also for herself.

After his own spate of tossing, Arnie rolled over to face Beth. "Are you okay?"

"How can we hope to locate Adrianna if the police haven't found her? And what if she's in danger? Can we get the help we need?"

"You've thought of all of this already, haven't you?"

"Yes, but right now it all seems so impossible."

Arnie put his arms around her and whispered, "You've made a believer out of me. We'll do what we can do." Then he started moving his arms—and his hands—and his lips. He was quite an expert, and it didn't take Beth long to start tingling and respond in kind. She didn't resist when Arnie's fingers traced her collarbone, then her nipples, her navel, and on down. Afterward, they both slept more soundly than they thought possible, under the circumstances, and were jolted awake by the alarm when it was still quite dark. In the early morning quiet-after-the-storm they showered and dressed for the long day ahead.

***

During the plane ride, Arnie made notes about messages he needed to leave for his assistant, agents, managers, and whoever else he was supposed to confer with over the next few days. Beth tried to read a paperback but gave up and started studying the map she had printed of St. Thomas and the surrounding islands. She had learned online that there were lots of little islands where one could go for a day or longer excursion and that there were boats, or perhaps cabin cruisers or yachts, which could be rented. They would have a rental car to help them get to places on St. Thomas Island or to ferries crossing to other islands, but an auto wouldn't help them get to a vessel on the sea if Adrianna was on a boat or ship. Problems to be solved!

At the first layover, Arnie made his calls, and Beth called Meg to tell her where they were and to ask about Psycho Cat. She found out the cat had prowled around the Knells' house during the evening, but late that night, when the storm was so loud, he had hidden in a clothes basket in their closet. Early in the morning, after the storm was over, true to character, the crazy cat came out of the closet in a feisty mood. He started hissing at birds in the tree outside the window. Then he ran across Meg and Paul in bed and leaped onto a window seat on the other side of the room. Now he was fed, Meg told her, Psycho Cat was not to be found, maybe sleeping in some private corner of the house.

Beth called home next to check the messages on their land line. There was a call from one of their duplex tenants about a tree that had fallen across his detached one-car garage. The top of it had come to rest on his car which was parked in front of the garage door with his wife's car inside. Not only was his car damaged, but neither car could be used to go to work. What should he do?

Without a doubt, it was handy to have an insurance man as your business partner. Beth handed her phone to Arnie so he could return the call and give the correct answers. Arnie learned that he and Beth had the same insurance carrier as their tenant, but different agents. Each policy covered different aspects of the accident, and the insurance company would have to send someone out to look at the situation. This would require calls to insurance agents, tree services, and construction companies to get it all arranged and would probably take Arnie all of their layover time.

Wow, this will keep Arnie busy. Travel downtime can make him so crabby.

Beth felt a little ashamed of herself for being glad about her tenants' wind damage, but at least certain specific steps could be taken to fix that mess, in contrast to the uncertainty of how to solve the mystery of Adrianna's disappearance.

When Arnie finished his talk with the tenant, he eyed the cell phone he was ready to return to his wife. This was the phone which had transmitted all of the bad news for the past several days. Before he handed it back to her, he reset the ring tone from the three organ tones to a pleasant bird song sound.

"Here you are," he said. "Maybe now you'll get better news on this phone." He chuckled at her skeptical look. "I'm not superstitious. I just don't like the way answering your cell phone makes you grimace."

"Thanks." Beth smiled and kissed Arnie on the cheek while she put her phone away. "I've meant to change that since Wednesday."

While Arnie made his calls during their layover, Beth attempted again to call Adrianna and to contact her boyfriend Max with the number Meredith had handed over. It was something she could do to calm her nerves. She'd tried various times in Kansas City, but she figured there was always a chance one of them would answer this time. She had no luck.

Chapter 15—Finding the Way

"If you run out of ideas, follow the road; you'll get there."
— Edgar Allen Poe

The first chance Beth and Arnie had to see the beautiful St. Thomas resort where she found such a bargain rate came on Monday morning. They had arrived after sunset Sunday evening and had taken a shuttle to their lodging; so they had only briefly glimpsed the grounds by moonlight. Waking to the calming sound of waves hitting the rocks below their balcony helped Beth believe they had made the correct decision to pay the extra and get a hotel on the ocean front.

One look at the impressive lobby in daylight convinced her. From the entrance, she could see a wall of glass doors on the opposite side of the hotel restaurant, open to a view of dazzling sunlight on white surf and seagulls on aqua water. Beth surmised the vegetation-covered hills, looking like floating green icebergs in the watery distance, were some of the other Virgin Islands.

Two glass urns, one filled with fruit juice and the other with flavored rum, invited guests to relax and begin their resort experience with a taste of the tropics. The lush upholstered furniture, deluxe flower arrangements, and attractive displays in the windows of gift shops fulfilled Beth's preconceived idea of a four star resort hotel. Beth and Arnie took some time to look around and wound up at the hotel café where they sat outside on a veranda overlooking the shallow beach and the water.

"This is the life," Arnie said. "Just think. I could be sitting in my office right now, surrounded by paperwork, talking to agents all day."

Beth sighed. "It's beautiful. I could almost forget why we came and enjoy relaxing here. We'd better get busy mapping out how we're going to find Adrianna, though."

"At least, let's take time for a nice breakfast. Then I'll let you come up with a search strategy using the local maps while I follow up on the calls to our unhappy tenant and to the insurance people to make sure that poor young man's car gets rescued from the tree branches today. How does that sound?"

"Like a plan."

Late morning, they caught a ride to the closest rental car office and set off from there in a subcompact to find Max and (Beth crossed her fingers) Adrianna. Arnie got in on the driver's side, leaving Beth to navigate.

"Make sure you let me know a long time before we have to turn," Arnie said. "I'm going to have to focus on driving on the left side of the road; turning into the correct lane will take concentration."

"I'd be glad to drive," Beth said, "and let you do the navigating."

Arnie looked sideways. "Not on your life. You have enough trouble stepping off a curb without tripping. Now, where are we going first?"

Beth grinned. She had no great desire to drive on the right side, let alone the left side of the street, in an unfamiliar place. "Well, Adrianna's mom gave me Max's address, cell phone number, and name of the bar where he works. You remember he came down here to work because he has a friend who works in a bar here and told Max how great it is. Max hasn't answered any of the cell phone calls I've made to him. At the resort I got directions to the bar, but the person I asked wasn't sure how to get to the apartment address Meredith gave me. Let's try the bar. It's a restaurant, too, and might be open at this time of day for lunch."

"Point me in the right direction."

The island was surrounded by beaches, but luck located their resort on the beach on the opposite side of St. Thomas from the Mermaid Pub where Max worked. Beth used the map given to them by the rental car company to find their way the short distance across the island toward the city of Charlotte Amalie and the protected harbor where cruise ships docked every few days. The ships spilled their huge passenger holdings onto the streets of Charlotte Amalie and into its shops, restaurants, and bars. Some passengers chose to take excursions, to partake of the water sports offered, or even to rent cars and explore the island on their own. Many of them shopped, ate, drank, and took in the sights from the harbor area. It was their good fortune, according to the resort concierge, only one ship was scheduled to dock there today, around 8:00 a.m. Maybe the tourists would be on their tours by the time they got to the harbor.

Beth surveyed the scenery from the passenger seat. "Oh, look over there!" She could see the bay and some other islands in the distance. The ocean views were intermittent because much of the road led through dense jungle-looking growth, past houses and buildings, some of them ramshackle. Off the main road, farther up on the mountainside and also down toward the sea, she could see beautiful white and beige stucco houses with the characteristic coral roofs of the island showing above the lush greenery. When they arrived at the summit of the road she pointed out a docked cruise ship, many smaller boats, and dozens of sail boats, with their floating swan-like appearance, in the harbor of Charlotte Amalie. "Ah, this is where the brochure pictures of must have been taken."

"Please, Beth, I can't look at the scenery while I'm trying to concentrate on driving here."

"Sorry, but the sun on the water is so sparkly. Even the buildings are the most colorful I've ever seen—blue, yellow, green, orange, aqua, and pink—lots of white, too, and all with coral roofs. No one goes for brick red and suburban beige around here."

"I see that. I guess the bright colors and coral roofs are a Caribbean characteristic."

"Uh, slow down a little. These roads aren't very well marked. We're going to miss the turn," Beth said, returning to navigator mode.

"I'm only going 25 miles per hour," Arnie said.

Beth looked down at her map. "You need to veer left at the next intersection."

She attended to her map until they spotted the Mermaid Pub near the waterfront, close to the cruise ship wharf. The streets were narrow and clogged with traffic. It took them a while to find a place to park, but they recognized the town was built for walking. Narrow paved alleys, lined with shops of all descriptions, led away from the waterfront. The streets extended up the hill toward the main road, Dronningens Gade, named by the Danish colonists in the nineteenth century, according to the tourist literature. Arnie finally found a parking area near the center of town, and they made their way back toward the bay, past various gift shops, to the pub.

Inside, the Mermaid Pub was dim after the bright sunshine, but they saw that the side facing the harbor was all open to the outside deck. It was a casual place where a pretty young waitress greeted them in a pleasant manner. She directed Beth and Arnie to choose any table.

"We were told Max Zeller, our acquaintance from Kansas City, works here." Beth said. "Is he working today?"

"There's no employee here by that name," the waitress said, "but I've only worked here a few weeks. A friend and I came from Ohio. There seems to be a lot of turnover. Most everyone here from the States will stay and work only a short time, I've heard. The bartender, Tim, is daytime manager and has been here the longest. If your friend worked here, Tim might remember him."

Beth and Arnie stepped up to the bar while they waited for their order. Tim was a smiling fellow, who looked to be in his late thirties or early forties. He had light brown skin, tanned darker by the sun, and must have had ancestors from almost every continent. The pub was not yet busy; so the bartender came right over.

"What can I do for you?"

"I'm Arnie Stockwell, and this is my wife, Beth. First of all, maybe you can help us find a friend. Do you know a young man from the States named Max Zeller? We thought he was working here."

"Not any more. He worked here for several months last fall. I haven't seen him much since then. Funny you're asking about him, though. Several weeks ago there was a guy in here asking about Max."

Beth and Arnie looked at each other for a second. "Do you know who the guy was or why he was looking for Max?" Arnie asked.

"No, it was busy in here at the time. So I told him what I knew and went on to the next customer. The guy asking was a big fellow, calloused hands, work clothes—possibly a construction worker. Maybe you know him?"

Beth went into the act that she'd practiced in her mind for finding Max in case they had to question people about his whereabouts. "Oh, no, we don't know who that was. We're from Max's hometown, and we promised his grandparents we'd look Max up and give them a report on his health and welfare. You understand. They don't get any more than 'fine' when they call and ask him how he's doing. Do you know where he's working now?"

"He might still be working at a bar called Mango Tango on St. John Island. It's right near Cruz Bay Harbor. Cruz Bay is the main town on St. John. You can take the ferry from here or from Red Hook on the East side of St. Thomas if you decide to go. The only reason I remember where he went is because he and his friend Smitty both quit at the same time to take server jobs there. We have plenty of young people applying for our jobs, but it's hard to find two experienced ones at the same time. Anyway, they both came back to have a couple of drinks one night on their day off and said they were getting worse money at Mango Tango than they did here. Cruz Bay's got some upscale shops and resorts but not as many cruise ship customers, you know?"

"Mango Tango in Cruz Bay, thanks." Beth wrote down the information. "So Max was interested in making more money?"

"They both were. Kids come down here from the States thinking they'll have fun, make a lot of money, live on a dime, and take home enough to go to school or whatever. That doesn't happen. It's expensive to live here, and what money they make goes mostly for living expenses and for partying. Most kids take it as a learning experience—work here for a short time, and then move back home. Max was more serious about making money. He played the tourists for big tips when he was here, but he must not have made enough to stick it out." Tim made a wry face. "Besides that, the Islanders who work here don't take kindly to a Statesider making more tips than they do, you know? Sometimes there's a little tension."

"Were Max and Smitty roommates?" Arnie asked.

"I'm pretty sure they were."

"I don't know if I've met Smitty," Beth said. "What does he look like, and what's his real name?"

"Smitty's a big blond, six-foot-something, real stocky, and... oh, yeah, tattoos all over his arms. He had a job waiting tables here, but he looks more like a football player or a hearty sailor than a waiter. He's pretty quiet, not outgoing like Max. His last name is Smith, of course, but I don't recall his given name. The manager would have it on his employee records. But we just called him Smitty."

Beth pointed to an entry in her notebook. "Can you tell us how to get to this address? This is the mailing address we have for Max. Maybe we can visit him there—so we can give his relatives a report."

Tim told them how to get to the address by referring to landmarks. "The streets aren't very well marked," he said, "but you should be able to find the building with my directions. Only thing is, Max and Smitty might have moved when they went to work on St. John. It would be a long commute by ferry."

Beth and Arnie followed the bartender's directions through Charlotte Amalie and found the rooming house. Beth stumbled on the rickety banister-free wooden steps leading to an open wood porch. Not surprised, Arnie caught and righted her. When they looked up, a crumpled figure stood in the open doorway. Beth's first thought: how did Eva Standish get here, wearing a Mumu? Only this woman had piercing dark eyes rather than Eva's light blue ones, and they didn't look as if they'd be peeking around doorways. These eyes made one stop and pay attention.

As predicted, the little landlady told them Max and Smitty had moved last winter. She didn't have their forwarding address. Beth and Arnie thanked the lady and turned to go down the steps, their faces registering disappointment.

"I don't like to see people sad," the ancient landlady said to their backs. "I have something which will lift your spirits and make all your troubles better."

Arnie turned halfway and looked around, keeping his hand on Beth's elbow. "Oh, well, thank you. We'll be okay once we find our friend."

"No, wait. Wait there for one minute," the old woman said. "Be back in the blink of an eye."

Beth and Arnie looked at each other and shrugged. Both had been raised to be polite; so they waited. The woman came back in a minute and a half holding out a little jar containing a blue-green liquid. Beth raised her eyebrows.

"Oh, I know, city people have lost the old ways. But I speak the truth. This is a love potion, and more. You only have to share this tonight, or later this afternoon if you want, and you will have lovely sex—erotic, delightful, sensual. Tomorrow, you will solve your problems, and all will be well. You'll see. Here, take it." She pushed it into Arnie's free hand. "You'll see. You'll find out."

Arnie glanced at Beth for a second, and she raised her eyebrows in a "why not?" look. He pulled out two dollars and gave it to the old woman. She grabbed the cash and cackled.

"What's it made of?" Beth asked, eying the small bottle of liquid the woman put into her hand.

"Ah, it has frog, pollen, coca, quail egg, honey, and algarrobina syrup from the carob tree. It is sweet. You will like."

"Uh, frog?"

"The frog is aphrodisiac. You'll see. Them boys, Max and Smitty, they didn't believe in it. But Max got some at last. He knows. He wants things better."

At the bottom of the steps, where Beth and Arnie arrived with no more mishaps, they saw two cats nosing each other. The felines scampered off under the landlady's porch, making noises deep in their throats, suggestive of a mating ritual. Beth laughed.

"Those two must have gotten hold of some of this love potion." Arnie pointed to an empty jar lying in the tall grass next to the porch. The two giggled all the way back to the car, where Beth stowed their own jar of magic potion in the cup holder.

Chapter 16—Getting Closer

"But surely for everything you love you have to pay some price."

— Agatha Christie, *An Autobiography*

Beth hadn't expected to spend the afternoon on the island of St. John. However, the ferry ride was exciting for a landlocked Midwesterner, the views of the Virgin Islands and the seascape proved terrific, and she learned that two-thirds of St. John is a protected National Park. The rental car remained parked at the ferry landing on St. Thomas Island; so on St. John they walked through Cruz Bay, the largest village on the island, following the directions they received at the dock. They strolled past the quaint Dockside Mall, through a small park surrounding the National Park headquarters, toward a relatively new shopping center built part way up the side of the tree-covered mountain which pinned the village against the sea. There they found the restaurant/night spot, Mango Tango.

Inside, the setting was more formal than the casual seaside ambiance of the Mermaid Pub in Charlotte Amalie. They were greeted by a slim young hostess, dressed all in black; her shiny golden blond hair tucked behind her ears fell to the middle of her back.

"A table for two for lunch?" she said.

"No thank you. We'll sit at the bar," Arnie said.

"Are Max Zeller and Smitty working here today?" Beth asked. "We are acquaintances from the States."

"Oh, y'all know Max and Smitty? They worked here for a few months, but they both up and quit a couple of months ago. To tell you the truth," she said in a whisper, and looked around to make sure none of the servers was listening, "it hasn't been as fun and lively around here since they left. Max, especially, was always making everyone laugh."

"I know what you mean," Beth said with a friendly nodding of her head. "We know Max through his relatives and promised to give them an update about him. This is where we thought he worked. Do you know where Max and Smitty went when they quit here?"

"I'm pretty sure they went to a construction job at a new condo project being built on St. John. Our head server worked with both of them and knew them better than I did. He's over there, and it's not very busy. I'll send him over here."

The waiter, a young dark-haired fellow with a light complexion, also dressed in black, shook hands with Arnie and Beth. His eyes smiled as he told them about the two young men. "I still see them once in a while. We planned to hike and dive together whenever we can get a free day or evening at the same time. It's only happened twice since they started working construction, because they work days and I work a lot of nights. The condo site where they work isn't very far, though. They work for a construction company based in St. Thomas—practically a local company compared to the outfits from the States which do most of the building here. Those condos are going to be fantastic, with views some people would kill for."

He cringed when Beth's head popped up suddenly and she gave him a shocked look. "That's only an expression," he said.

"Can you give us directions to the construction site?" Arnie asked. "We'll go over there and see if we can steal Max away from his job long enough to say hi."

***

"This is incredible," Beth said, as they trudged up a narrow, unpaved road on the side of a wooded hill toward the construction site. "No wonder the police haven't been able to locate Adrianna

89

down here if we're having this much trouble even finding Max's current job." She was glad she wore her hardy walking shoes today rather than the strappy sandals she brought for resort wear. They both wore hiking shorts and quick-dry short-sleeved shirts, hers pink and his white. The quick-dry aspect was coming in handy as much as they were sweating in the heat and humidity. Beth started wiping her brow with a tissue about a fourth of the way to the condo site, and despite her sturdy shoes, she stumbled over a rock while doing so. With barely a break in his stride, Arnie caught her before she fell.

"We're getting closer to finding him," he said, "and, as far as we know, the police and F.B.I. don't know the connection between Adrianna and Max like we do. Whether we find Max or not, we're going to have to give the police the information we have; you understand that, don't you?"

"I know. This idea seems more absurd the farther we go, even to me. I thought I'd have good news for Meg by now. I hope we find Max at the top of this hill and he can lead us to Adrianna today."

***

However, Beth was to be disappointed again. When they reached the construction site, they asked about Max Zeller and were told he was not there. They did find friend Smitty, burly, shirtless, and sweating buckets. He seemed pleased for the break no matter what the reason. They learned his name was Darrel Smith and confirmed that he was the one who had tantalized Max into moving to St. Thomas. Smitty told them Max had been pining for his girlfriend ever since he got to the Virgin Islands but was determined to make some money before he went back home.

"They kept in contact, and she showed up last weekend," Smitty said. "Max took off work this week so he and Adrianna could go camping in the National Park on St. John Island. He borrowed the camping equipment from our project chief. Max makes friends with everyone he meets."

"Do you know how we can contact him, their camping location, or if he has a new cell phone number?" Arnie asked. "We'd really like to see them while we're here."

"I don't know where they camped. They might have moved around. He has the same phone number he always had, but a lot of cell phone services aren't covered on St. John, especially back in the national park. The project chief might know how to find them. He was offering to lend them the use of his cabin, too, when Max was talking about Adrianna coming."

Beth was not yet jubilant, but at least she was relieved about one thing. No wonder Adrianna hadn't answered all of the calls they had made. She probably couldn't use her phone. However, she had answered her father's e-mail last Wednesday or Thursday, the one he sent before he knew she was a suspect for the embezzlement. She must have been in town at some point last week.

"Can you introduce us to the project chief?" she asked. "We're hoping he'll tell us where Max is now. Like my husband said, after all this hunting, we'd really like to see him before we leave the island."

"The boss isn't here today. His main office is on St. Thomas." Smitty gave them the boss's name and the address and phone number of the office. "He might be there unless he's at another job site."

They gave Smitty their contact information to use in case he learned any more or thought of some other way to contact Max. Then they set off in a rather dismal mood for another round of Hide and Seek. At least that's how Beth was starting to perceive their quest.

***

To get back to the ferry landing, Beth and Arnie took the shortcut Smitty told them about on a trail which led across the mountainside through the dense forest. It was a natural surface trail winding up over the side of the mountain which sheltered Mango Tango and the village of Cruz Bay. Sticky heat and slow going posed the possibility that this "short cut" would take longer than the road they had taken to get to the building site. They were delayed even longer when they had to take refuge under a thickly foliaged tree as the hot sunshine was replaced by a sudden drenching shower. Precipitation from one cruel black cloud turned the bright green forest dark and menacing, the path slimy and slick, and the air momentarily chilly. However, the rain lasted only about fifteen minutes, and the warmth returned with the sun. By the time they reached the end of the trail at the edge of the town, Beth and Arnie were practically dry, with only rain-frizzed hair and some mud-spattering to show for their adventure.

"That was a new experience," Beth said when they emerged from the forest trail onto one of the village streets. "It could have been so much worse if one of us had slipped and fallen into that mud. I must have been paying attention to my footing for a change, or I would have taken a tumble, for sure."

"I'm not sure I didn't," Arnie said, looking at his muddy white sneakers and the streaks on his legs and shorts. "I'm going to have to dip these shoes into the ocean and let them dry before I can pack them."

Beth smiled and clucked absently. She felt the need to not let Arnie be aware of the anxious feeling in the pit of her stomach during the walk back toward the ferry landing. To be this close to Max and to know Adrianna was with him, but then to have to run down this construction boss and maybe get another detour was too much. She remained quiet and subdued on the ferry ride back to St. Thomas. While en route, she tried to make a call to Meg's cell phone back home, but she didn't get through. At that point, Arnie could tell she was about to have a melt-down.

"Remember, Beth," he said, "we've only been here one day, and we know Adrianna is nearby and is safely camping or maybe staying in a cabin with Max."

"At least we're sure hoping she's safe with Max," Beth said.

Chapter 17—Feeling Threatened

Let me tell you something, Spencer. You are talking about a perfectly normal dog as if he's possessed. You've been seeing too many Stephen King movies.

- Marcus Boswell, *Murder She Wrote*

Late that afternoon, back in St. Thomas, Beth and Arnie learned Max's project chief would not be available until the next morning. The brusque receptionist who answered the phone at the construction company office had no idea where Max Zeller might be and would not give out the boss's personal number. All Beth could do was to ask to be put on the chief's appointment list for first thing the next morning.

After returning to the resort, Beth finally got a call through to Meg. She told her sister everything there was to tell about their search for Max and Adrianna in the Virgin Islands and then had to repeat it all when Paul got on the phone. The rest of the evening Beth tried to resign herself to waiting, and Arnie suggested they take advantage of the resort. They took a dip in the pool and relaxed in the spa. Then, while the sun set over softly rolling waves, she and Arnie walked along the beach and marveled at the intermixed colors on the horizon. But, even as they watched the stunning array drop out of sight millimeter by millimeter, unexpected thoughts of the day's revelations and disappointments caused Beth's insides to churn. It was as if someone were periodically sticking a pin in a voodoo likeness of her.

She knew Arnie was attempting to calm her, but Beth wasn't sure his earlier statement claiming "Adrianna is safely with Max" was justified. After all, they had learned of Max's obsession with money and that the condos he was helping to build were enticing but obviously above his means. Perhaps he was the force strong enough to make Adrianna steal money from Renfro Construction. Everyone here was taken with personable Max, and Adrianna certainly hadn't let his influence slip away over the past nine or ten months.

They ate a late dinner at a torch-lit outdoor bistro on the beach; fresh cashew-coated Mahi-mahi cooked to juicy perfection, steamed vegetables, and rice made for a tropical feast.

"I'm going to have to ask the waiter the name of this house white wine," Arnie said. "It's perfect with the fish, don't you think?

"Arnie," Beth said, "Do you honestly think Max's boss, or crew chief, or whatever title he has—do you think he'll believe we would go to the trouble of going to his office to find out about Max if we're merely friends of his grandparents? I mean, don't you think we need to tell him something a little closer to the truth? Especially since Smitty told us he's been involved with Max's preparations for Adrianna coming to the Islands."

"Good point," Arnie said. "Normal vacationers who are just acquaintances wouldn't be chasing Max into the woods, or wherever, when they know his girlfriend is visiting. Smitty and the other co-workers didn't probe into our reasons, but a boss might not be so accepting."

"So maybe we admit we're looking for Adrianna?"

They finally decided they would tell at least a partial truth. They would say they needed to find Adrianna because there was a small emergency situation at home and her parents had not been able to contact her. Since Beth and Arnie were going on vacation anyway… They doubted that the construction project chief knew that there was a BOLO on the Islands for Adrianna, or he would have turned her in by now. Wouldn't he?

They went to bed early that night, partly because they couldn't think of any more to do, but mostly because they were tired of all the hoping and doubting, all the hunting and speculating.

"Where's that love potion?" Arnie asked. "Wasn't it supposed to make everything okay by tomorrow if we used it tonight?"

"No kidding," Beth said. "We need some kind of help. I put it over on the desk. Maybe we need to sip it, frog being an aphrodisiac and all."

They both half sat up to look toward the desk, but neither could spot the bottle in the dark. Beth giggled at the thought of drinking such a concoction. She turned to Arnie and slowly stroked his chest down, down across his abdomen. "I'll go get it," she said. Then she kissed his skin in the wake of her caress.

"Well, we really don't need help having passionate sex," Arnie whispered into her hair. Then they proved it.

Their lovemaking helped them sleep, but for Beth, the sated feeling was temporary, and after a couple hours of troubled dreams, she opened alert eyes. At first she was alarmed. What woke her? Maybe the smoldering doubts which had been haunting her dreams erupted into a blaze and startled her awake? She lay in the dark, listening to Arnie's soft snore, trying to count sheep, relax her body, think peaceful thoughts, anything to fall back to sleep. Finally, she became aware of a dim murmur of voices, almost like an echo, coming through her window. Curious, and not at all drowsy, Beth climbed out of her side of the bed, careful to not wake Arnie, and went to the open balcony door.

Below her on the beach, two men, two shadowy, burly, menacing-looking males, stood facing toward the hotel, one gesturing and one flashing a light toward the rocks at the bottom of the hotel directly beneath the room balconies. What on earth were they discussing? They wouldn't be considering climbing the rocks and burglarizing someone's room from the balcony? Her French doors stood wide open all night to let in the wonderful breeze and the sound of the waves. Probably most of the other rooms had open balcony doors, too. The moon was only a crescent. Burglars could climb unseen.

Beth stepped to the side, behind the curtain, sticking her head around only enough to watch. What should she do? She could call the front desk. They would have security people who could go check these guys out, wouldn't they? Or, was she imagining danger because they'd been tracking Max and worrying about Adrianna's disappearance? After all, this was a resort. Maybe those men on the beach had been partying until all hours and were out there marveling at how the hotel was built right above the rocky shoreline. How foolish she'd feel if she called for help and caused some innocent vacationers to get into trouble.

As she watched and wavered about what to do, the fellow with the flashlight turned toward his companion and tilted the light toward their feet. Boots. They were wearing the kind of boots she had seen the construction workers wearing on the job that afternoon. The men looked as if they were arguing or at least debating—maybe whether the climb was possible? Climbing on the rocks in those boots made sense, but shimmying up onto the balconies? Debatable.

In the next moment, the flashlight was extinguished, and Beth squinted to try to distinguish the faces. The moonlight was thin on the beach, and all she could make out was that one of them was a big blond guy. Wait. Big and blond? Like Smitty? The two started climbing the rocks. The big one clicked on his light and shone it up the wall of the hotel right onto Beth's balcony. She pulled her head behind the curtain. Had they seen her? Her heart thumped.

Before she could decide what to do, Beth peeked out with one eye and saw the men jump off the rocks and stride away toward the end of the hotel's beach. She continued to look for several minutes after they disappeared from her sight; and then she stepped cautiously out to survey the area from the darkness of the balcony.

"Beth?" Arnie called from the bed. There must have been enough light from the star-blanketed sky for him to see her silhouetted out there. "What are you doing?"

"Shh," In a soft, nervous whisper. "Come on out here, and I'll tell you, but don't make any noise.

"Do you see anyone down there?" Beth asked in an undertone.

Arnie looked around. "No one. Why?" He put his arm around her. "Did you have a bad dream?"

"No. I mean, I guess I did, but that's not..."

She turned toward the inside, pulled Arnie with her, closed and locked the doors, and pulled the drapes together with a snap. Arnie sat sleepy-eyed on the bed while Beth paced around the room telling him every detail of what she had seen.

"Beth, you really think it was Smitty?" he said.

"Well—well, I can't be sure. It was too dark, and they were too far away for me to see their faces. But both of them were big and wearing construction-worker style boots. And one of the guys was blond like Smitty. We told Smitty where we are staying. Remember? Arnie, he could have brought someone along to help him shut us up."

"Baby, you've been watching too many detective shows. Smitty sounded and looked like a good friend to Max. Consider this; the hotel could be adding on or remodeling, and those guys were out there discussing how they'll be able to work on top of that rock pile."

"Must I remind you? We are essentially in the *middle* of a detective mystery. And why would two construction workers be out there in the dark talking about how they will be working here?"

Arnie glanced at the alarm clock sitting on the bed stand. "It's only quarter to one. They might have gone out drinking after work, gotten drunk, started talking about their next big job, and wandered over here. I don't know. I know they are gone, though, and you should come back to bed and try to get some sleep."

Chapter 18—Conferring with the Boss

"'Is there any point to which you would wish to draw my attention?'

'To the curious incident of the dog in the night-time.'

'The dog did nothing in the night-time.'

'That was the curious incident,' remarked Sherlock Holmes.'"

-Exchange between Inspector Gregory & Sherlock Holmes –*Silver Blaze*

The name plate on the door read "T.M. Blakely, President." Beth and Arnie introduced themselves. It was necessary for Beth to raise her chin a few inches as she shook hands in order to look into the weathered face of the sturdily built, well-groomed, gray-around-the-temples, middle-aged man who wore jeans and boots.

"Sit. Sit. What can I do for you today, Mr. and Mrs. Stockwell?" he asked with a sociable smile.

"We…" Arnie and Beth started to speak at the same time. Beth motioned for Arnie to continue. "We apologize for taking your time. We were told you're the crew chief for a condo development on St. John, not that you're the company president."

"For that project, I'm both. I'm acting as the developer, the general contractor, the project manager, and, at times, the crew chief. We're known for being laid-back on the Islands, but in some cases we can do as much multitasking as you Statesiders. The condo development is my pet project, one I've had in mind for a long time. I purchased the land a few years ago and not until now have had the time and spending power to develop it. Have you seen it? It's got one of the best views on the Virgin Islands."

"We were at the job site yesterday," Arnie said, "and you are entirely right about the view; it's fantastic."

"Thank you. Now, tell me, how I can help you?"

"We went there to find one of your employees, Max Zeller, and were told by his friend, Smitty, that you might know where to find him and his girlfriend, Adrianna. All he could tell us was that they went camping with your blessings—and with some of your equipment. We need to speak to Adrianna."

Beth noticed that Blakely looked them over with a sharp eye for a split second before he answered. "As a matter of fact, I might be able to help you. Can I ask you why you want to find them? I've known Max only for a couple of months, and I only this week met his girlfriend, Adrianna, but I am fond of them both. Adrianna and I hit it off immediately, especially since she works as a project manager at a construction company. The two of them are off on a romantic get-away after not seeing each other for some time. If you only want to say hi, then I'd rather keep their retreat a private one just for them."

Beth appreciated Blakely's caring sentiments. She hadn't expected such a personal interest. She said, "I'm Adrianna's aunt, actually her step-aunt, and we need to find Adrianna to tell her about an emergency situation at home. We thought she might be with Max, and, when that was verified by his friend Smitty yesterday, we came here to ask for your help. We aren't here to keep her from reuniting with Max. We merely need to inform her about the situation, and we haven't been able to get her by phone or e-mail."

"In that case, of course I'll help. I won't ask for specifics, but I hope the emergency isn't a matter of life and death. I'm not surprised that you couldn't contact them by cell phone. Unless you have a radio transmitter, they are out of reach—staying in my personal little cabin hideaway on a small island some miles from here. They planned to stay there for the rest of this week, and I'm set to pick them up on Saturday. They have a radio like this one here in my office for emergencies, and it emits a loud signal which should alert them unless they're out on the water. Let's see if we can get them on the radio."

This was the second construction company owner Beth had met in the space of a week and one of the only two she had met in her life. She couldn't help comparing them. They both had the look of success and the smooth talk typical of men used to practicing public relations. However, T.M. Blakely seemed much more eager to help. Of course, Herb Reynolds might have seemed less sympathetic because he believed Adrianna robbed his company. Beth stored that thought away as she heard a male voice answer the two-way radio.

T.M. explained to Max that Adrianna's aunt and uncle were here and needed to tell her about an emergency at home. The disembodied voice asked through the static, "Are you putting me on? What would an aunt and uncle of Adrianna's be doing here? They would have just called in case of an emergency."

"No, no, seriously, get Adrianna on the radio. Tell her that Arnie and Beth Stockwell are here from…"

"Kansas City," Beth said.

"…from Kansas City and need to talk to her."

They could hear in the distance Max calling Adrianna and her incredulous voice telling him it was impossible that Uncle Arnie and Aunt Beth were in the Virgin Islands looking for her. No one from home even knew she was here. How could… Then she spoke into the radio. "This is Adrianna. Mr. Blakely, are you kidding us? Are my relatives really here?"

With a nod from T.M. and a quick demonstration of how to use the talk button, Beth stepped up to the radio, attempting to keep her voice calm. "Hi, Adrianna, this is Aunt Beth. Sweetie, this isn't a joke. Arnie and I are here to tell you about an emergency back home, and we need to talk to you in person. Can you get back to St. Thomas today?" She looked questioningly at T.M. He nodded.

"What emergency? Is it Poppa or Meg or my Mom or...?"

"No, honey, everyone is okay. This is about you."

"Aunt Beth! Is this a ploy to get me back home and away from Max? Did Poppa and Meg talk you into doing this? Because—if so, it's too late!"

For a long moment, Beth was speechless. She didn't expect this reaction. She began to address Adrianna's accusation. "No," she said, "no, no, this isn't a trick. Your Dad and Meg like Max. If they criticized him, it was only to support you when he left and you seemed so lonely. We..."

Arnie stepped up and took the control from her. Beth noticed him watching Blakely, and he had apparently made the decision to trust him and more fully explain their true mission to Adrianna, even if this man overheard. "Adrianna, this is Uncle Arnie. We're not here because of you and Max. We're sorry to interrupt your rendezvous, but something has happened at Renfro which puts you in jeopardy, and it has to be addressed immediately. Everyone has tried to get in touch with you by phone and e-mail for the past several days, probably since you've been on your island with Max."

Blakely left the room without being asked and closed the door without a sound. Arnie glanced at the door, looked relieved, and continued with more explanation. "Adrianna, you've been accused of a crime. We need to see you in person in order to explain it all. Is there a ferry from where you are, or do you have access to a boat? We'll hire a boat and come to you, if need be."

After a short silence on the other end Adrianna asked, "A crime? What kind of crime? At Renfro?"

"We really need to see you in person. This open radio isn't the way to tell you."

"Well, okay, Uncle Arnie. But we only have a little putt-putt boat here for going out a short way, and we have to wait for Mr. Blakely to come back here next weekend and pick us up in his big boat to get back to St. Thomas."

Beth had been standing next to Arnie hugging herself tightly enough to make red marks on her arms with her fingers, listening with such intensity she forgot to breath. Finally, she leaned around Arnie and pushed the talk button. "Adrianna, we'll find out from Mr. Blakely how to get there and be there as soon as we can. We have a lot to tell you."

When Beth opened the door, she found T.M. Blakely conferring with his secretary, a tall, stocky, middle-aged woman who looked as if she might be more comfortable on the job at a construction site than sitting at a desk. Blakely told Beth and Arnie he surmised this emergency required quick action and he had rearranged his schedule so he was free to take them over to his cabin where Adrianna and Max were staying. The secretary was scrutinizing the Stockwells with disapproving interest. Blakely motioned them back into his office.

"Thank you, Mr. Blakely, for your kindness." Arnie said. "We don't want to inconvenience you. We can rent a boat and get there on our own if you'll give us directions."

"You're welcome, and please call me T.M. It's not an inconvenience. I wish to help."

"We don't want to involve you in this, T.M." Beth looked at Blakely's face. He smiled in a kind manner and looked her in the eye. She decided to trust him further. "You could be accused of harboring a fugitive. We're here to bring Adrianna back to Kansas City with us so she can prove herself innocent of a criminal act of which she's accused. You've already helped us find her, and we're grateful, but we don't want to get you in trouble."

"I think you're putting yourselves in the same uncertain situation. And I'm willing to take the chance. I don't know her as well as you do, but I don't think Adrianna is a criminal, either."

On the way to the dock, Beth called Meg and left a message saying they had located Adrianna, she was safe, and they were on their way to see her. She decided to wait for Adrianna to call and talk to Paul.

Chapter 19—Cruising to the Island

"One of the saddest things in life is the things one remembers."
— Agatha Christie

The Cornerstone wasn't the biggest cabin cruiser at the docks, but it impressed Beth as one of the prettiest. T.M. assured them that it was one of the fastest. It was painted blue and white and had a deck polished to such a high shine Beth could see her worried face reflected back at her. The pilothouse was enclosed, and a spacious cabin provided the comforts of home below deck.

Beth and Arnie lounged and watched the aqua water split into white foam on each side of the bow. They could see several of the small islands in the calm sea, possibly some of the same they had noticed from St. Thomas. The bright sky and fluffy white clouds belied the tension Beth felt, but the regular rhythm of the engine propelling the boat through the water toward Adrianna helped steady her nerves.

Beth not only appreciated the beauty of the aquatic world on the trip over, but she also accepted with eager relief the sympathetic help being provided by T.M. Blakely. Arnie, on the other hand, told Beth they should not put too much faith and trust in a stranger. A certain amount of tension developed between the two men until, half-way through the trip, Blakely motioned for Beth and Arnie to step inside the wheel-house.

"I realize you may think it strange—for me to leave on a work day to help you with a problem which is none of my business, and I want to tell you why I'm doing it," Blakely said. He turned to look at them with a frown of sincerity, while they stood contemplating the fancy dials, before he returned his focus to the rippling waves.

"It's so good of you to explain," Beth said. "In fact," she said and glanced toward Arnie, "we did wonder a bit."

"You see," Blakely said, "I had a son, a young man who, I'm afraid, was terribly spoiled by his mother and me. We paid his entire tuition plus room and board for a fine university in the U.S. and gave him a great deal of spending money besides. After he graduated and returned to St. Thomas, I started grooming him to go into our family construction business, which I started as a young man about his age."

"Uh-oh," Beth said.

"Exactly… My son had learned some wild habits while away. I don't know how he ever earned his degree, because drinking, drugs, and drag racing had become his true occupations of choice. He developed the habit of—I can't call it working, but—coming into the office for half days and then taking off on one of his fast vehicles. He started hanging with the crowd of young people from wealthy families who come to the Virgin Islands on a whim to work and party—mostly party."

T.M. took a deep breath. "At only 25 years of age, he died as a result of a motorcycle accident on one of the lonely mountain roads on the Island, in the middle of the night, after overindulging at a party. I was left," Blakely said, "with pain and anguish, to always wonder if I could have prevented the behavior that led to the accident."

T.M. told them he had seen in Max the son he had wanted. Max was experienced in construction work, but, more importantly, he worked with dexterity, confidence, and intelligence. He didn't drink on the job like some of the crew, and he kept everyone in good spirits. Blakely declared he was determined to have not been a bad judge of character to have believed in Max and his charming girlfriend. Being wrong about them would reinforce the thinking he despised--that he was somehow responsible for the death of his son, whom he had loved and trusted, too.

The cabin cruiser sped along through the sparkling water, its occupants silently anticipating the approaching meeting. For some reason, T.M.'s revelations about his son renewed Beth's faith in her step-niece. The ability to steal from Renfro wasn't in Adrianna's nature, she was sure. Beth reached into her purse and pulled out the notes she had written about the people connected to the case, Adrianna's good friend Abby, Abby's boyfriend Joey, Adrianna's mother Meredith, the company president Herb Reynolds, Meg, Paul, and now Max. They all had close and loving relationships with Adrianna. Had some circumstance or pressure turned one of these people into a criminal, or was the culprit someone she hadn't found yet? Perhaps it was another bookkeeper in the firm, the accountant, the floosy blond at the desk next to Abby's, or even Abby's boss, Mr. O'Neill. Anyone in the company with access to the records could have transferred funds on paper and taken advantage of Adrianna's absence to put the blame on her.

Then there was still Max. Beth hadn't talked to him yet, and he was the one with, seemingly, the most influence over Adrianna. Adrianna was here with Max—Max, who was intent on finding sources of money. The missing money might be here, also. Did Adrianna, like Tolstoy's Anna Karenina, fall for a handsome, charismatic adventurer and, for him, give up her family, her reputation, her home? And her cat! Psycho Cat—the thought made Beth smile in spite of herself. Adrianna wouldn't leave him behind, would she? But then again, Anna Karenina had left behind her cherished son to go with her lover—leading to that tragic downfall.

The cabin cruiser approached a dock on a small island. They would very soon see Adrianna and Max and get a better feel for why Adrianna kept her whereabouts unknown. T.M. had radioed ahead; as they approached the dock they saw Max standing ready to help tie up the craft. Adrianna stood slightly behind him with a severe look on her face. No big smile to greet them today. At Adrianna's feet, Beth spotted a tiny long-haired, mega-whiskered tabby cat with white feet and stomach sitting on its haunches in a prissy manner with its head cocked, seeming to be in sync with Adrianna's wariness at the approach of this group.

Adrianna and Max were both dressed in shorts and tee-shirts with sneakers on their feet. Max, more muscular than Beth remembered from the brief encounters she'd had with him, was deeply tanned. His teeth looked particularly white and his eyes emerald green on his strong-jawed face with its day-old stubble of beard. Adrianna bore the rosy look of having spent time in the sun after a long winter. She had pulled her dark hair back in a ponytail; the auburn highlights glinted in the sunlight.

"Aunt Beth, Uncle Arnie, can you tell me what this is all about? Mr. Blakely, do you know what's going on? This is the most bizarre thing that's ever happened to me." Adrianna called from the dock before they even got off the boat.

While Blakely threw the ropes in and Max secured them, Arnie helped Beth off the side of the boat and then jumped off himself. Adrianna stepped over to hug them, and while she was greeting Arnie, the kitten grabbed Beth's attention. Its ears flattened, it slunk toward the end of the dock. Weird for a cat to position itself closer to the water if it was nervous, in Beth's opinion. However, with a quick glance, she saw T.M. and Max approach from the land end of the dock after tying off the front of the boat. Maybe the pounding of their footsteps had spooked the little cat?

Max stopped next to Adrianna to be reintroduced and shake hands with Beth and Arnie, but T.M. went to the end of the pier. "Where'd this cat come from?" he called out as he hovered over the tiny fur ball, huddling on the outermost board of the long dock.

"Mittens belongs to the caretakers," Adrianna said. "She's a kitten they brought over with them yesterday because she seemed too insecure to be left at home with their dog. When I took such an interest in her, they offered to leave her with me until they come back on Friday. We keep her outside so she won't get fur all over your house, but whenever I'm outside, she's my little shadow."

Adrianna turned her attention back to her relatives with a little private cat lover's smile, seemingly certain her explanation would suffice. T.M. didn't reply. Instead, he started climbing a short ladder into the back of the cruiser where he had stored a cooler full of drinks and snacks. Beth turned toward Adrianna, ready to start addressing her concerns. But in that split second before her eyes left the scene, did she see T.M.'s foot slide sideways and knock the kitten into the water off the end of the high pier before he bounded up the ladder? It had to have been her imagination. Kittens are always getting underfoot, in the way, and accidently stepped on. T.M. seemed oblivious, concerned only with accessing the gate at the top of the steps.

"The kitten!" Beth screamed and pointed to the place where Mittens had recently been hunkering.

They all looked and started toward the end of the dock. Adrianna sprinted ahead. She dropped to her stomach and reached out toward the small soaked body which had resurfaced, was wildly treading water, and was about to be rushed under the pier by the incoming waves. The water was deep here, for the sake of the boat docking, and the tiny kitten was sure to be drowned or smashed into one of the pilings before it could swim the long stretch to the rocky shore.

Max hesitated only long enough to kick off his sneakers before diving into the sea. He came up, shaking the water off, and looked around for the kitten. No blob of fur was apparent on the bright waves.

"She's under here. Can you find her?" A note of panic in her voice, Adrianna pointed under the dock. "Mittens," she called.

Max swam into the darkness and stayed there longer than Adrianna could take it. "Max? Max!" She went to the side, dropped onto her stomach again, and leaned as far over the side as she could without falling off, her ponytail almost dragging the water. "Come on out. Don't get yourself hurt."

Max swam out directly below her. In one hand he held up what looked more like a big-eyed jellyfish covered with seaweed than a cat. Adrianna reached down for the animal, and Beth and Arnie each took an arm and helped her to her feet. She picked the seaweed off while cooing to the dripping creature, and then wrapped the scrap of life into the bottom of her tee-shirt. Meanwhile, Max swam to the lowest end of the dock where he climbed out and made his way back toward the group, wringing out his shirt as he walked.

"Hey, Max, great rescue." T.M. called from the yacht where he had the cooler at the top edge of the ladder. "Can you two guys take this cooler from me so I can climb down?"

The kitten wriggled its way out of Adrianna's shirt, jumped to the deck, shook herself, and then loped the length of the dock past the approaching Max and along the path toward the gardens as if being chased by a nightmarish black German Shepard.

"She'll be okay," Beth said. "She'll probably find a sunny spot to dry off and then lick herself clean before she conks out for a long afternoon catnap."

Chapter 20—Connecting at the Cabin

"The impossible could not have happened; therefore the impossible must be possible in spite of appearances."

— Agatha Christie, *Murder on the Orient Express*

"We'd best sit down for this," Beth said when Adrianna brought up the subject of being accused of a crime. They walked toward the house in silence and found wooden lawn chairs on a huge flagstone patio facing the sea.

"Hold on for one minute, and I'll bring out some glasses for drinks and some plates and napkins for the snacks I brought along," T.M. said. "This has been some kind of day for all of you, and you've got to be starved."

"It'll give me a second to put on dry clothes, too," Max said.

Adrianna turned her head toward the retreating men and looked irritated.

"Did someone refer to this mansion as a cabin?" Arnie said when the two men left.

Through the glass patio doors, past the comfortably decorated living area, the lanai in back of the house was visible. A large swimming pool enclosed by a screened cover was surrounded by bamboo furniture. Bright chair pads, mosaic table tops, potted plants, and fountains screamed luxury. Another screened-in terrace, from which one could see the water on the other side of the island, ran along an entire side of the house off of the kitchen and dining areas.

"I don't want to wait anymore," Adrianna said, ignoring Arnie's bemused question and the absence of Max and T.M. "Please, tell me what the heck happened at Renfro and what crime I've been accused of committing before I start screaming in frustration."

Beth sat on the edge of her chair, took a breath, and began. "First, let me assure you that, as far as we know, you're simply wanted for questioning. A large sum of money has been stolen from Renfro, and it was money from your last big project. The reason we came all this way to find you is because we couldn't contact you."

Max appeared in the doorway in time to hear this pronouncement. He sat down next to Adrianna without comment.

Beth said, "Your disappearance and the fact that you didn't return phone calls and e-mails from us or from the police made your absence appear more and more suspicious. We were all afraid you'd be picked up by the police before we could talk to you. Your parents are worried sick."

"My mom, too?" Adrianna said.

"She means your Poppa and Meg," Arnie said. "Your mother gave Beth some information which helped us to find you, and I'm sure she's worried, also."

Beth explained more about the embezzlement, how it was discovered, and why Adrianna was a suspect. Pausing to nod a thanks to T.M. when he reappeared and handed out bottles of water and soda and set out snacks, she went on to describe her conversation with Herb Reynolds and his explanation about why Adrianna was incriminated.

"We don't know if the police have enough evidence to arrest you, but it'd be best if you could tell them your story," Beth said. "At least Arnie and I now know why you didn't get our messages here on this island. That's a start."

Adrianna sat through all of this informational speech as if frozen. When the lengthy explanation was finished she looked out at the sea, then at Max. Her expression was one of disbelief.

Max put his arm around her. "Adrianna is completely innocent, you know, not only of the crime, but also of the lack of communication. I was the one who convinced her that she was right not to tell her dad and step-mother all about us yet, and I was the one who brought her out here—where we haven't been able to get or return messages for a few days."

Adrianna looked at Max with intensity and then gave him a weak smile. "It's not your fault, Max. I didn't want to tell Dad and Meg because I don't think they approve of Max very much. I wanted to make sure we really are getting back together before I told them." Max drew her closer.

The group sat without speaking for several minutes. Seagulls flew around the white sandy shoreline in the clear, bright air, and a cool breeze blew off the water. It would be nice to let Adrianna and Max stay here, safe and comfortable. Beth knew, imagined they all knew, staying was impossible.

Finally, Arnie broke the silence and spoke to Adrianna. "Back home, I thought Beth was a little crazy to want to fly here and find you. I figured your return was up to you and the police. I still think we're nuts, because I'm not sure how we're going to get you back to Kansas City without getting us all in trouble. But you know you have to go back and clear yourself as soon as possible. Right, Adrianna?"

Adrianna didn't hesitate. "Absolutely," she said. "I'll change my airline return ticket and fly out as soon as we can get back and arrange for it."

"I know I'm piling bad news on bad, but I have to tell you that you might be listed on the airline passenger lists as a person of interest wanted by the police, and you could be picked up at the gate," Arnie said with an apologetic look.

"If that happens, I'll be ready for it." Adrianna raised her chin to a determined angle so that everyone present believed her.

Chapter 21—Flying Home to Face the Frenzy

"Mysteries force a man to think, and so injure his health."

- Edgar Allan Poe, *Ne Pariez Jamais Votre Tête Au Diable Et Autres Contes Non Traduits Par Baudelaire*

It appeared to Beth that T.M. Blakely, the owner of a successful business and possessor of impressive personal paraphernalia, was used to skillful decision making. From what she had seen of him so far, however, passionate Beth couldn't help speculating that in certain situations T.M.'s heart ruled. She had noticed him listening without comment and watching the four people ponder their situation.

He must be so full of concern he's sitting there thinking about the best course of action to take to help all of us in this situation.

At last, T.M. said. "Adrianna, I might be able to keep you from being picked up by the police until you're safely home and ready to talk to them. As I told Arnie and Beth, I've had my share of disappointment and reason to deal with the law on the behalf of a young person. I should back away from this whole thing, but I have this feeling that you're worth the involvement. Several of the island law enforcement officers are friends of mine. I'll ask them to put you in your aunt and uncle's custody until you reach Kansas City.

"Mr. Blakely, I don't know what to say. You are incredible for believing in me and—and for giving us so much—so much help." Adrianna got up and hugged her benefactor.

"There's a caveat, though," he said, "It would help me if Max stays around to work on the condos for a while. I'm going to Miami next week to select certain items for the building project. He's one of my best people, and, you know the saying, 'While the cat's away, the mice will play?' I need him to make sure that doesn't happen while I'm gone."

Max balked. He said he didn't want Adrianna to leave and face this without him. Adrianna took him aside. Beth could hear the two whispering heatedly and then more quietly before they came back to the group on the patio and agreed Max would stay at least until Blakely returned from his purchasing trip. Later, while Beth helped her pack, Adrianna told Beth she didn't want to get the decision to stay with Max tangled up with the emotions she was sure to encounter while trying to clear up the theft allegations. Beth was taken aback. She put her hand on Adrianna's arm.

"Sweetie, if you can think so clearly throughout this entire affair, you won't have any problem," she said, and hoped she wasn't being too optimistic.

They spent the rest of the afternoon eating a little, packing, and closing up the cabin. It was later than they had planned when they finally were able to cruise back to St. Thomas. The sea water was smooth, and the match-lit sunset over the sea burned into a blaze of hot pinks and oranges radiating into the cool purples and grays of the clouds on the western horizon. Beth caught her breath as she stood at the rail to watch while the embers burned themselves down to an orangey-pink glow.

"Look at the sunset, Arnie, isn't it glorious?"

"Nice—lovely," he said, pulling her close to his side and gazing at her shining face as well as at the sky.

Splendor, nightfall, peace, darkness, drama… Normally, Beth felt she'd like to grab hold of a paintbrush or at least a camera to capture such contradicting grandeur. Now, instead, in the quiet, accentuated by the slap of water on the sides of the craft, Beth's mind began racing with worries about the immediate future. When she studied the faces of her companions, she noticed that they all looked deep in thought, also. For a few minutes, she considered leaving Adrianna's welfare in the seemingly very capable hands of T.M. Blakely and going home with Arnie the next day to her ordinary, serene existence. The truth was that she was not only nervous, but she was scared. It wasn't only for Adrianna's sake; she and Arnie could well be snagged and hauled into custody, too, or be hurt by some unknown booted criminals. How could she handle such a situation?

T.M. played some soft CD music, and after a short time Beth could see Adrianna and Max standing at the bow whispering and caressing. A few words drifted back to her. Max seemed to be assuring his 'Anna that everything would be okay. Beth and Arnie sat side by side with their arms around each other and watched the colors fade from the sky. Gradually, Beth's escape instinct began to fade.

"I think we're lucky to have T.M. helping us," she said in a whisper into Arnie's neck. "This is the correct way to do it—to get Adrianna back home before taking her to the police, right?"

"I'll all work out," Arnie said. "It's hard to know exactly the best moves since we've never had to deal with anything like this. But I'm glad you decided to take this trip. We found our girl, safe and sound." He kissed Beth on the forehead.

On shore the evening was busy. Blakely went to his office to make phone calls to his law officer friends. Beth and Arnie headed back to the resort to pack. When Beth called home to let Meg and Paul know what was going on, she could hear the jubilation in their voices.

"Adrianna called us already," Meg said. "She started crying when she was telling us how sorry she was to have made us worry. Then I started crying and told her how sorry we were that she felt she couldn't tell us about Max. All in all we almost drowned our phones. So I didn't get all of the details. Adrianna said she'd call Meredith, too, and we let her brother know she's okay."

"She's fine so far. Now we have to get her back there to prove her innocence".

"Paul knows of a good lawyer he's going to contact."

"A lawyer, absolutely, good thinking, and have you heard from the detective?"

"Detective Rinquire came by last night to find out if we'd heard from Adrianna. At that point, of course, you hadn't found her yet. But he kept looking around as if he were looking for evidence that she might be hiding out here. Finally, we offered to take him on a tour of the house to prove she wasn't here. He backed off and admitted that there was no indication that she had returned from the Virgin Islands yet."

"Well, I guess you'd better call and tell him Adrianna is on her way home, but it might take her a couple of days to get there. As soon as we know whether we can get Adrianna on our flight tomorrow morning, I'll call to let you know when we'll be there. After I talk to Adrianna a little more, I'll be able to tell you if she has any ideas about someone else the detective should check out as a suspect."

"I'm glad she's with you, Beth. We already told her, but tell her again that we love her—and you, too."

As it turned out, Blakely arranged everything with the police and went online with Adrianna's information to cancel her return flight and purchase a ticket for her on Beth and Arnie's flight. Adrianna and Max spent the night on the cabin cruiser, thanks to Blakely's continuing generosity. Beth couldn't know how the two lovers slept, but her night was a little stuffy. She refused to leave the windows open to the balcony of the hotel, and she woke up at every slight noise. No one appeared on the beach or tried to break into the room, but she felt a little groggy the next morning.

The Stockwells picked Adrianna up at the dock on the way to take the rental car back and catch the shuttle to the airport. Max waited for them to arrive before leaving to ride the ferry to St. John where he shared a small upstairs apartment with Smitty. He acted cheerful and encouraging. For Adrianna's sake, Beth assumed.

"You'll be back home this afternoon, tell them your story, and call me by tomorrow morning with the good news that you've been cleared," Max told Adrianna. She replied with a big kiss and thanked him for his confidence. They lingered together holding hands for a few minutes.

Taking the cue, Beth discretely followed Arnie into the cabin to help retrieve Adrianna's luggage. "I'm worried about Max not coming back to Kansas City with us to corroborate Adrianna's story," she said. "I know that's not going to happen now, but doesn't it seem a little weird that T.M. is relying so heavily on Max since Max has only worked for him seven or eight weeks?"

Chapter 22—Addressing the Issues

'Eliminate all other factors, and the one which remains must be the truth.'

- Sherlock Holmes Quote, *The Sign of Four*

Adrianna wouldn't be seated near Beth on the flights. They might not have much time to talk after they got home, what with her parents and getting back to work, and... Did they put people in jail when they were only suspects? Beth hoped not. In any case, during the ride to the airport she attempted to fill Adrianna in on all the details of her visits with Adrianna's mother, Meredith, her boss, Herb Reynolds, and her bookkeeper friend at Renfro, Abby West. Adrianna was not stopped at security by police officers or airline personnel, probably thanks to T.M. Blakely's influence with local law enforcement. The smooth arrival and check-in gave them a bit of time to sit and talk before boarding.

"Adrianna, how did you meet Max?" Beth asked.

"He was the supervisor of a crew for one of the subcontractors on a job for Renfro. I talked to him when he came into the office one day to check on some billing problems. That was when I was still working in the accounting department. We started talking, and I found out he was going to business school at night while working at his job all day. We started talking about school and such, and, well, we clicked."

"Does he know anyone at Renfro?"

"He knows Abby West. Max and I hung out with Abby and her boyfriend at the time. In fact, Max introduced Joey, a guy he knew from work, to Abby on a blind date. He met some of the other Renfro employees briefly when I invited him to a company TGIF at the Brooksider Bar one time. That's all I can think of."

"Do you have any idea who might have wanted Max's contact information enough to bribe and threaten your mother?"

"No. I don't get it. Why did the guy need Max's address, and why didn't he ask one of Max's friends or me?"

Adrianna considered her own questions. "Oh, yeah, the man was trying to frame me. He probably doesn't know Max's friends and couldn't ask me because it would have made me suspicious. It might be someone who doesn't know me personally," she said, half to herself. "But Max hasn't been contacted by anyone, and how did that guy know I was going to visit Max at this time? I didn't even know myself until the project was done."

"Your mom didn't give a very complete description of the guy to whom she gave Max's information--medium height and weight, darkish hair--but she did say that he has a mustache and a large tattoo on his upper arm which extends to right below his elbow. Does that ring any bells?"

"I know several guys who have tattoos on their arms. I work with people in construction, you know. Well, not all construction people have tattoos," Adrianna said with a crooked grin. "Lots do, though. Max has one; it's on his upper arm. But I can't think of anyone who has a mustache *and* the kind of tattoo you described. I'll think about it; maybe someone will pop to mind."

"How about Abby's boyfriend, Joey?"

"Joey Zitelli? Yeah, he has tattoos. I can't remember how far down on his arms. I know I could see them when he wore tee-shirts. He could have a mustache, too. I haven't seen him for months. What do you know about Joey?"

"I visited Abby at her apartment after I found out about the theft. He was there. It looked as if he lives there."

"Well, that's news to me. I haven't hung out with Abby for a while, but she broke up with Joey several months ago as far as I knew. They must have made a big leap in their relationship in the past couple of months if they're living together."

"Would Joey and Max have remained in contact after Max went to the Virgin Islands?"

"I doubt it." Adrianna thought for a moment. "Abby and Joey met through Max, but Max and Joey were really just acquaintances from working construction together—not good friends like Abby and me."

"What happened to your friendship with Abby?"

"I'm not sure. It might be my fault because I've been so busy with work since I've become a project manager that mostly I want to veg with Psycho Cat when I have time off. I begged off a few times, it's true, but we still hung out sometimes. Then, she became a little—I don't know—distant, like she was trying to push me away. I finally gave up on asking her to do things after her attitude changed. I thought maybe we became friends simply because we worked together, and now she doesn't feel comfortable around me. And we no longer have Max and Joey to double date with, and...stuff like that."

A serious look crept into Adrianna's eyes and onto her lips a wistful smile. "I remember that first double date. The guys planned to take us to a movie and then out for drinks, but Abby suggested we take in a summer festival in Raytown, her hometown. You know, it's about twenty minutes from midtown. Anyway, we went over there and had a great time going on the carnival rides, eating brats and cheesy fries, and acting silly. It's how Abby was, always made things fun."

"Do you think Abby could be the company embezzler?"

"No!" Adrianna said, "I'm pretty positive that Abby is honest and very dedicated to doing her job well. Um, I guess she would be in a good position to do it...being in the accounting department." Adrianna looked troubled at that thought. "There's another bookkeeper, though, the one that took my place. Have they investigated her?"

"I'm not sure, but I think they've investigated everyone at the company in any position to have taken the money. Unfortunately, as I told you, you seem to be the prime suspect at this point."

Adrianna didn't respond. She frowned and studied her hands. Beth, Arnie, and she were sitting in the gate waiting area at the airport, and Adrianna looked as stiff as the plate glass windows through which they could see the runways outside. Would Adrianna maybe need a strong drink or two or a sedative to get home without shattering? Beth saved that thought and took the time to ask a few more questions while she had the chance.

"Who in the company could have created false subcontractor accounts in your name? Who had access to your social security number?"

"The company executives who hired me would, I guess, and the ones who write the payroll checks and administer the health insurance forms. That would include Abby, of course. Our accounting, payroll, and human resources departments are administered by the same person. Pete O'Neill is in charge, but the bookkeepers actually print the checks. I did that job at one time."

"Mr. O'Neill, your former boss, right? Does he have any reason to steal money and implicate you?"

"He…" Adrianna looked down and blushed a bit. "I don't think he would do anything like that…but…well…when Max first left, Pete O'Neill came on to me big time. I mean, he was pulling me aside to talk and leaving me private little notes. He even sent flowers to my apartment. I went out with him a couple of times. That kind of attention is hard to resist. But I wasn't interested. He's not my type, and he's old. He's like, forty or so, divorced, and pays child support for two kids. Besides, I'm not the only woman he flirted with at Renfro.

"When Pete O'Neill was interested in me, and I became his confidante, he told me about his mother, who raised him alone. He said she was always concerned with attracting men and never paid much attention to him. Those men gave Pete gifts and vacations, but they took his mother's attention away from him. I think after that, even while he was married, Pete plied his charms to attract every woman he met, trying to fill the void his mother left. Then he used each woman until the next one came along. Some women, though, became infatuated with his charisma and kept trying to lure him back. Allison, Renfro's front desk receptionist, is one who still pines for him."

"Ha. I wondered about that," Beth said.

"He seemed okay with my turning him down, and we remained pleasant in the office. Then I got the promotion to project manager, and Pete wouldn't even talk to me anymore. Maybe I make more money than he does or he's envious or something. Actually, I work harder than he does, and I don't feel bad about making more money. But I do feel bad about losing contact with my friends in the accounting and human resources office. Anyway, I think they're good people. I can't see any of them being dishonest and evil enough to steal that much money and blame it on me."

Adrianna squeezed her eyes shut and pressed her lips together; it looked as if she was trying not to cry. Beth patted her arm. This new role as interrogator was emotion laden. How did police investigators do it all of the time without being empathetic? Maybe they were moved but trained to suppress their feelings and concentrate on the facts. She remembered how Detective Carl Rinquire seemed to soften up after he met and talked with Adrianna's dad and step-mother. Beth took a deep breath and continued her questioning. She wanted to get as much information from Adrianna as she could, while she could.

"Your boss, Herb Reynolds, certainly has access to your information. Can you think of any circumstances which might cause him to steal from the company?"

"That seems very implausible. Money stolen from the company weakens the company finances, and the company is his livelihood."

"That's true. He's a joint owner of the company, right?"

"Yes. His retired business partner, Alex Frommer, is claiming to not be receiving his negotiated share of the profits. Mr. Reynolds denies that allegation. I can't envision it would help the matter to steal from the company. Besides, if he did it, why would he try to implicate me? He's always been more than fair with me."

"You haven't had any run-ins with him since you took your new position?"

"No. I've handled a couple of important jobs, and I've heard only praise. He isn't a person who is really friendly and personal at work, though. And I think he's been preoccupied with the problems and threats of a lawsuit from Alex Frommer the last few months. Hmm, a lawsuit; that would be a reason to need money.... No, he's a good man, my boss and mentor. I normally contact him when I need advice or help with the job. I've actually been in charge of two of the biggest money-making projects lately."

What was she missing? Beth hoped she could put all of this together during the flight. She should have taken notes like a real interrogator, but didn't, not wanting to upset Adrianna any more than necessary. Beth had wished a light bulb would go on and she'd know who the real suspect was after talking to Adrianna. Instead, Adrianna had mostly praise for each of them. Was there something she said that pointed to any of them? Any or all of them could have some small motive. Or was it someone else, someone Beth hadn't met? She thought about her experiences here on the islands, and the two construction workers on the beach in the middle of the night, the ones who had scared her silly, came to mind.

"Adrianna, can you think of anyone here who has caused you to mistrust them, anyone who might have influenced Max to get you down here when it would make you seem guilty?"

"No, everyone here has been very nice to me."

"How about Max's friend Smitty? What do you know about him?"

"Smitty? Well, he and Max were friends before I met Max. They worked together for several years before Smitty decided he needed to take a break and decide what to do in life. He's a little shy, and we didn't double date, but I met him in Kansas City. He seems like a nice guy. I blame him a little for getting Max to leave Kansas City, but ultimately it was Max's decision." Adrianna was silent for a moment or two. "Coming to the Virgin Islands was probably good for Max," she said with a serious look. "He has decided that the partying gets a little tiring after a while and that money isn't going to be tossed to him like beads at a Mardi Gras parade."

But has Smitty decided the same thing? And did he talk Max into making another attempt to make easy money fast by collaborating with someone at Renfro to embezzle and launder construction company money?"

During the first leg of their flight home, Beth started recording new information gathered from Adrianna. Halfway through, she dropped the pen. She lunged for it, bumped her head on the seat in front of her causing the passenger in that seat to glare back at her through the opening between seats, and spotted her only writing instrument just before it rolled under her seat. Beth said a weak, "Sorry," and proceeded to feel for the pen with her foot. She couldn't reach it. Arnie was snoozing beside her, and there was no room to lean down and look for it. She decided, for the ninety-ninth time, klutzhood is a curse, closed her notebook, and took a nap.

Chapter 23—Returning to Reality

"Poirot," I said. "I have been thinking."
"An admirable exercise my friend. Continue it."
— Agatha Christie, *Peril at End House*

The Stockwells and Adrianna breezed through the short layovers and arrived at Kansas City International Airport Thursday evening with no incidents of being stopped or questioned beyond the normal security gate screenings. It was early evening by the time Beth and Arnie drove Adrianna to her condo apartment.

Inside the doorway, Adrianna stopped, her eyes grew wide, and she hugged herself as if to keep from shaking. Beth saw Adrianna begin to hyperventilate and thought she might faint. No wonder— scattered rugs, piled books, overturned cushions, half-open drawers, and framed pictures lying on tables. She put her arm around the young woman's shoulder and reminded her that first Psycho Cat and then the police had disrupted her well-kept home. Adrianna nodded, closed her eyes for a minute, carried her bags into the bedroom, and returned to the front room, a forced calm on her face. She made her obligatory call to Detective Rinquire while Beth and Arnie were still there for moral support. The detective wasn't on duty, but she left her name and number for him to call back.

"I've got a little stay of execution," Adrianna said. "Ew, poor choice of words. Maybe Poppa and Meg will bring Psycho Cat home. I need my furry friend to grant me some of his courage so I can face this."

She called her father, who wanted to see her right away. Adrianna agreed. "Bring Psycho Cat with you, please," she said. "I miss that little rascal."

Meg and Paul arrived within minutes. "We jumped in the car and came right over," Meg said after the hugs and kisses. "We've been ready for your call ever since you left St. Thomas."

Adrianna lifted Psycho Cat into her arms and stroked him. The cat put his paws on her shoulder and nuzzled her ear. Then he switched shoulders and purred against the other side of her head. Everyone laughed, and Beth sensed one small knot of tension begin to loosen a bit. Adrianna set her kitty on the floor. He wound his way around her legs a few times, rolled at her feet until she gave him a tummy rub, and then calmly sauntered to the sofa and jumped onto his favorite napping spot on the back cushion.

Beth and Arnie stayed long enough to help answer a host of questions from Adrianna's parents. When Adrianna told her folks she was waiting for a call back from Detective Rinquire, Paul reminded her the criminal lawyer to whom he had been referred by his attorney said they should wait for a lawyer to be present before Adrianna gave any statement to the police.

"Why?" asked Adrianna. "I don't have anything to hide."

"It seems that if the police have circumstantial evidence against you, they'll ask questions which will cause you to make incriminating statements. That'll give them reason to hold you. Richard Montorlee, the lawyer, needs to talk to you first so he can give you advice and can speak for you at the interrogation."

"When the police find out Adrianna wasn't hiding from them," Meg said, "they'll look for the real thief."

Would they, or do they think they have found the guilty party and will simply turn it over to the prosecuting attorney to prove Adrianna did it? Beth wasn't so sure, but this wasn't the time to say so.

As Beth and Arnie got up to leave, Meg was preoccupied with hugging Adrianna every few minutes and asking what she could do, and Paul was all serious business doling out the low-down on how to protect her rights. They all looked up and thanked the Stockwells for finding Adrianna and bringing her home. Beth hoped Paul and Meg would leave soon and let Adrianna get some rest.

Arnie drove the short distance to a Deli in Brookside for sandwiches to take home. Knowing Adrianna had nothing in her refrigerator or cabinets, Beth started to worry again that Paul and Meg wouldn't think about feeding Adrianna.

"Your sister not thinking about feeding Adrianna," Paul said, "is like Bill Gates not thinking about computer software. It's like Warren Buffett not thinking about investments. It's like…"

"Okay, Okay, you're right. I'm just being a mother hen. Let's go home and crash."

Chapter 24—Arresting Development

"We were about to give up and call it a night when somebody threw the girl off the bridge."

- John D. MacDonald, *Darker Than Amber*

The next morning, after Arnie left for the office, Beth donned her walking shorts and set out on the mostly dry Trolley Track Trail. After the big spring storm the night before they left for St. Thomas, the weather had turned warmer, and the outdoors looked and smelled sparkly fresh. Maybe a fast walk would help relieve the tenseness she felt in her shoulders and neck. Waiting to hear about Adrianna's conversation with Detective Rinquire felt like waiting for a fish to latch onto her fishhook—she'd never had luck with that.

Strenuous exercise was starting to help her unwind when a bird sang from her vibrating pants pocket. Beth's heart beat faster. She took a deep breath, put the phone to her ear, and answered with a calm voice. After all, it could be the Roofing Company calling to arrange a date to patch the damaged garage roof at the duplex. The new ring tone didn't portend bad news.

However, nothing could have negated the expectation forecasted by the new serene phone tone more cruelly than the call Beth received. A hysterical-sounding Meg shouted across the air waves as soon as Beth answered. "Beth, we've been here for an hour and they have Adrianna in some room. They won't even let us see her, and now they're accusing her of *murder*! The lawyer is supposed to be on his way, but he's taking too long and..." Meg's voice broke.

"Meg." Beth spoke barely above a whisper, her heart pounding. "Is Paul there? Let me speak to him, please."

"Beth," Paul said, "I shouldn't have let Meg call you. This isn't your problem, and you've done too much already."

"No, Paul I'm way too involved at this point, and I want to be there for Meg and Adrianna. Please tell me where you are and what's happened, even if I can't help."

"Okay. You're right. You deserve to know. I hope this lawyer is worth his salt. He seems to be taking his time getting here. Or maybe we're just too anxious.

"Anyway, here's what we know. This morning, the police picked Adrianna up at her condo. They brought her to the police station in handcuffs and are questioning her now not only about the embezzlement, but also about the murder of a bookkeeper at Renfro, Adrianna's friend Abby. Adrianna called us as soon as they let her. Meg found a substitute for the classroom, and we rushed right over to the station. They interrogated us about how long we were at the condo last night and what we knew about Adrianna's whereabouts after we left.

"We were there from when we saw you—about 6:45—until maybe 8:00 or so. Meg wanted to go get groceries and make us all something to eat, but Adrianna begged off and told us she was going to unpack and have a pizza delivered while she waited to hear back from Detective Rinquire. We didn't think he'd call until this morning; so we left her to rest until today. As far as I know, she didn't hear from the police until they rousted her out in the early hours of this morning."

"Oh, Paul, I'm so sorry. Do they seriously think Adrianna had something to do with a murder? How was Abby killed? When did it occur?"

"Apparently, she was strangled sometime between 7:00 and 10:00 last night. Her boyfriend found the body, and there was a note and maybe a phone call record that implicates Adrianna as the murderer. The timing is the reason we can't be any kind of alibi. I only hope Adrianna remembers what I told her about not answering their questions until the lawyer is present. There must be a way she can prove she got a pizza and stayed home last night."

"There's got to be. The doorman would have had to let the pizza delivery person into the building and then call Adrianna to let her know it was there. Paul, would you like for me to come to the station and help calm Meg?"

"Might not be a bad idea. I'd like to be free to talk to Adrianna's lawyer when he gets here, and Meg is so wound up she'll be making judgmental remarks to the wrong people without thinking."

Beth jogged back home, took 5 minutes to change clothes, jumped into the car, left a message on Arnie's work phone, and was at the station within 25 minutes. By then the lawyer had arrived. Beth told the reception clerk she was there about the Adrianna Knells case and was allowed into the room where her relatives were waiting. Paul introduced her to the lawyer, Richard Montorlee, a black man with graying temples. The attorney wore horn rimmed glasses, a dark pinstriped suit, a white shirt, and a red tie. He so impressed Beth with the way he took control of the situation that she was lost for words and, after a brief greeting, she sat down with her arm around Meg to listen to his conversation with Paul.

Montorlee had learned the particulars of the arrest from the police. He listened to Paul's account of the events of the morning and assured them Adrianna could be held for only 24 hours without conclusive evidence against her.

"What kind of evidence is conclusive?" Beth asked.

Richard Montorlee glanced over at Beth and then addressed all of them. "They need something which puts her at the murder scene."

Beth could feel Meg stiffen against her.

"Things like blood samples which have her DNA, matching fingerprints on a murder weapon, or an eye witness who saw her there."

"They don't have any of those, I'm sure," Paul said, "since Adrianna was nowhere near the crime."

"I suggest you all go get some coffee and a snack, and I'll let you know more as soon as we get through the interviews," Montorlee said.

Was this guy smooth, or what? Beth decided *interview* was his euphemism for interrogation. She envisioned Adrianna sitting in a chair with a bright light shining in her eyes blocking her view of the muscle men standing on either side of the room, while the interrogator harangued her with unanswerable questions which would make her confess to all the killings in the Kansas City area during the past three years. Beth had to rub her forehead to clear away such thoughts.

Montorlee went to talk to Adrianna, and the three frightened relatives waited in chilled silence punctuated by the sounds of phones ringing, machines clicking, and voices rising and falling from behind walls and partitions. Meg wiped her eyes occasionally. Beth sat on one side of her sister, patted her hand, and whispered now and then, "Everything's going to be okay."

Paul perched grim-faced on Meg's other side. He got up every five minutes to ask the policeman at the desk when they would know anything. The desk sergeant was polite at first, but after the fifth time, he raised an eyebrow and in a firm tone told Paul that he should exhibit some patience and stop bothering him. Paul opted to get coffee for the three of them then sat down stiffly to sip his.

"I need to call Meredith to let her know what's going on," Paul told Meg and Beth. Meg nodded her head in silent agreement.

"You don't really know what the charges are yet," Beth said. "You should wait until we know more."

Paul agreed in a flash and sat back in his chair with lowered shoulders. Beth hoped the news he would have to tell muddle-headed Meredith later would be better than the news he had now.

Chapter 25—Waiting

"The worst of all was to be faced with the interrogation technique of Thirty Seconds. The interrogator would say something and you had to respond quickly, without once repeating yourself or using the personal pronoun. Very few dissidents could last the full thirty seconds, and a refusal to comply was taken as equal proof of dissidence."
- H.M. Forester, *The Dissidents: A Novella*

After what seemed to be an eternity, but was probably only 45 minutes, a somewhat grim and tired-looking Detective Carl Rinquire, wearing khakis and a sports shirt, brown loafers and a huge technical-looking wristwatch, appeared in the waiting area. Paul, Meg, and Beth popped out of their seats.

"Are you finished with Adrianna?" Paul said. "Can we take her home?"

The detective shook his head toward Paul and Meg, looking rather sad, in Beth's opinion. Then he turned toward Beth.

"It's good you came down here, Mrs. Stockwell," the detective said. "I need to ask you a few questions."

Beth had been expecting this, since Paul and Meg were questioned earlier. She nodded toward her relatives to let them know she was fine. Beth followed the detective through a door and tried to imagine how she would feel if she were being accused of a crime. She imagined she was being led to an interrogation room similar to the ones she saw on television detective shows, rooms with stark concrete block walls, plastic chairs, and metal tables. How scared

Adrianna must be. Then Beth realized she might herself actually be accused of the crime of harboring a fugitive. Egad. Adrianna might not be the only one in danger of being locked up.

"I understand you have been with Adrianna the past few days," Carl Rinquire said after they were seated.

The detective sat behind a desk in a room that looked like an office—no bare cement wall or hanging light bulb—and Beth sat in a chair with a padded seat pulled up in front of the desk. Relieved, at first, she then began pondering if they were being recorded or watched. She glanced around for evidence of a recording device or a two-way mirror.

"My husband and I were with Adrianna parts of the last two days," Beth said. "After we located her in the Virgin Islands on Wednesday, we brought her home the next day. That is, yesterday." She wanted to remind him that they were able to find Adrianna when law enforcement couldn't and that they should be commended, but she avoided the urge. With this thought in her mind, however, she was able to stay poised even though the ensuing questions seemed harsh and repetitive, especially the ones about why they had *contrived* to avoid the police at the airports. She was sure this detective was trying to make her say something which would incriminate Adrianna. She wished Adrianna's attorney, Richard Montorlee, was with her.

"So you had no contact with Adrianna after about 7:00 last evening?" Carl Rinquire said finally.

"That's correct. But if Adrianna did order a pizza as she told her parents, the doorman at the building would be able to verify it was delivered. He'd also know whether or not Adrianna left later last night. Even if she left by the back door, he would have been able to see her on the video monitor at the front desk."

"Okay, sure, we'll check that out. By the way, good job finding your step-niece."

Beth smiled and nodded. Even after the badgering questions, the detective seemed like a decent fellow. He escorted her back to the waiting room where Paul and Meg were still sitting, and then left.

"I think my account about why we were in the Virgin Islands and why we brought Adrianna home the way we did must have matched Adrianna's version well enough to satisfy Detective Rinquire," Beth said in a whisper.

Other than that she kept her comments to herself. The way Detective Rinquire had responded to her idea of checking with the doorman at the condo building made her think he had already checked. The police were doing their jobs, but, as far as she knew, Adrianna was still the primary suspect.

A morning's tiresome wait in the police station gave Beth time to speculate about the motive someone would have to kill Abby West. Abby's name topped her list of possible embezzlers. A bookkeeper had the easiest access to the accounts. Abby had reason to need money and apparently had a grudge against Adrianna. It didn't make sense that someone would kill her—unless she had an accomplice who wanted all of the money. Joey, her boyfriend, maybe? Of course, the police must be investigating him as another suspect for the murder.

Paul tossed his third coffee cup into the trash bin right before Richard Montorlee appeared to tell them the police were still looking at Adrianna's alibi and the evidence.

"If everything in her story checks out, she will be released this afternoon," Montorlee said. "I have other work to do back at my office, but I'll be in to handle the details as soon as I hear from the police. The three of you should go get some lunch and try to unwind."

Montorlee's voice and expression were controlled, kind, and confident. Paul shook the attorney's hand and made sure they had each other's direct cell phone numbers. Meg gave him a weak handshake but took a shaky deep breath before she could get out a "thank you for your help." Beth mumbled a quick thank you to the attorney from her seat when he looked her way. She'd wait until Adrianna was cleared of all suspicion before she'd praise him.

Chapter 26—Remaining Under Suspicion

"One doesn't recognize the really important moments in one's life until it's too late."
- Agatha Christie

Late that afternoon, as Richard Montorlee had anticipated, Adrianna was released. As soon as she left the police station, Beth contacted Arnie for the second time to tell him the details of her KCPD experience.

"Paul asked the attorney to get together with the family this afternoon in order to help us understand this whole thing and what's going to happen," Beth said.

"Good," Arnie said. "I should have been at the police station with you."

"No, I'm fine, but they might question you at some point, since you went to the Virgin Islands, too. The detective accused me of conspiring to get Adrianna past the police. I guess you would be the one I conspired with."

Richard Montorlee's law office was located in downtown Kansas City, far enough north of the police station, their work places, and home that he agreed to convene with the family in Brookside. Beth was able to reserve a meeting room at the East-Gate Condos since she was a condo owner. It was almost 4:30 by the time they all sat down—Paul, Meg, and Adrianna on a sofa, Beth, Arnie, and Richard Montorlee in armchairs—in the party/conference room. The long room, decorated in a contemporary style, included stuffed sofas and easy chairs, a kitchenette with bar seating, and a long dining/conference table. In these surroundings it was easy for Beth to imagine they were having a little family gathering and they'd be serving iced tea, fruit, and cookies.

The first words out of the attorney's mouth destroyed that feeling like an ice pick popping a balloon. "You must understand that Adrianna is free pending more investigation," he said.

Beth watched the family. Adrianna looked at Mr. Montorlee much as a diligent student will gaze at her professor, eager to get more information. Paul and Meg glanced from the attorney to Adrianna and back again, like body guards, ready enough to learn the dangers ahead, but more than ready to jump in to help their charge if needed. Arnie appeared concerned and possibly puzzled, from the look of the furrows in his brow.

Montorlee continued. "The police don't have enough evidence to hold Adrianna right now. Her alibi checked out. The doorman opened the door when the pizza was delivered and spoke to Adrianna when she came down to the lobby to retrieve it around 8:30 P.M. He was on duty until midnight and saw no evidence to indicate Adrianna left the building. The video from the security cameras verify his story. Also, no fingerprints from the crime scene match Adrianna's."

"Then why is she still under suspicion?" Beth asked.

"Police are always suspicious. They figure an assailant will find a way to sneak past a security camera and will wear gloves in the commission of a crime. Besides, they still have a phone call, made from Adrianna's phone to Abigail's phone about forty-five minutes before the crime, and a note, ostensibly typed on Abigail's computer and printed on her printer, which says she and Adrianna stole the money. Abigail's boyfriend, Joey Zitelli, handed the note over to the police and said he found it on the bedroom dresser after he found the body in the living room."

Adrianna spoke up at that. "I did call Abby last night at around 8:00, right after Dad and Meg left. It was stupid of me. I wanted to hear from her what was going on and why I'm being blamed. Abby was one of my best friends, and I guess I thought she'd be on my side even after all this. I told her I had to stay put until I heard from the police, and she said she'd call me today and meet me to tell what she knew. I-I can't explain the note or how…" Adrianna's voice broke.

"Wouldn't Abby's boyfriend be a prime suspect?" Arnie asked. "He supposedly found the body and a note no killer reasonably would leave lying around as evidence."

"Exactly what the police thought," Montorlee said. "However, the boyfriend said he found the note in an envelope addressed to the police under Abby's cell phone when he picked it up to call 911. It was typed and printed from her laptop last evening at about 8:45, right around the time she was killed, maybe right before. Joey also identified the silk scarf which was used to strangle the girl as one that belonged to Adrianna. Adrianna has admitted to it being her scarf."

Everyone looked at Adrianna. She nodded in silence.

Montorlee said, "Joey works an evening shift and didn't find the body until about 1:00 a.m.—well after the time of death. His coworkers have verified he was at work all evening and was never gone more than five minutes or so at a time, not enough time to have gone back to the apartment and committed the crime."

"The police showed me the scarf," Adrianna said. "It did once belong to me. I gave it to Abby quite a few months ago when she admired it because it suited her coloring so much better than it did mine."

"Well, now how would Joey know the scarf belonged to you if Abby had been wearing it for several months?" Meg said.

Adrianna replied softly, her eyes lowered. "Joey saw me wearing it before—I mean, when we were all—that is, Abby and Joey, Max and I were doing things together all the time. I gave it to Abby after she and Joey broke up. Abby told me on the phone the night she—last night—that she hadn't worn the scarf for ages. She told me she was getting it out while we were talking on our phones and said she was going to wear it to work the next day. Joey probably never saw her wear it; he only saw it on me." She paused and looked around at the family as if explaining to herself as well as to them. "Now she'll never…"

Montorlee broke in. "Neither the scarf nor the letter are substantial evidence enough to hold Adrianna for more than questioning. The letter was typewritten and not signed."

Another reason to admire Mr. Montorlee, he had experience enough to know when to cut off the dialog when it started to become maudlin.

"However," Montorlee said, "the police won't eliminate any suspect until the killer is found, especially when circumstantial evidence points to Adrianna. Even though she would ordinarily not be strong enough to strangle a struggling woman the size of the victim with a scarf, the girl was bludgeoned first with a blunt object, reducing her ability to fight back. There was a heavy skillet on the cabinet near the body, but there were no finger prints. The evidence they have points to Adrianna as the main suspect for both the embezzlement and the murder. The thinking goes like this: Adrianna talked to Abby, her accomplice, last night. Abby threatened to tell all. Adrianna went over there to confront her and, when she wouldn't yield, killed her in a rage."

Beth couldn't help admitting to herself the plausibility of that angle. Adrianna could have snuck out last night and done this, after she told all of her family to go home. She looked at the young woman and then at her stepmother.

Maybe my perfect sister isn't always successful, after all, if she raised a murderer.

Yikes, what am I thinking? This isn't about trying to find a frailty in my sister; this is about Adrianna, almost a daughter to me.

She believed with all her heart Adrianna was innocent, period. And a certainty--they must help Adrianna prove her innocence beyond a doubt rather than waiting for a jury to look at the evidence and decide her guilt or innocence.

Beth said, "So what needs to be done is to find the real thief and the real murderer. If Joey didn't kill her, then someone else must have learned about Adrianna's return and about Abby planning to meet with her. Were there any other calls to or from Abby's phone last night?"

"Apparently only one to Joey," Montorlee said.

"Do they have any idea where the stolen money went?" Arnie asked.

Arnie was definitely getting into the investigative mode and no longer suggesting Beth leave the detective work to the police. Beth gave him an appreciative look. His was an obvious question she hadn't thought to ask.

"Adrianna?" Richard Montorlee looked at her.

"It's okay," said Adrianna. "These are my family members. They've done so much to help me already. I want them to know everything, no matter how bad it sounds." She faced them. "The police found out that when the false vendor accounts in Kansas City were closed down, the money was electronically transferred to several banks in St. Thomas, into accounts opened with my social security number. Someone withdrew the entire amount, in a series of large ATM and teller transactions."

"Max!" Paul spoke the name as if he were spitting out rotten meat.

Adrianna gave her father a hurt look. "No, Poppa. Part of the money was withdrawn while I was there. I was with Max every minute, and we didn't go to an ATM. Max used cash and his debit card once to buy the groceries we needed, and that was it. Besides, the ATM withdrawals could have been made anywhere in the U.S., not only at an ATM in the Virgin Islands."

"Then where does that Virgin Islands connection come in? Is it just a coincidence?" Meg said to the general gathering but while looking at the attorney rather than at Adrianna.

"It would be a huge fluke for it to be a coincidence. The police are going to investigate the Kansas City connections, and particularly the

Renfro connections, of anyone in the Virgin Islands who may have learned about Max and Adrianna's relationship."

"That could be almost anyone in St. Thomas and St. John," Arnie said. "Max is quite the friendly one."

There was a general nodded agreement to his statement. "Hmh," Richard Montorlee snorted. Must have been to prove he understood the humor. But he didn't seem prone to levity when it came to representing a client. "It may take some time and effort," he said. "The police are looking into the matter, too, but if any of you find out something which will help, please let me know as soon as possible." He handed one of his cards to each of them, made an appointment to talk more with Adrianna the next day, and left.

Beth, Arnie, Meg, and Paul escorted Adrianna up to her condo. While Adrianna manipulated the key in the lock, Beth noticed the door to the neighboring condo open a crack, and Eva Standish peeked into the hallway, a folded piece of paper in her hand. Beth smiled and waved a friendly greeting. Eva pressed the paper into Beth's hand and then closed her door abruptly. *Bad people can be two-faced* was printed on the note in shaky handwriting. Beth stuffed the note into her pocket without showing it to anyone.

Inside the apartment, they were met by a wound-up Psycho Cat. Adrianna caught him as he loped across the room and picked him up to caress and kiss. From her arms, he jumped to the floor and ploughed across the top of the sofa and to the top of a bookshelf where he could sit and regard them all from a kingly position. He soaked up the attention, admiration, and chuckles of appreciation his actions garnered from everyone in the room. If only the momentary lightheartedness could have been bottled and sipped repeatedly over the next few days.

Chapter 27—Planning the Next Move

"Hercule Poirot: I am an imbecile. I see only half of the picture.
Miss Lemon: I don't even see that."
- Agatha Christie

That evening, before Adrianna had finally shooed everyone home, Arnie was called to the police station for questioning. Beth went with him, and, while sitting in the waiting area, she rummaged around in her purse for the small notebook in which she'd been jotting names and ideas about the embezzlement for the past week and a half. She'd remembered to put another pen in her purse, and she wanted to add the new development—murder. Much of what she needed to know might be in the Caribbean, but she couldn't spend the money to revisit the Virgin Islands. Maybe she should rethink all of the memos she put together about the people and places they visited in St. Thomas and St. John.

Adrianna would most likely call Max, tell him all about her experience today, and ask what he knew. He might be picked up for questioning by the F.B.I. or by the Virgin Island police and not be reachable. Max seemed like a trooper, though, and a capable one, at that. Right now he could be scoping out the Caribbean culprit who was in cahoots with the Kansas City killer. She read the notes she had for Max listed under *Suspects* and then, with only a little hesitation, added Max's name to her list of *Helpful People*.

Arnie came out of the interrogation room, immediately grabbed Beth's arm, helped her regain her balance when she almost lost her footing, and led her to the car. "Whew." He sighed. "That was an experience I'd rather not have again. I thought I might remember some part of our trip or something Adrianna said in a different way than you did, and then we'd be thrown in the pokey."

"I guess it turned out okay, didn't it?"

"Your guess is as good as mine. But at the end the detective thanked me for my time, and we shook hands. That's a good sign, I think."

"Was it Detective Rinquire?"

"Yes. He's the one who questioned you and Adrianna, isn't he?"

"Right. I'm guessing this is his case. He's the one who came to Meg and Paul's house the first time we learned about Adrianna being sought for questioning. I guess it's his job to be hard-nosed when he's interrogating someone. Maybe now all of us have been questioned and have the same story he'll be more apt to search for other suspects."

"Do you know if they have any neighborhood witnesses who saw someone at Abby's apartment last night?"

"I don't know, but it's a good question. Maybe Adrianna knows, but I'm not sure how much the police told her about their investigation. Perhaps her lawyer gets all those details."

Arnie drove. Beth gazed out of the car windows at the city. The beautiful evening made it hard, even for two people in such tense and reflective moods, to be depressed. The year progressed toward summer; Daylight Savings Time had added an hour of sun in the evening; the amount of sunlight was increasing by several minutes a day; and the rain from the week before had helped turn their particular part of the Earth into a lush garden. The warmth of the late afternoon sunshine, the scent of the blooming clematis, lilies, and lilacs, and the beauty of the bright green avenue medians and parks lifted Beth's spirits. She started feeling invigorated enough again to keep on looking for the answer to this confounding mystery, even though she didn't have a clue how to proceed.

"Arnie," she said, "I was reviewing my notes while I was sitting in the waiting room at the police station. There's definitely a connection between the theft and the murder, don't you think?"

"Absolutely."

"And there's got to be a connection between the criminal here and a collaborator in the Virgin Islands—probably the person who was looking for Max several weeks ago at the Mermaid Pub. There's a conspiracy."

"I agree."

"Well, the guy who visited Meredith, the so-called Tom Collins, the guy with the mustache and tattoo, is involved somehow. He could be not only the thief, but also the murderer. I wonder if he works at Renfro or if he's directing someone who works there. If we could learn who he is and give him up to the police…"

"Good thinking, sweetie, but how're we going to do that?"

"I have no idea, but maybe Adrianna can help."

Beth's focus on the problem was interrupted as soon as she arrived home. She had been either out of town or at the police station since Sunday, and now there were several messages on the answer machine. The first was from Adrianna. Flowers from Pete O'Neill had been delivered to her after the family left. The bouquet was accompanied by a note. Despite their differences, it said, he didn't believe she had embezzled the money from the company or committed murder; after working with her, he knew her good character.

Beth returned the call to find out what Adrianna thought about this unexpected gesture. Adrianna was grateful someone from the company had reached out but was perplexed it had been Pete O'Neill. Knowing him, she speculated he had some ulterior motive, but she couldn't figure out what it could be. He couldn't possibly believe she'd change her mind and agree to date him, could he?

Beth advised Adrianna to enjoy the thoughtfulness of the flowers and try to relax. She knew Pete O'Neill didn't have a mustache when she saw him in the accounting office. Well—he could have shaved it, and he could have a tattoo. It was unlikely she could now visit Renfro again and ask to talk to him, though. Even that sweet little receptionist, Allison, would deny her request after a murder had been committed. Besides, what could she ask him? *Did you visit Meredith Knells and threaten her?* This line of thinking would get her nowhere.

The other messages on her machine had to do with a rental issue which needed to be addressed. Landlady duties didn't wait for personal problems to be solved. According to the insurance agent's message, the company's representatives had inspected the hole in the garage roof made by the tree during the storm last weekend. He suggested they put a temporary patch on the hole until a roofing company could fix it.

Her tenant left a message which said only part of the fallen tree had been removed by the tree service, and he urged that the rest of the tree be removed. He said the tree would grow above the garage again and cause trouble in the future. It sounded correct, but Beth needed to look at the problem before making a final decision. Scattered showers appeared in the weather forecast for the weekend. She persuaded Arnie they should go to the duplex while they still had a bit of daylight. They could nail a piece of plywood over the hole in the garage roof and figure out what needed to be done with the tree.

The fix-it job required a ladder, which they transported in their trailer hitched to the back of their SUV. Once there, they set the ladder up against the front of the detached garage. Arnie worked at nailing the patch over the hole, and the tenants came out to chitchat about the storm's devastation. The young man whose car had been squashed showed them pictures he had taken of the huge branch lying across his car. Those pictures, taken from different angles for the enlightenment of the auto insurance agent, cinched the decision to have the rest of the tree removed to prevent future garage and car disasters.

Problems like this one popped up several times a year in the rental business. Beth and Arnie always handled them in their stride. Beth felt comfortable assuring people everything would be all right when their plumbing acted up on the second floor and ruined the ceiling of the living room below or when a tree fell onto their car. She felt uncomfortable whenever she had to deliver bad news or turn people down, such as when she had to call and reject a rental application because the applicants had horrible credit scores. She didn't like those calls, but when such a call was necessary, she turned the applicants away with the explanation that hers was a small business and they would surely find another place with a larger rental company.

Beth decided she needed to use the same firm but gentle technique in her search for the criminal trying to frame Adrianna. Her first task should be to knock on doors, uncomfortable as that would be, and look for a witness in Abby's building who might have seen or heard something helpful. Maybe she'd find someone who would talk to her even if they wouldn't talk to the police, or maybe there was someone the police had missed. People seemed to warm up to her fairly fast and would tell their life's stories if she took the time to listen. It was worth a try.

Their refrigerator was almost empty, but Beth and Arnie were tired of eating out and didn't want to spend time grocery shopping that evening. Beth found some chicken breasts and frozen vegetables tucked into the door of the freezer and some quick cooking rice and canned tomatoes in the cupboard, perfect for a satisfying casserole. At 9:30 p.m., Arnie was watching a show on TV, and Beth was trying to read when the phone startled her. It was Adrianna.

Chapter 28—Talking the Situation Through

"There is nothing like looking, if you want to find something."
- J.R.R. Tolkien, *The Hobbit*

"**A**unt Beth ," Adrianna said, "I just got off the phone with Max. He didn't pick up when I called him earlier, but later he called me back. It's a good thing we have unlimited night and weekend minutes on our phones, because it took me a long time to tell him about what happened today. I mean, last night and today. Oh, I'm babbling—Abby's murder…"

"I understand, dear. Did you tell Max about the bank accounts in St. Thomas where the stolen money was deposited?"

"Yes. And he was taken in for questioning today about the stolen money. That's where he was when I first called. They have no evidence connecting him to the accounts; so they couldn't hold him. They didn't try to connect him to the murder. He was completely unaware Abby was killed until I told him, and you can imagine how upset he was to learn I'm a suspect.

"Thursday and Friday he worked at the construction site. You remember Mr. Blakely asked him to supervise the condo building site where he's been working? If he had all of that money, do the police think he'd be working so hard? The police pretty much let Max know he is still under suspicion and should stay around because they'll be keeping track of his activities. Max wanted to jump on a plane immediately and come home to be with me anyway, but I talked him out of it."

"How did you do that?"

"I told him I need for him to check out all of the people he's had contact with in order to figure out who might have opened and cleaned out those bank accounts with the stolen money. I mean, his friend Smitty is from Kansas City. He might have a contact at Renfro, and he certainly knew about my relationship with Max. He could have used us as scapegoats. And if not Smitty, there are a number of other people he has worked with who are from the Midwest or may know someone here."

Fantastic. Adrianna had the same idea as she did about how Max could help. She had some of the same doubts about Smitty, too, even though Beth had not told her about her nighttime scare at the resort on St. Thomas. Beth found her notebook and opened it to the pages she filled during the trip to the Virgin Islands.

"I have some people in my notes he can question," Beth said. "There's Tim the bartender at the Mermaid Pub, the odd little landlady of the rooming house where Max lived, Max's friend Nate Jones, nicknamed Tat because of his tattoos, the bartender at the Mango Tango on St. John, and maybe some of Max's current construction buddies. Oh, and then there's T.M. Blakely. He could have mentioned Max's situation to a business buddy who then set up the scheme with a co-conspirator at Renfro."

"Okay," Adrianna assented, "I wrote those down. I'll give the list to Max when I talk to him tomorrow. I'm sure he's already thought of most of these people. He's going to start snooping around even yet tonight. I think he's glad he can help."

"Remind him to be very, very careful. There's already been a murder. It looks as if these crooks are capable of anything. They're not only greedy; they're evil."

"I did tell him to be cautious, but Max reminded me that he's a pretty good actor. He's good at Poker, too. He can fake people out with a dopey depressed look on his face which everyone believes. Because of the murder I really think he realizes the seriousness of being especially surreptitious."

"Good. It must be a tight-knit community of locals there, judging by the way Blakely was able to get us so smoothly off the islands by making a phone call. The police may be suspicious of Max because he's an outsider."

"Aunt Beth, they're not going to find anything shady about Max. And besides, if they're watching him, they'll be close by when he needs them."

"I know. But I don't want Max to get into a dangerous situation or to put you in more danger."

"I'm going to talk to Richard Montorlee tomorrow. Maybe he'll have more information about what the police are doing. Right now I need to call Poppa. I told him I'd let him know what Max had to say."

"Another quick question or two, please," Beth said.

"Shoot."

"Uh—"

"There I go again. Who knew my vocabulary was thick with murder slang?"

Adrianna's comment caught Beth off guard. She hesitated for a tick. She didn't know whether to laugh or to try to console Adrianna whose usually good-natured kidding now sounded sardonic. She bit her lip.

"It's okay; you keep that sense of humor about this whole thing. It's a whole lot better than getting depressed," Beth said. "I wanted to ask you something. Do you know if the police found any witnesses who might have seen someone go into or out of Abby's apartment Thursday evening?"

"Mr. Montorlee told me they asked the neighbors but didn't find anyone who saw anything."

"And have you told your mother any of what has happened?"

This time it was Adrianna who paused before answering. She had always hesitated to talk about her mother. Beth regretted asking, after what Adrianna had been through today. But she said, "I called her last night to let her know I got home. I left a message. She was probably at work, but she left a voice mail on my cell phone today while I was still at the police station. She said she's glad I'm okay. I didn't call back tonight because she'll still be working, and I don't think I can describe my ordeal today in a voice message. Besides, I've got to think about how to tell her about this—uh—new development."

Beth had been hoping Adrianna had asked her mom more about the mysterious man who had paid for Max's address and then threatened to hurt her if she told anyone. Maybe the identity of *Tom Collins* was something she and Meg needed to discover. Adrianna had enough to worry about. However, Beth needed something more to jog Meredith's memory.

"I get it," she said. "Hard to tell anyone, but especially your mother, that you are suspected of such a thing. Just one more question. Do you happen to have a photo of the people you work with at Renfro, maybe a group picture or pictures from a party?"

"No. I can't remember us ever having a group photo taken. Maybe Meg has some. She always takes her camera to everything, and she might have some pictures from one of the holiday parties she and Poppa attended. Why do you want a photo?"

"Well, if the embezzler is one of the employees, someone may recognize her or him from a photo."

"Oh, Aunt Beth, you're not going to go looking for witnesses, are you? I don't want you to get hurt."

"I'm thinking ahead. That's all. I'll let you go so you can call your dad."

Chapter 29—Worrying and Losing Sleep

"Once upon a midnight dreary, while I pondered, weak and weary,

Over many a quaint and curious volume of forgotten lore—

While I nodded, nearly napping, suddenly there came a tapping,

As if someone gently rapping, rapping at my chamber door.

"'Tis some visitor," I muttered, "tapping at my chamber door—

Only this and nothing more."
— Edgar Allan Poe

Beth, who had gone to bed exhausted a bit after 10:00 the night before, was up early Saturday morning dressed in her walking clothes, sipping coffee near the bay window in the breakfast room. She watched the top edge of the sun peek above the horizon and then, bit by bit, gather all of its pink and orange rays into one dazzling orb. By 6:00 a.m. its shimmering light was beginning to warm Kansas City, like a quilt gradually warming cold feet on a winter's night.

By the time Arnie appeared in the kitchen in his boxer shorts and tee shirt, yawning and squinting at the light filtering through the blinds over the sink, Beth had read through much of the newspaper. Arnie liked to sleep in on weekend mornings, but he didn't seem surprised to see Beth up and around already.

"I heard your groans and howls during the night," Arnie said. "Were you having murder and mayhem nightmares? Or, were you saving Adrianna from being locked up?"

"I'm sorry," Beth said. "I hope I didn't keep you awake all night. All I remember is waking up feeling exhausted, but I don't know whether someone was after me or what."

Arnie came to the table with his coffee cup and laid a gentle hand on her shoulder. "Don't worry about me. I go right back to sleep. Seems as if you need to unstress, though."

"Yeah, maybe I'll get out on the Trolley Track Trail and walk off some of the edge. Wanna come?"

Arnie put his cup on the table, sat down, and pulled the newspaper over. "Go ahead. I'll do some jogging later. Take some time to shake it off. Remember, this situation isn't all bad. Adrianna hasn't been arrested for the murder, and they've got some good people working on the case. You don't need to assume the burden."

He held his arms out to her. She stood, came over with a grateful smile, gave him a hug and a kiss, picked up her walking shoes from where she had left them beside the table, and padded to the front door to put them on. She felt relieved Arnie understood. He knew she needed some time by herself to think, and he was willing to give it to her. That, or he was tired of listening to her whine about the whole thing. Either way, she intended to hit the trail, put the pedal to the metal, so to speak, and listen to her muscles moan for a change.

It was the end of April. There was still a slight chill in the air when Beth started walking south on the smooth flat trail. Only two other people approached. Par tradition, she said good morning to each of the runners as they sped by.

Even out here alone, she couldn't seem to focus her thoughts toward a solution to the crimes and what she could do to help uncover the criminals. Beth had always been impatient, and she knew she wouldn't sleep properly or get rid of that tight empathetic feeling for Adrianna until the case was solved and the murderer was in prison.

As she walked south on the trail, gray clouds crept between her and the warming sun. She zipped her light windbreaker up to her chin and shivered.

At the Quick Trip in the Waldo shopping district, she watched a young mother scramble to steer two boys, one a toddler and one pre-school aged, into the store. The boys, wearing matching bright green and white striped shirts and khaki pants, trotted like puppies, bumped each other, ran circles around their mother, and giggled with hilarity at their own antics. Their mother finally maneuvered the two inside. Beth turned her head to look through the store window as she passed and could see the mother shunt the boys to each side of her and take their hands firmly before she headed into the stacks of convenience store merchandise.

This must be a single mom who needed to purchase some basic item, training pants or a bottle of milk for the children, before she exhausted herself running her Saturday errands, having only Saturday to accomplish them because she worked ten-hour days during the week for low pay. She had been forced to take the boys with her, there being no one with whom she could leave them, her husband having left her for a wanton woman.

Beth shook her head to clear it. Now she perceived nasty problems in everyday situations. Probably the young mother had merely stopped for gasoline, with her kids in tow, and was buying them a treat.

Near the end of the trail, Beth turned around and headed north, north toward home. North also led toward the condo building, where Adrianna was either sleeping in or not sleeping at all. That sad thought gave her the impetus to get started, even without having fully developed a plan. She dialed her sister's phone number.

Beth had to hold her phone to her ear while she talked. She had not found the necessity of purchasing Bluetooth earphones made for hands-free, constant wireless connection. Her power-walk slowed almost to an amble while she talked over strategy with Meg. She passed through the small but hip Waldo shopping area, barely noticing the folks scurrying to and from cafés, drug stores, and antique shops.

Not until she reached the section of trail which ran parallel to her own street did Beth finish her conversation and resume her pace.

Two minutes later, her knees turned to jelly and she stumbled to a stop. She had spotted a man who appeared to be peeking through a front window of her house and then slinking—yes slinking, no other word for it, slow motion, bent over, arms drawn in, glancing back over his shoulder like a fox on the prowl—toward the far side of the house. The man wore a baseball cap and a long-sleeved jersey, and Beth thought she noticed a mustache when the man turned. It could have been a shadow. *Wait, turn around again!* But, then he was gone.

Beth crept off the trail, staying behind some bushes which separated the public median from the street. She crouched down and peered through the foliage toward her house while she phoned Arnie. It took a few rings before he picked up.

"Where are you?" Beth said in almost a whisper.

"What do you mean, where am I?" Arnie said. "You called home, and I answered."

"I mean what part of the house?"

"In the den, at the computer. Why? What's wrong? Why are you whispering?"

"Arnie, listen. There's a man outside the house. He looked in the front window and then went back toward the garage. I'm across the street behind the bushes, but can you peek through the back windows without being seen? He looked as if he's, you know, casing the joint to find out if we're home. It could be the guy who threatened Meredith. Maybe. I don't know. Anyway, I'm scared to come home if he's still around."

"Hold on," Arnie said. "I looked through the kitchen and breakfast room windows. I'm going to all the windows downstairs."

"Be careful he doesn't see you."

"Why? If he sees me he'll know someone is home and will be scared off, if this really is a bad guy." There were pauses as Arnie went from window to window. "I don't see anyone out back or on either side of the house," Arnie said after a few minutes, "but the person you saw could have been a meter reader. The meters are on the driveway side of the house. He could have cut down through the back yards to other houses."

"Well, he looked as if he was creeping…"

"There's no one here now. You can come on across the street. I'll watch from the front door."

Beth jogged across the street and to the front porch. Her heart still pounded in her chest, and she expected a mustachioed man to jump out from the side of the house at any minute. Arnie roamed the whole back yard with her and pointed out the utility meters until Beth felt relatively safe again. However, her mind picture of the man peeking through her front window couldn't be shaken. Was it really a snoopy meter reader, or had she seen a peeping *Tom Collins?*

Chapter 30—Lacking Patience

"The secret of getting ahead is getting started."
- Agatha Christie

Later that morning, Arnie left for his jog, and Beth drove out of her garage into bright warm sunshine, the morning clouds having dissipated or blown off to the east. Meg was expecting her, and Beth hoped she had located all those photos she had taken at Renfro events.

Ten minutes later, an almost cheerful Meg greeted her at her front door. "I found all of these photos," she said, holding out several envelopes full of prints. "There are quite a few people in these pictures I don't know. Maybe I was introduced to some of them, but I don't remember who they are. Anyway, you know me, the record keeper. I took the pictures and kept them because I thought someday Adrianna would like to look back at the folks she worked with at her first job after college. You should see how many pictures I have of her and her brother's friends from their school days. Anyway, maybe one of these includes an image of the evil maniac who's trying to frame Adrianna for the crimes, assuming that someone will be able to recognize the person from these snapshots."

"You take excellent pictures, Meg," Beth said, shuffling through the first batch of photos. "I recognize a couple of people in these whom I saw for a few minutes when I visited the Renfro offices the week before last." She looked up from the pictures. "Have you heard from Adrianna this morning?"

"I haven't talked to her," Meg said, and sighed. "Paul called her about half an hour ago. She was getting ready to talk to her attorney, Richard Montorlee, today. I mean, she was probably preparing mentally more than physically. Then Paul called the attorney to ask if the police had found any more evidence. Mr. Montorlee told Paul the detectives weren't working on the case all night and we need to be a little patient. Paul said he had to bite his tongue to keep from reminding the lawyer we aren't paying him to tell us to be patient. He went on to work. He wants to try to concentrate on his jobs while he waits, mostly to keep him from thinking about Adrianna's plight."

Beth lifted her eyebrows. "Oh, be patient, be smatient—I'm of the opinion that patience isn't going to help Adrianna."

Meg nodded and looked sad. "It's too bad no one could find the real crook before Abby West was killed. She could still be alive, assuming the two cases are related."

"They must be related. It would be a far-fetched coincidence for the murder to be some bungled break-and-enter when Abby and Adrianna are so connected to the Renfro case. There's the note and the scarf. No mention of anything stolen. There's little doubt, as far as I'm concerned, the theft and murder are connected, and there's at least one very evil character out there."

"So let's get going to find out who it is."

Meg slipped on a windbreaker and dropped the photos into a large colorful carry-all, orange with stylized multicolored flowers, which made her look as if she were going shopping in Key West. Beth drove them to the apartment complex in Kansas City's Westport neighborhood where the murder was committed.

Upon entering the door to the hallway, with its numbered doors and stucco walls, plain but clean, and lacking a lobby, Beth almost lost her nerve and turned back. She had only a vague idea how to approach the neighbors to find out what they knew. There was a chance one of them had a nosy streak, like Eva Standish. If she could find that person and ask the correct questions the right way, she might find out some good information. Such a person would surely have talked to the police already, though. It wasn't reasonable that she would find someone who had seen or heard something if the police didn't.

"Well," she said and took a deep breath as if preparing to dive off a cliff into cold water, "We're already here. We may as well give it our best shot."

Chapter 31—Giving It Our Best Shot

"'Never laugh at live dragons, Bilbo you fool!' he said to himself,
and it became a favorite saying of his later, and passed into a
proverb."
- J.R.R. Tolkien, *The Hobbit*

After the brief doubt-laden pause in the downstairs hallway, Beth and Meg huddled briefly to discuss their strategy. They decided the best canvassing plan would be to start with the apartments closest to Abby's and work their way toward the farthest ones. It was Saturday morning, hopefully not early enough to disturb those who slept in on weekend mornings, but not so late that people would be started on their Saturday outings.

Meg and Beth eyed the open stairwell, shot each other determined looks, and filed up to the second floor, Beth in the lead. The first doorbell they rang, at the apartment door to the right of Abby's, produced no answer even after they waited, hands clenching purses for dear life, for what seemed like an eternity. They went to the door on the left; Beth expected, almost hoped for, a similar response there.

However, a barefoot young man in jeans pulled a tee-shirt over his head as he opened the door. Immediately, Beth's face assumed a look of humility and friendliness, and she used a pretense similar to the one she had used in the Virgin Islands to excuse her probing.

"I'm sorry to intrude so early this morning," she said, "I'm Beth, and this is my sister Meg. We're friends of Abby West, your next-door neighbor who was killed. Her parents are so distraught that the murderer hasn't been found; so Meg and I thought if we talked to her neighbors we might find a witness, or someone who has an idea who the killer might be."

Perhaps a young professional, by his look and demeanor, the young man gave them an indulgent smile. Beth had the feeling he considered them two harmless older ladies who could be blown off, but should be treated politely. She with her zippered pink cardigan and shoulder bag and Meg with her wild carry-all bag and pleasant face must remind him of his own mother or aunts.

When he hesitated, Beth played on that persona. "We wanted to do some little thing that might help, because we feel so terrible about Abby and bad for her parents. Sometimes people will tell a person's friends what they wouldn't tell the police—little things that might not seem to mean much or things they remember later after the police have left."

The young man nodded, "I'm afraid I can't help you. Like I told the police, I was at a bar in Westport listening to music with friends and didn't get home until after 11:00 that night. When I came in, the police were all over the building and had the crime scene blocked off." He squeezed his eyes shut as if in pain. "But I saw the body inside the open door. It was, you know, purple-looking and bloated. I could tell because she was nearly naked. Her legs were apart." He shivered. "And I clearly saw her face, Abby's dead face, I mean. Her tongue was hanging out, her eyes were open and popped, and her neck, ugh—red and black and..."

He stopped and looked embarrassed. Meg held a hand to her chest and appeared pale. Beth felt light-headed, as if she might faint.

"I'm—I'm sorry. I didn't have to be so—so graphic. I don't want it to bother your sleep like it does mine. Um," he said, "The police questioned me then. I haven't lived here long—less than two months—and only knew the couple well enough to say hello in the hallway, not well enough to know who might want to hurt them— her. I figured it was a domestic situation or a break-in. But I bought a new chain lock for my door to install this weekend."

"I understand, but have you heard any quarrels or seen any visitors who seemed suspicious or unusual?" Beth asked, straining to appear calm and in control.

"I guess I heard a little yelling one weekend morning. It didn't sound angry, just loud. But that's a hazard of apartment living. I turn up the TV or something when I hear noise on either side of me. I believe Joey works in the evening until late. And I'm not here much, either. I didn't notice any visitors except for one; a young lady was leaving when I got home—could have been a sister or a friend. Sorry, ladies, that I can't give you any more help. The woman who lives on the other side of that apartment might know more, but I saw her leave with a suitcase early Friday morning. She said she was going to her parents' house because she's scared to stay here until the killer is caught."

"Was anything stolen; did the police seem to think it could have been a burglary?" asked Meg, still with the hand on her chest.

"I don't know, but the questions the police were asking suggested they were hoping for me to identify someone Abby might have known. It sounds as if you think it was someone she knew, too."

"Could be," Beth said. "I was in the apartment only once, but I didn't see anything very valuable—at least not valuable enough to induce a burglar to go to the middle of the building and pass up apartments where no one was at home in order to get to Abby's."

"True, unless they had a stash of drugs, or something. I didn't see any evidence of drug use, though," he said.

"Do you know of anyone in this building who may have known them better?" Beth asked.

"Try the apartment at the end of this hallway. The lady there has a kid, and I saw Joey throwing a baseball with him outdoors a couple of times." He gave Meg an apologetic look. "Um, again, sorry for my description of the murder victim. I didn't mean to uh, gross you out. It's only that it's been so much on my mind since that night."

Sticking to their original plan, Beth and Meg tried the apartment directly across the hall first and then every door in the hallway until they reached the end. Each person they asked either had not been home or had been watching television or something similar at the time of the murder and had seen or heard nothing unusual. At one apartment, two girls, who rented the apartment as roommates, lived there long enough to know Joey had lived there only about two months and Abby had been dating someone else before. They had never met Abby's old flame but were surprised when Joey moved in. Their eyes shone as they prompted each other to remember things about their unfortunate murdered neighbor.

"When one of our friends roomed with us for a short time, she saw an older guy go into Abby's apartment. She said the guy wasn't old enough to be her father but was still pretty old. We thought she could be seeing a married man," one of the young women said. Her roommate nodded her head and raised her eyebrows.

"Did you get a look at him?" Meg asked, ready to reach for the photos in her bag.

"No," the one girl said and looked at her roommate who this time shook her head.

"Do you think that guy might have killed her in a jealous rage or something?" the second roommate said, her eyes wide at the thought.

Beth ignored the rhetorical question. "Does your friend who saw him live close by?"

"She got a job in Chicago and moved there. It's been five or six months ago when she saw the guy. I doubt if she'd be able to remember what he looked like, anyway."

"But maybe she would remember one helpful detail."

Almost bursting with enthusiasm, one of the girls found their friend's cell phone number on her list of contacts. She dialed the number but found that it was no longer in service. Disappointed, Beth wrote down the absent friend's name, in case it might help the police, and thanked the girls for their time.

From inside the apartment at the end of the hallway, the sleuths could hear loud music with a heavy beat. They rang the bell and knocked a couple of times before the music ceased and the door was answered by a fit woman in her thirties wearing exercise clothing and wiping her brow with a towel. She listened patiently to their story before she shook her head.

"I'm sorry. I didn't see anything, and I really don't want to get involved."

"But we learned from another neighbor that you have known Beth for quite a while and that Joey played catch with your son. Don't you want to help all you can to find the murderer?" Meg said, sounding incredulous. "We're not the police. We're friends who are trying to do the right thing. You don't have to do anything except tell us whatever you know which might help solve her murder and give closure to her family." At least, Meg, in her distress, remembered to stick with the façade Beth had created—that they were friends of Abby's family.

The woman started to close the door in their faces, her eyes sparking with indignation toward this little lady with her strange bag who presumed to stand there and lecture her. She paused, however, when her son walked up behind her. He appeared to be nine or ten years old and had straight brown hair cut short so that his ears looked large. He held his open, sincere-looking face up to his mother and put his hand on the arm she was using to close the door.

His body was half hidden behind hers, as if he was a shy three-year-old, but his young voice was firm. "Mom, Mom, I saw that other guy, the old one, come here that night."

"Hush, Trent," said his mother.

"Mo-om, I didn't tell the police because you said we shouldn't, but someone's gotta know," Trent said.

"Was the 'other guy' the one who used to come here to see Abby before Joey moved in?" Beth asked. She bent her knees to sit on her heels so she would be at the little boy's level.

"Yeah, I saw him that--you know--*that* night." Trent got it out before his mother used her door-shutting arm to pull him behind her.

"Now, you see. I'm not having my only child be a witness for a murder. You can find someone else. There's probably another person out there who saw something that evening. I'm not putting him through police questioning and trials."

The lady didn't attempt to close the door again. She stood there looking defiant, willing them to go away. Young Trent stepped out from behind her, and she put her arm protectively around his shoulder. The little fellow gazed up at her with intensity, like Beth imagined Psycho Cat might look at Adrianna when he wanted to say something important but couldn't. His mother looked down at him thoughtfully but shook her head.

Beth glanced at Meg. Meg looked calm and collected on the outside, but she knew her sister was turbulent on the inside—taking a minute to collect her thoughts and decide how best to approach the mother's understandable attitude. Meg had been on teachers' association committees and had argued at school board meetings against raising class sizes when there were budget shortfalls. She was active in her local political meetings. This was a gal who could reason with pre-teens and with their parents. There must be something she could figure out to say which would convince Trent's mother to let him speak. In slow motion, Beth rose from her crouch to a standing position and waited to let Meg speak.

Meg looked her adversary in the eye and spoke politely. "I understand that you are a mother and are protecting your child. We weren't going to tell anyone who we are, because we thought people might be more open if we pretended to be friends of the victim. Actually, I am the mother of a young lady who is suspected of murdering her best friend Abby. No one else has been found with any information leading to a different suspect, and I'm so afraid that my daughter is in danger of a false accusation and arrest. I'm pleading with you to let me help protect my child. I have some photos in this bag. If you could let Trent look at them and see if he recognizes the man he saw, we'll try as hard as we can to use the information without telling the police where we got it. I don't want you or your son to be in a dangerous situation, either. Please, will you let him look at them?"

Trent looked up at his mother again. "Is it Okay, Mom?"

"You won't give the police or anyone his name?"

"Not without your permission."

She considered, sighed deeply, and gave her son a hug. "Okay, Trent, let's look at the pictures. I know what the man looks like, too. Even though I didn't see him last Thursday, I'm pretty sure Trent would recognize him if he saw him that night. I don't know his name, do you, Trent?"

"No," said the boy, "but I was out in the courtyard taking some trash to the dumpster when I saw him come in through the gate and go up the stairs to Beth and Joey's apartment. It was late. You know, like around 8:00, and the sun was already down. So I couldn't see him real well, but I know it was the guy that used to come see Abby."

"We were never introduced to the man," his mother said as she contemplated a package of photos she took from Meg, "but we saw him come around some evenings and on the weekends for several months. Abby acted really private about him. She did say they worked together, and I thought maybe there was a rule against dating a co-worker in her company; so I didn't pry. After Abby started seeing Joey again she seemed so happy to introduce us to him, and this spring they've been out in the courtyard and to the park with us a couple of times."

Trent's mother's shoulders relaxed. She told them her name was Lisa and asked them to come in so they could set the pictures down on the table to see them better. They all took a seat. Trent put his knees on the chair and his elbows on the table, eager to get started. Lisa looked ready to become involved as well. Of course, many of the pictures included Adrianna, whom Meg identified to them as her daughter, and many of them showed Abby standing next to or close to Adrianna. Beth noticed Lisa's eyes growing moist when she held a picture of Abby by herself, dressed in a lovely winter party dress.

"These were taken at some company holiday parties and summer barbeques," Meg said. "Be sure to look at the people in the background," she pointed out to Trent. "I didn't know I was going to need pictures of everyone who worked at the company when I took these, but for Adrianna's memory book I tried to get most of the employees into at least one shot."

Trent took his appointed task very seriously. One at a time, his mother studied each picture then set it down in front of Trent, holding back only one to reexamine. He picked each one up and studied the faces, squinted, and bent forward until his nose was ten inches from the table in order to see the faces in the background. After thorough scrutiny, he stacked most of the photos face down in a neat stack. One picture was left face up next to the stack, then another, but Trent went on through the rest in a concentrated manner before he spoke.

"I think the guy is in these two pictures," Trent said after he had looked at every one.

"And this could be him, too," Lisa said, holding out the picture that she had kept back. "Remember, though, I only ever saw him from a distance when he visited Abby's apartment."

Beth and Meg took the pictures and held them up with three hands, two of Meg's and one of Beth's. In one of the two snapshots Trent handed them, the man was in the midst of multiple revelers at the company's annual summer barbeque. In the other he was half turned away from the camera in a group of people toasting at the winter party. Lisa gave them a group photo with everyone facing forward. The man she identified stood on the far right-hand side in the back row. The people were in summer clothes and all had big, goofy smiles. Meg seemed to remember taking the picture last summer, and at first she thought the man could be Herb Reynolds. Beth thought the image in one of the pictures looked vaguely like Pete O'Neill. They decided they weren't sure who the man was.

"Thank you so much. This may not be our killer, but at the very least he should be able to tell the police what Beth was doing right before she was killed," Meg said. She gave both Lisa and Trent a spontaneous light kiss on the cheek before leaving.

Chapter 32—Picturing the Possibilities

"Many homicidal lunatics are very quiet, unassuming people.
Delightful fellows."

*- Agatha Christie, And Then There Were None: A Mystery Play in
Three Acts*

In the passenger seat, Meg sat with three photos on her lap. She stared at them as if all of a sudden she would have proof positive as to the identity of their primary suspect. "This looks like Herb Reynolds, but I'm not entirely sure," she said. "No, it looks like a slimmer man in this shot. I sure can't imagine Herb having an affair with anyone, let alone a young girl like Abby. I hope he's not the former boyfriend."

Meg continued scrutinizing the photos but couldn't seem to come to any conclusions. In one winter photo, the man wore a dress shirt, in the other, a sweater with long sleeves. In the summer shot, one of his arms was behind the person beside him, and the other was outside of the picture's edge. The elusive tattoo Beth kept hunting could not be seen, if it was there. In all three photos, the face was turned or partly obscured.

"What'll we do now?" asked Meg.

"What we should do is take these pictures directly to the police or maybe to Richard Montorlee," Beth said, frowning at the street ahead when the traffic light turned red.

"We can't. I promised Lisa I wouldn't give Trent's name to the police or to anyone. What will we say—I took these photos a couple of years ago, and we believe this man—whom we can't exactly identify—embezzled Renfro money and killed Abby? What kind of proof would we have? Besides, Trent and Lisa weren't exactly positive this is the guy. Didn't you hear them say 'I *think* this is the man' and 'this could be the man' when they gave us the pictures?"

"I know. Believe me I know. It's the same kind of promise I made to Adrianna's mom—that I would tell no one where I got my information about Max. The first thing we need to do is take these pictures to Adrianna and find out if she can identify the man in the photos. Maybe she'll know what motive he might have, and we can take that to the police without having to break our promises."

Meg called Adrianna, who didn't pick up. She left an eager-sounding message for her step-daughter to call back as soon as possible to help with a clue.

"Come to think of it," Meg said, "I believe Adrianna is with her lawyer this morning. It could be like a doctor's office where you have to spend an hour in the waiting room before it's your turn."

Beth rolled her eyes and nodded.

Meg's tone became flat, and she gazed out the side window. "Adrianna is going grocery shopping after her meeting. I told her I'd go for her, but she wants to have something to do. She's so tired of sitting around waiting to hear from Max and her lawyer. I could hear the tremor in her voice last night when she admitted she wasn't even sure she'd be able to go back to her job after her vacation time ends next week."

The day remained sunny after the threatening clouds had shadowed Beth's early morning walk. She felt full of energy and as brilliant as the sunshine reflecting off of the white stucco buildings they passed south of the Old Westport area. After gearing up to interview people in Abby's apartment building, she felt an impetuous determination to work out this new dilemma at once.

"Okay, I have an idea," she told Meg. "The killer is likely to go to the wake and the funeral, especially if he, or she, works at Renfro. The person wouldn't want to raise suspicion by not going. At least, well, that's what I've learned from detective shows. Seems logical, though. Have you checked the paper yet to find out if arrangements have been made for the visitation?"

"No, I didn't even take time to glance at the front page this morning."

"I didn't either. Let's find a newspaper and get something to eat while we wait to hear from Adrianna."

Bagel sandwiches and iced tea were welcome refreshments, and Beth ate with gusto. The sapping of all the mental and physical energy and tense shoulders from unaccustomed sleuthing gave her a big appetite.

On the obituary page of the *Kansas City Star*, plucked from the bistro counter, the sisters found the information. The funeral events for Abby would be observed in the Catholic tradition. There would be a "Vigil for the Deceased" service at 4:00 P.M. Saturday, which was this very afternoon. It was part of the wake, scheduled for 3:00-5:00 at the Rosewood Funeral Home. A funeral mass would take place Sunday afternoon at Abby's parents' church, with the burial service to follow. The notice in the paper listed a big family of survivors, mother and father, siblings, grandparents, and other extended family members.

Reading about Abby's short life, and those left to mourn, made Beth sad and even more frightened for Adrianna. Only an evil and incorrigible person—those words didn't even suffice in Beth's opinion—could take a young person's life, whether for the sake of greed, jealousy, rage, or even fear.

It was noon when Adrianna returned her step-mother's call. From what Beth could hear from Meg's end of the conversation, Adrianna's morning must have been discouraging. The sisters had too much to tell Adrianna to elaborate over the phone. Meg, after a quick consultation with Beth, asked if they might meet at the condo, bring Adrianna a bagel sandwich and a drink, tell her all they had learned, and find out what the lawyer said.

***

"You're a handsome, furry, nice kitty," Beth said in her baby voice. She kneeled on the carpet of Adrianna's apartment to rub the upturned tummy of Psycho Cat. Beth rather missed the capricious creature, even though he had lived at her house for only a few days.

Adrianna returned to the living room after storing the rest of her groceries in the kitchen and grinned at the sight of the cat being made over by her aunt. She placed her hands on her hips when she caught her step-mother sitting on the sofa fluffing pillows and then straightening a stack of magazines on the coffee table.

"What are you doing, Mama Meg?" Adrianna said, and smiled. "Don't you think I keep my place tidy enough?"

Meg's hands flew to her lap, and she looked contrite. "No, I mean, yes. I'm sorry. Your apartment is spotless. I guess I'm nervous and need to stay busy is all."

Adrianna sat down and put her arm around her step-mother. "I was kidding," she said. "I know how you are. In fact, I start tidying up when I'm nervous, too. I must have learned it from you."

The condemned consoled the grieving parent. Beth had noticed Adrianna's slip into childhood jargon with "Mama Meg." Meredith had always been Mom or Mother, but Poppa Paul and Mama Meg starred in the role of real parents. Was Adrianna feeling vulnerable enough to give up? Beth hoped not. They needed to get this thing solved.

"So what did Richard Montorlee have to say?" she asked.

Adrianna told them there was not much news from the lawyer. The police were rechecking the evidence gathered at the murder scene, but she still remained the primary theft suspect and also a possible murder suspect. Finally, at her step-mother's urging, Adrianna sat down to eat her sandwich while Beth told her about their sleuthing at Abby's apartment building.

Meg came over, sat down, and placed an envelope containing the three photos picked out by Trent and Lisa on the table in front of Adrianna. She tapped her fingers while Beth described the morning's events. Finally, Beth indicated the pictures they wanted Adrianna to consider.

"We need you to identify the man our witnesses pointed out as being Abby's visitor. None of the images are very clear, but we hope you'll be able to recognize him." Beth was careful not to use Lisa or Trent's names, even to Adrianna. She would hide their identities unless forced to reveal them. Even then, she decided, she'd let Meg try to get Lisa's permission first.

With a huff and a slight shake of her head that said *well, finally*, Meg laid out the photos from the envelope. She used the end of a pen to point out the image in question on each one. Adrianna examined the three pictures then looked up with a short, dismissive laugh.

"This is interesting, but it's not conclusive by any means. Listen to me. I'm talking like a lawyer. Your witnesses identified two different people. These two--and she indicated the figure in the winter photo and one of the summer photos—are pictures of Pete O'Neill, the director of Human Resources and Payroll. The other one is Herb Reynolds, don't you see? They resemble each other. Only Pete is a little younger and has a red tint in his hair. Like you said, the men are in the background, and it's not easy to differentiate unless you know them well. Herb Reynolds never wants to have his picture taken; that's probably why you didn't have him in more of your photos."

Beth and Meg grabbed the snapshot in question and bent down to look so fast they bumped heads. "Ohmygosh," Meg said in a whisper, rubbing her bruise, "after Li... I mean the witnesses picked these three pictures, I didn't even think to make sure they were all of the same man. And I do see now, this one is Herb, for sure."

"Well, he has his head mostly turned away. It's reasonable we didn't pick up the difference," Beth said. "But I can see how our witnesses could mistake one for the other. Adrianna, do you know why either one of them would be visiting Abby?"

"Hmmm, Abby broke up with Joey soon after I was promoted. Then she stopped being friendly to me. I had a notion maybe Pete O'Neill came on to her after I turned him down, and she was embarrassed to tell me they were dating, because she was his second choice. But I didn't know for sure. It was just a thought. Pete went out with every single gal in the company who was willing.

"Abby wouldn't discuss with me why she broke up with Joey or who she was seeing. She must have been short on funds after Joey left. She likes nice things. So it could have been Mr. Reynolds, since he would have lots more money to spend on an affair than Pete.

"Oh and there's another thing," Adrianna said. "I heard Herb Reynolds and his wife separated last month. The separation is understandable if Mr. Reynolds was seeing Abby on the sly." Adrianna put her elbows on the table and her face in her hands.

Adrianna's world was quaking, and it seemed every time she thought the last brick had fallen, another aftershock rolled in. Beth didn't want Adrianna to lose her confidence under the amassing pile of rubble.

Beth said, "I know someone else who might be able to help us identify the Thursday night visitor. Adrianna, please call your mother and tell her we need to talk to her as soon as we can get there."

After talking to her mother for some time and explaining several times why they needed to see her, Adrianna clicked her phone shut. With a frown on her face, she told them her mother had *sort of* agreed to their visit. Meg set her jaw and shook her head. Beth felt like rushing over there and punching Meredith in the gut.

Chapter 33—Confronting the Truth

"If you confront anyone who has lied with the truth, he will usually admit it - often out of sheer surprise. It is only necessary to guess right to produce your effect."
- Agatha Christie, *Murder on the Orient Express*

Fresh and sunny, people flitting about tidying their lawns like birds fluttering around their nests in the treetops, the spring day was meant for lightheartedness. Beth attempted to think positive thoughts as she drove her somber companions toward Meredith's apartment. She reconsidered Adrianna's mother's reaction with a little more charity. Meredith may have slept until noon after getting in at 3:00 or so in the morning. Adrianna woke her with the phone call. After they explained the situation in person, Adrianna's mother was likely to be eager to help—well, maybe not eager, but perhaps willing.

She noticed a mother watching her youngster learn to ride a tricycle up and down their driveway. Huge smiles blossomed on both faces as the mother rejoiced over her child's expanding ability to use his muscles and to control a bit of machinery. Beth wondered if Meredith ever had that kind of experience with Adrianna.

***

"I guess Tom Collins could be one of them two guys. About the same look. 'Course, without that gorgeous mustache, it's hard to tell." Meredith said. She held each photo at arm's length, then close to her face. She threw them onto the table. "Those aren't very good pictures. Besides, it was a few months ago when I saw him, and I was a little plastered by the time he…" She glanced at her daughter.

"I know, Mom. You gave him Max's contact info, and he threatened to hurt you if you told anyone," Adrianna said.

Meredith turned on Meg. "Shit. You promised not to tell anyone about that," she said. "I should have known better than to trust you two b…"

"Mother!" Adrianna said.

Meg stayed mute, but inner conflict showed on her face. It was surely a struggle to keep from lashing back at the woman, but she had never in her life said anything negative to Meredith or about her to her daughter.

"Meg didn't tell," Beth said. "When Arnie and I flew to the Virgin Islands to find Adrianna, I had to explain how I located her and why you were afraid to tell the police where she was. Anyway, since you were the only one who had a clue Adrianna had gone there to visit Max, she could have easily guessed how we found out."

"Yeah, you think you're a hero?" Meredith said. "If you hadn't gone and brought Adrianna back, she'd be safe hiding down there right now. And I wouldn't have to worry about someone finding me and beating me up—or worse. Say, how'd you find out in the first place that Adrianna was gone? I thought you weren't going to tell anyone you were leaving, Adrianna."

"It was my cat, Sylvester," Adrianna said. "He needed tending, and Meg always takes good care of him."

"Cat you nicknamed Psycho? Good name. Cat must be like the step-relatives." Meredith mumbled her jibe to the table top with a scowl on her face and didn't look at Adrianna.

Adrianna stood up from the table and stood with her arms crossed, as if daring anyone to oppose her purpose. "You're right. If it hadn't been for the kitty announcing my absence, I'd still be with Max. But I don't want to hide out. I want to prove my innocence."

"No one here is trying to be a hero," Beth said, "and no one's at fault, either, except for the bad guys who stole money and murdered a young woman. We need to concentrate on finding out who did those things. Meredith, we can't see any tattoos in these photos, but can you describe the tattoo you saw on Tom Collins' arm for Adrianna? Maybe she will recognize having seen it on someone."

"Uh, I don't remember exactly," Meredith said. "It was a design, and it came about to his elbow. That's all."

The memory lapse seemed strange, because if there was one area in which Meredith Knells was a connoisseur…it was tattoos. All kinds of tattoos covered her body—her hands, arms, feet, legs, stomach, back, and neck, not to mention places Beth would rather not see. Some of the tats were rather artistic, in Beth's opinion, but all of them together reminded her of a jammed flea market.

Beth knew Adrianna, on the other hand, averted her eyes when she saw a tattoo on someone's body, and she exhibited none on her own. Single piercings, only, in her ears—at age twenty she had decided to get her ears pierced, but only because she had received, from an unobservant college boyfriend, a pair of pearl earring studs which she wanted to wear to a dance. Since then, Adrianna always wore studs or small hoops in her ears. When Beth and Meg talked about their wrinkle creams and hair products, Adrianna admitted to using only shampoo, cleansing cream, minimal make-up, and classy earrings each day.

Pureness of body image, a one-drink limit of any kind of alcoholic beverage, aversion to medicines and drugs of any kind— those were some of the characteristics Adrianna had assumed. She never talked about it, but Beth thought Adrianna strove to differentiate herself from her mother and maybe to be a role model for her.

It made sense Adrianna would not be able to describe or remember tattoos, but Meredith? The entire visit was a disappointment in terms of gaining more information, but at least Meredith seemed happy to see her daughter back home and safe. The two had exchanged huge hugs when Adrianna walked in, and the faded mother closed her hand over Adrianna's for minute when the four women first sat at the table. Maybe Adrianna would remember her initial greeting rather than her mother's self-centered attitude now.

Finally, Beth looked at her watch. "Thanks for looking at the pictures," she said to Meredith. "We need to go so we can make it to another appointment this afternoon."

Meg nodded, but Adrianna cocked her head and frowned as if wondering if the remark was an excuse to leave. Beth led the way to the door where she turned back to Meredith.

"Have you heard any more from Tom Collins since we talked to you last week?" Beth couldn't believe she hadn't remembered to ask that question earlier.

Meredith looked at the floor and spoke so softly Beth had to lean in closer to hear what she said. "He, uh, called me during the afternoon on Thursday before Adrianna got home. Told me Adrianna was on her way and warned me again not to tell the police or anyone about him." She looked up at the three women and begged, "You still aren't going to tell the cops anything about the information I gave the guy and about the money he gave me, are you?"

"That means this—this creep knew I was coming home even before I got here," Adrianna said, wide-eyed. She paused. Then something seemed to click. It was as if she hadn't until just then grasped the entire connection between the theft here, her trip to the Virgin Islands, and the accusation for the murder of her friend. Adrianna crossed her arms and tilted her head. "Did he offer you more money to continue to keep your mouth shut?"

"Picked up an envelope with my name typed on it at the bar. Four hundred dollar bills were inside," Meredith mumbled.

The three women paused, mouths open. Adrianna looked as if she would say something, but she shook her head instead and closed her lips tightly. She turned on her heels and sped down the hallway without looking back. Beth and Meg followed.

Meredith yelled at them from her doorway, "He threatened us again. He said I could get hurt, or he would hurt you, if I rat on him. What was I going to do?"

They heard her again, following them and screeching as they were about to leave the building. "You're not going to tell the police about this, are you? I don't need them cops poking around here...Adrianna. I'm trying to protect you, too! Meg! Beth, you're not..."

Chapter 34—Going Forward

"One of us in this very room is in fact the murderer."

- Agatha Christie, *And Then There Were None*

Adrianna stood by the back door of the car until Beth unlocked it. She lunged inside and sat perfectly still, her arms again folded across her chest and her lips tight. Beth got behind the wheel and glanced in the rear-view mirror. She saw tears in Adrianna's eyes. For several minutes no one talked. Beth turned the radio down to the bare minimum. Cheerful pop music created an uncomfortable vibe, considering the mood of the car's occupants. Complete quiet was distressing, too, though.

At last, Adrianna opened up. "I called Mom Thursday evening right after all of you left. I told her everything that had happened. She never once mentioned she had been contacted by anyone. It would have made a difference when I was talking to the police and Richard Montorlee, to know someone knew I was coming back and was calling to intimidate my mother."

Meg was visibly seething, but she was still careful what she said about Meredith. "It's partly our fault," she said. "We made the promise to your mom to keep her secret in order to get Max's contact information. We did that because, at that time, we only wanted to find you. Promising not to tell was the only way we could get the information. She understands that some man threatened both

176

of you with violence, not the implication that someone in the Virgin Islands must have told that vile person you were on your way home."

"She understands the money," Adrianna said.

Neither Meg nor Beth commented further. Beth glanced at her sister as she drove. Meg sat staring straight ahead, working her fingers together in her lap as if warming them up to direct a choir. Beth wondered what music she'd choose. She decided they needed to move on. Concentrating on recriminations and lost opportunities wasn't going to help.

"Adrianna, you call your lawyer and tell him what you learned today. This time, we didn't make any promises to your mom to keep the information about the threats to ourselves, and Mr. Montorlee can counsel you what to do. If he thinks you and your mother are in danger, you can both come to my house and stay. Maybe the police will guard the house."

"I'll call Mr. Montorlee," Adrianna said, "and thank you for the invitation, but I feel safe at the condo building with Chuck and the other security guards. After all, Chuck told the police I stayed in and had pizza the night of the—the—murder."

Beth and Meg shot each other skeptical glances.

"Have you talked to Max yet today?" Beth asked.

"He called early this morning before going off to work. He said he'd talk to as many people today as he could, but he has to work until 3:00 this afternoon. That's 2:00 our time. Then he'll go out later this afternoon and evening to try to find any of his acquaintances who might have a tie to Renfro or know who does. He'll call this afternoon, I think."

"Good. Then, there's another duty we need to attend to today. I know this will be hard for you, Adrianna. From the newspaper obituaries we found out the wake for Beth is from 3:00-5:30 this afternoon. We should go and watch the visitors. There are bound to be people from Renfro. And the murderer, if he is one of the two men in the photos or anyone else from Renfro, might be there for the sake of not arousing suspicion with his absence. Joey will be there, too. I know he has an alibi for Thursday night, but if he's involved in any way, you might be able to tell by how he acts. Meg and I don't know these people well enough to read their faces."

"Aunt Beth, everyone from Renfro will look at me with suspicion. They all probably think I embezzled money from the company, and for all I know they may even think I killed Abby."

"You can go there with your chin up, Adrianna, because you know you've done nothing wrong. And if people shun you, we can sit and watch how they interact with each other. Do you think you can do that?"

"I do want to pay my respects to Abby's family and to—to say goodbye—because Abby was my friend." Adrianna raised her chin and uncrossed her arms. "I can handle it," she said.

Beth realized Adrianna was a lady who made her living interacting and negotiating mostly with men in the construction business. She should be able to deal with the people at the wake.

Chapter 35—Attending the Visitation

'Come, Watson, come!' he cried. 'The game is afoot. Not a word!
Into your clothes and come!'

- Sherlock Holmes Quote

-The Adventure of the Abbey Grange

Beth hurried home to change clothes after dropping Adrianna and
Meg at their respective domiciles, and she found Arnie holding the
kitchen door from the garage open for her. Sometimes he reminded
her of a faithful dog, loving and watchful. Beth rushed toward him
and stumbled up the steps. He grabbed her before she could fall and
gave her a hug. Earlier, she had called to let him know she was taking
Adrianna and Meg to see Meredith. Now, she pulled herself away,
walked with him into the kitchen, dropped her purse on the counter,
and brought him up to date on her morning and the plan to attend
the visitation for Abby.

"If Meredith and Adrianna have been threatened by some
unidentified person who could, by the way, very well show up at the
funeral home," Arnie said, "then I don't think you three women
should be going there by yourselves. If you're determined to go, I'll
go with you."

"Thanks, Hon," Beth said. "But we'll go in and leave from the
front parking lot where all the people will be coming and going, and
we'll merely sit through the visitation and the Vigil service. Nothing
can happen to us in front of all those folks. It'll be safe. You would

get too antsy. Meg and I will appear as two lady relatives there to support Adrianna."

"I know, but..."

"Richard Montorlee will be the only person, besides us, who will know Meredith broke down and told Adrianna about the phone call she got while we were on the way home. The bad guy made threats and paid money to keep Meredith from shooting off her mouth about him. He has no idea Adrianna knows about him."

"I understand, but..."

"Also, as far as the killer knows, Adrianna is the only suspect for the crimes. At this point he wants to keep her alive so she can take the fall."

Beth could see Arnie wavering. He didn't care for weddings, funerals, or long ceremonies of any kind.

"Okay, you're right," he said at last. "A funeral home packed with people is probably a safe place. I want you to stay aware of the people around you, though, and keep your cell phone in your pocket ready to press your speed dial for me if you see any suspicious activity. I'll be right here watching the game on television while I finish the paperwork I brought home this weekend, and I can call the police and be there in a few minutes."

"Agreed," Beth said. "And if it makes you feel better, I was thinking, it's probable Detective Carl Rinquire or one of the other investigating officers will be there to watch for suspicious behavior. He'd protect us, too."

"Makes sense," Arnie said.

***

At 3:05 P.M., Beth, Meg, and Adrianna arrived at the funeral home in Beth's car. Beth wore her dark gray herringbone suit with a black shell under the jacket. She stashed her phone, set on "vibrate only," in her jacket pocket as she stepped to the pavement.

Beth had complimented Meg on her soft navy-blue dress when she picked her up, but neither of them found the right time during the dark journey to tell Adrianna how stunning she looked.

The young lady wore a dark gray straight skirt with a tailored black silk blouse and gray pearls. Tiny matching pearl earrings, thick auburn hair swept up off of her neck, and her long dark lashes all contributed to Adrianna's striking appearance and caused the people heading to services to turn and gaze at her with appreciation. In her general demeanor, Adrianna seemed unconscious of her attractiveness and reacted to everyone with a disarming friendliness and openness that made her lovable. Beth hoped those qualities would help protect Adrianna during this potentially formidable funeral home visit.

The parking lot was nearly full. The aging funeral home, despite its long, low red brick exterior and its newly poured concrete drive, revealed its years of use in the tiny chips of paint missing from the wood of the door and window frames. More than twenty people were waiting outside one of the chapels to sign the visitor book, many having already entered.

"Wow," Meg said, "This is the biggest crowd I've ever seen at a wake."

The foyer was spacious, the windows were meticulously clean, and the furnishings, wood framed upholstered chairs, wooden end tables, pottery lamps, and a soothing pastel landscape painting, were inviting. However, the moldings and wallpaper were slightly faded, and there was a faint smell of aging carpet and heating vent dust in the air. The funeral home sat near a busy street with the cemetery extending for several acres behind and to both sides of it. There was a Catholic Church across the street, and Beth imagined Abby's ancestors had been interred in the consecrated grounds of its cemetery for decades.

On the way in, Adrianna nodded at someone who stared at her from the guest book signing line. Rather than return the nod, the woman turned immediately to whisper to a companion who craned her neck around to look curiously at Beth's polished young step-niece. Adrianna straightened her shoulders and took her place in line between Meg and Beth. For the first time during the duration of the wake, Beth regretted dragging Adrianna into this fishbowl.

"Oh, isn't that pretty?" Meg said when they stepped from the lobby into the chapel. "I guess the flower arrangement I ordered is among the dozens of others around the casket. Abby must have lots of friends and family."

"She has a huge family," Adrianna said. "She was a sweet person who attracted people. I bet some of her high school friends are here, and there are probably church friends and neighborhood friends from childhood, besides the people from work."

"The woman up front getting all the hugs must be her mom," Beth said, indicating a middle-aged, short, round woman sitting in the front pew wearing a plain black suit. Every so often the grieving lady plucked a tissue from a box beside her, dabbed her eyes with it, and jammed it into her suit jacket pocket. It was a wonder the pocket accepted all that paper.

"It's so great funeral homes these days celebrate the life of the deceased by displaying photos and DVD shows of the person's life. I've only met Abby twice, but the video makes me feel as if I've known her since her childhood."

"Do you want us to queue up with you in the reception line?" Meg asked Adrianna.

"Well, I…" Adrianna said. "I never met Abby's family."

"Really?" Meg said, with the shocked expression of a woman used to meeting and visiting with nearly all of her children's friends.

"We'd be putting her on display up there," Beth said into Meg's ear.

"Oh good grief, of course we would," Meg said, and turned to her step-daughter. "I'm sorry, Adrianna. I didn't mean to put you on the spot. Me and my darned penchant for doing what's expected—I didn't think about how going through that line would make you feel."

"Don't worry about it," Adrianna said with a small smile. She pointed to the pew on their left, second to the back of the small chapel. "Let's sit here so we can watch the people and head out early, if—you know—if we decide we should."

Meg walked into the row and took a seat. Adrianna started to stand aside, but Beth motioned for her to go in and sit in the middle so she'd have support on both sides.

Beth and Meg glanced through the programs they had been handed at the door for the service to be held at 4:00. Adrianna sat folding and unfolding her pamphlet while looking around at the people in the chapel like a trapped gold fish gazing at the occupants of a room from its fish bowl. Unlike a fish, Adrianna was able to clamp her eyes closed briefly when her scrutiny slid past the casket.

Protestant visitations Beth had attended included no formal speakers. Always interested in learning about the rituals and beliefs of others, she looked forward with interest to witnessing the Catholic observance of the "Vigil for the Deceased." According to the printed schedule, there would be certain prayers, music, and spokespersons to speak in remembrance of the dead girl. The Funeral Mass, the formal funeral service, was to take place Sunday afternoon at the church, as the newspaper had indicated.

Some of the visitors, when they left the front of the chapel, gathered in small groups and talked together in muted voices. Others sat alone or in groups on the pews and looked around or prayed silently. Beth's group spoke in whispers.

"Do you see anyone else from Renfro besides the snippy gals who ignored you in line?" Beth asked Adrianna.

"Oh, you noticed," Adrianna said. "No, I saw them pay their respects and then leave. No one else has shown up yet. I'll tell you what, when the service starts I'll nudge you both if I see anyone from Renfro come in. Okay?"

Meg asked Adrianna why she never met Abby's family members. After all, Abby had been to Meg's house several times over the few years the two young women had been friends. Adrianna, looking blankly into space and shaking her head in regret, whispered she didn't know for sure why, but it never happened.

"Once we were going to go to a greeting-card-making party at the home of one of her sisters. But at the last minute, Abby made an excuse she had something else to do. I got the feeling she was really hesitant to introduce me to her family." Adrianna sighed. "I hope she wasn't embarrassed by me or, worse, I hope I didn't give her the impression I'm a stuck-up suburban bitch and would snub her folks. That's a possibility. The way she acted toward me after I got the promotion."

Meg patted her step-daughter's hand. "Now, Adrianna, don't become self-deprecating. You are not the bad guy here. All you need to do is watch for the Renfro people as they come in." She squinted and gave her step-daughter a devilish smirk. "Don't worry, Sweetie, if anyone else gives you a sideways look and starts whispering, I'll give her my teacher glare."

Renfro was not a huge company. At a few intervals, Adrianna directed attention to colleagues who came in twos or threes to show their respect. Meg whispered names when she recognized some of the Renfro employees.

At one point Beth said, "Oh, that's Allison, the front desk receptionist who helped me talk to Abby."

After paying her respects at the front of the chapel with another young employee, Allison spotted Beth and her companions in their back pew, raised her eyebrows in surprise, grinned, and gave them a silly wave with her fingers as she walked by on her way past them toward the exit. Beth nodded. She mused about how the three of them would be the topic of an earthy dialog between Allison and her companion all the way home.

None of the Renfro people stayed long. They came, paid their respects, and left. Adrianna wrote their names and jobs on a small tablet she held behind her purse on her lap. Three administrative assistants, two project managers, some clerical staff, and a couple of their spouses came and went, some of them aware of Adrianna's presence and some not. To her consternation, Beth didn't see Detective Carl Rinquire, and neither Herb Reynolds nor Pete O'Neill made an appearance.

At one point Beth heard Adrianna catch her breath.

"What is it?" Meg asked.

Beth, following Adrianna's gaze, looked behind her pew and out into the foyer. Joey appeared to have entered through a door from an adjacent room, maybe an office. He frowned as he talked to someone dressed in a long white linen robe with tapered sleeves. The robed gentleman wasn't wearing the stole and vestments of a priest. Beth imagined he was a lay minister or an assistant priest, maybe a deacon. The two were speaking quietly but earnestly as they entered the chapel and proceeded up the center aisle. They did not appear to notice anyone until they reached the front and the minister turned toward the crowd.

"Please take your seats," he said, "for the Vigil Service."

People quietly took seats. Joey sat down in a front pew in front of the podium rather than in front of the casket where most of the immediate family sat.

Certainly, Beth decided, this service wasn't nearly as formal as the Funeral Mass would be on Sunday, but it definitely was long on ritual. Thirty minutes into the service, Beth was becoming antsy. She squirmed a bit and pulled her feet out of her pumps to stretch her toes. She noticed Meg and Adrianna changing positions a few times, also. Well, at any rate, the procedural, with its time-honored prayers and music, must be comforting to the family.

It was quarter till five before the minister announced, "Andrew West, brother of the deceased, will say a few words in honor of his sister."

Andrew, obviously an older brother of Abby's who favored his mother with his short stocky build, spoke briefly about Abby's happy childhood, her humor, spirit, and ambitions to better herself by taking business classes.

"I'm sorry for not being a better speaker," he said, "but I think I speak for my whole family when I say how much we all loved and respected Abby. Her death has been so hard for us because she was taken at such a young age. My parents never thought they'd outlive any of their children."

The sound of sobbing acknowledged appreciation of the speaker's words better than thunderous applause.

Next, Joey was introduced. "Joseph Zitelli," the minister said, "was Abigail's closest companion and friend in the months before her death."

Joey took a whole minute to look up, rise from his seat, move slowly to the podium, situate his notes, survey the audience from one side to the other, and clear his throat. His voice was deep and clear when he finally spoke. In plain language he told about his affection for Abby. He said she was so full of life and always wanted to do more; at that point he had to clear his throat again. Referring to their breakup that lasted several months, Joey revealed he had been heartbroken and a man without purpose until they reconciled. Since then, they had been busy planning their wedding and honeymoon and planned to use the money they had both been saving.

Joey lifted his head, looked out at the audience with an angry frown and said with fierce determination, "Now we have to find the murderer who ended my sweetheart's life as well as mine, and bring that criminal to justice."

The minister quickly stepped up to the podium and placed himself in front of the microphone with a look of disapproval. Beth guessed the ban on mentioning the murder was what they had been discussing when they entered. Joey meekly took his seat, but Andrew West reached across the aisle and patted his shoulder when he sat down, and it was easy to see the nods of approval from the rest of the family as they leaned forward and watched him sit down. It looked as if they wanted to give him the withheld ovation.

Chapter 36—Exiting Danger

"I felt that I breathed an atmosphere of sorrow."

— Edgar Allan Poe

A cacophony of sound permeated the small chapel as soon as the service ended. The undertones were forgotten. Most everyone stood up and moved around. Some left; some continued to visit with each other and probed to find out what their friends thought of Joey's outburst. A few latecomers made their way in and proceeded to the front to pay their respects to Abby's immediate family and to Joey, who had joined them. Renfro president, Herb Reynolds, was in the latter group. Adrianna nudged Beth and Meg when he walked in alone near the end of the service before Joey spoke.

"There's Mr. Reynolds. He's sitting over there," Adrianna said under her breath after the service ended, her hitchhiker thumb indicating the far side of the chapel, opposite theirs. "I was beginning to think he wasn't going to show up."

Herb's sports coat and tie with casual pants suggested an attempt to upgrade his Saturday work at the office attire for this occasion. It didn't appear he had noticed Adrianna and her family. In short order, he took his place at the end of the small line of people gathered to greet Abby's family, smiled, and exchanged a few indiscernible words with a young couple and their child who stood in front of him. Beth, watching him carefully, wished she had the ability or experience to be a better judge of how nervous or guilty behavior looked. She saw

Herb look briefly at the casket and then away. That is exactly what she would have done. Herb Reynolds looked pretty normal. Of course, he could be a good actor.

"I don't think we're going to learn anything new by watching people here," Beth said, "and we're the only ones still seated, except for the family. Are you two ready to leave?"

"Yeah," Adrianna said, and picked up her purse. "I've already seen a few people look at us like they're wondering who we are and why we're still sitting here. Let's go."

"I'm ready," Meg said.

The three started to stand and turned to look toward the aisle when Adrianna sat back down with a plop and tugged Beth and Meg down with her. She looked down and acted as if she was digging into her purse for something.

"I saw Pete O'Neill and the new bookkeeper enter the chapel door from the lobby," Adrianna said. "I don't really want to run into them on the way out."

Beth looked toward the isle and studied the passing profile of the man who looked so much like Herb Reynolds, the man she had met briefly during her Renfro visits—comparable height, weight, build, and even haircut. In spite of the similarities, however, it was fairly easy to tell them apart in person—probably the reason Beth had not noticed before how much they looked alike. Herb had more gray in his hair and more pleasing, regular facial features than Pete, whose nose was more prominent and whose eyes, at least from this angle, looked small and squinty.

Beside Pete, his hand moving from her elbow to her lower back, strode a young blond female. She wore a little too much make-up and, in Beth's opinion, clothes too tight to be worn on such a solemn occasion. When the pair was out of earshot down the center aisle, Adrianna said, "That gal is dressed to be a pick-up at a local tavern rather than to attend a funeral. She's the new bookkeeper, hired to help Abby. She worked at Renfro for only a month before I took my trip to the Virgin Islands."

"Mr. O'Neill seems to be acting awfully friendly with her," Meg said.

"He's a "womanizer"—probably why he's divorced."

They watched as Herb Reynolds introduced himself to each family member and expressed his regrets. He was almost through when Pete O'Neill, now holding the hand of his bookkeeper protégée, leaned over to greet Abby's mother, still sitting in her pew. Beth saw Herb look up and notice his two employees. She was too far away to see any change of expression on his face, but she noticed he shook hands with the last of Abby's siblings and then sauntered past the podium to the side aisle on the far right.

Herb leaned against the wall, crossed his arms, and observed. Adrianna had dipped her head, but Beth was sure she saw Herb pause and drop his arms as his gaze rested on Meg for a few seconds. Perhaps he recognized the pretty head between Meg and her, also, but he continued sweeping his regard around the room until he again turned toward the group at the front.

Pete O'Neill and his companion must have found very little to say to the family, even though they had both associated with Abby every work day, for several years in O'Neill's case. They fired off their condolences as if in a hurry to catch a train, or a dinner reservation, and then turned and started toward the door. As they did, Herb Reynolds, with a scowl, pushed himself away from the wall and started toward the center aisle through one of the empty pews. Pete stopped when he noticed his boss coming. His face turned a startling bubblegum pink, and he whispered something to his companion who immediately clicked away in her stiletto heels toward the restrooms.

Beth sat transfixed as the two men spoke heatedly to each other in low voices. She saw Herb nod in her group's direction. Pete turned and stared, then turned back to Herb. Beth grabbed her purse and Adrianna's arm, got Meg's attention, and jerked her head toward the door. However, before they took two steps toward the center aisle, a voice called out from the side aisle behind them. They had been too busy watching Pete O'Neil and Herb Reynolds to notice Joey Zitelli make his way up the side of the chapel shaking hands and accepting hugs along the way.

"Adrianna, Mrs. Knells," Joey said. "I didn't see you here until now. I want to thank you for coming." He saw Beth turn with the others, and recognition hit. "You're the lady who..."

"Joey, this is my Aunt Beth," Adrianna said.

"You have a good memory of faces. I visited your apartment to talk to Abby when Adrianna was missing," Beth said. "I'm so sorry for your loss."

"Joey," Adrianna said, "I hope you don't think that I..."

"I don't know what to think," Joey said, lowering his eyes. "Honestly, I don't know why anyone could have murdered my Abby, but it's hard for me to accept that you would have done it."

"You have no way of knowing whether to believe me, but I didn't steal money from the company, either," Adrianna said, "and I hope we'll soon be able to prove it."

"The truth is," Joey said, "my neighbor told me about a visit she had from two women. From what she said, I think one of them women must have been you, Mrs. Knells."

"What all did she tell you?" Meg asked.

"She said she identified Abby's old boyfriend from some photos you showed her and that he was at our apartment complex the night of Abby's... Anyway, he could be the killer. Have you shown the pictures to the police? Do you know who he is?"

"Not yet, to both questions. The identification was a little foggy. There were two men identified in the photos, men who look somewhat alike," Meg said.

"Do you know the name of Abby's old boyfriend?" Beth asked.

"No. I wish I did," Joey said. "She wouldn't tell me. I think she worked with him, and she was embarrassed. Do you know who it was, Adrianna?"

"No," Adrianna said. "Abby didn't share that with me, and like Meg said, there were two men in those photos. We're not sure which one it was, if either, and of course we aren't positive one of them was involved in the murder. He may have visited that evening for some sound reason."

"Abby seemed very upset after the embezzlement came to light—so much that she took time off work. Maybe the guy came to reassure her, especially since they may have had a romantic connection," Beth said.

"Maybe, but I'd like to get my hands on the guy. I'd find out what he knows."

"We're going to give our photos to the police and let them work on it, Joey," Meg said.

Beth noticed Joey's eyes straying to the center isle behind her and turned her head to see Pete O'Neill and Herb Reynolds standing near, maybe within earshot. They stopped talking and took off toward the lobby when they saw Joey and Beth look their way. There was no telling how much of the conversation with Joey they had overheard, if any. She turned back to the group.

"Did you recognize the men who just now walked by?" Beth asked Joey.

"I think one of them, I'm not sure which one, is—uh—was Abby's boss at Renfro, the head of the Accounting Department. I met him once before our break-up. Why?"

"Oh, no reason. They seemed to have been standing there scrutinizing our group."

"I don't know," Joey said. "I noticed them right before you looked back. Maybe they were curious about Adrianna and her family being here."

Adrianna's eyes grew large, and she fumbled to collect her purse and the order of service off the bench. "We'd better let you get back with the family, Joey, and let people honor Abby rather than watch me."

All three women saw Herb and Pete face each other in conversation on one side of the lobby as they passed through. When they started across the drive toward the parking lot, Beth glanced back and saw both of the men exiting the front door of the funeral home. A spike of adrenaline made her heart pound so hard she felt as if she were heading to the guillotine to the beat of drums.

Beth quickened her pace and motioned to Meg and Adrianna to hurry. She rolled her eyes and pointed her thumb backward to indicate they were being followed. The car was on the far side of the lot. She looked back and saw Herb and Pete in the parking lot heading straight toward them. How were they going to get to the car, crawl inside, and drive away before the two men caught up? And what would the men do if they did catch up?

As Beth was about to run and pull her sister and step-niece with her, a man opened a car door in front of them, got out, and approached. The three women kept walking and were prepared to slip around him when he spoke a cheerful greeting, "Well, hi there. I was hoping to talk to you inside, but I'm glad to be able to see you before you leave!"

Before Beth could bolt, he grabbed her elbow, a little too firmly. As Meg and Adrianna slowed to protect Beth, he took Meg's elbow with his other hand and whispered in a gruff voice, "I'm a police officer here to keep track of things. I saw the men following you. Pretend you know me, and I'll watch until you get safely to your car."

Beth remembered seeing this man stand off by himself for a short time and then blend in with the crowd in the lobby when they first entered. During the service, she recalled, he sat in the back pew opposite them with some other folks.

She relaxed a little and tried to keep her voice from shaking. "Oh, my goodness, Mark, it's been a long time. Meg, remember Arnie's friend from work? You met him at that one party at our house. Mark, this is Adrianna, my niece. Do you know the West family, too, Mark?"

"The family has been my neighbor for years. It's sad about their daughter," the policeman said in a voice which could be heard across the parking lot.

The ladies nodded.

"Well, I won't keep you. I just wanted to say hi. Tell Arnie we need to get together again soon. Listen, the parking lot is almost empty. I'll watch until you get to your car."

"Thank you, Mark," Beth said. Then she added in a soft aside with a grateful look, "Thanks a lot."

She chanced a look back as they reached the car. Herb Reynolds was getting into the driver's side of a car, and Pete O'Neill was headed back into the funeral home. The plain clothes detective had scared them away. Or…maybe they had come out into the parking lot to continue their contentious conversation and weren't following the three women after all. Beth was feeling more confused than ever as she pulled out of the parking lot.

In the car, Meg and Adrianna, with nervous energy, talked about what Herb and Pete could have heard. They came up with possibilities of grim outcomes which could have occurred in the parking lot if the policeman had not appeared. By the time they had laid out their plan of escape in case they were kidnapped, they were in a fighting mood and no longer nervous. Beth didn't know whether to laugh or to go straight home and lock all of them inside with Arnie's baseball bats at the ready until the killer had been found and put in jail.

Chapter 37—Gathering Clues

"For in the long run, either through a lie, or through truth, people were bound to give themselves away ..."

- Agatha Christie, *After the Funeral*

Beth watched Adrianna through the rearview mirror while she drove. The fire in the young woman's eyes burned down to ashes. Adrianna set her mouth, stared out of the window for a minute, and then began searching through her purse.

"Listen," Beth said, "after that encounter at the Funeral Home and my hysterical panic attack, I'm a believer. There's danger out there. Whether it's from Herb Reynolds or Pete O'Neill or Tom Collins, I don't know. Anyway, Adrianna, I don't feel comfortable leaving you alone in the condo. You know I have a great guest room, and you can stay until the police catch this criminal."

"Or you can come home. You know we have a security system. You and Psycho Cat can stay as long as you need to, and you can sleep in your old room," Meg said.

Adrianna responded in a rather offhanded manner while she directed most of her attention to the re-activation of her cell phone which had been off during the wake and had migrated to the bottom of her handbag. "Listen, there was an officer at the Funeral Home today, wasn't there? Richard Montorlee must have informed the police about the threat to Mom and me. There's twenty-four hour security at the condos, and the police can be there in a nanosecond whenever they're needed. I'll be fine."

She looked up and grinned at Meg as her phone searched for the cell tower signal. "Besides, Psycho Cat is as good as a security system. He'll let me know if there's any reason for me to dial 911. I'll put it on a speed dial number, and I'll sleep with my cell phone."

As soon as the phone service activated, Adrianna checked her messages while Beth and Meg waited silently. She clicked the phone off and announced that her lawyer had indeed reported to the police her mom's fear of physical danger and wanted her to call him back so he could hear more details. Adrianna recounted all she remembered about her mom's story to Beth and Meg to make sure she recalled Meredith's encounters exactly as they did.

"According to Meredith," Meg said, "the man who called himself Tom Collins approached her in the bar at the restaurant where she worked. He seemed to know all about you, your mother, and Max."

"That's right," Beth said. "And he knew flattering your mom and getting her drunk would get him an invitation to her apartment where she would be more vulnerable."

"Hmmm," Adrianna said, still looking at her phone. "Max would know those things, and, uh, Abby would have. I guess Joey could have learned about my mom from Abby. I don't know how Pete O'Neill or Mr. Reynolds or anyone else at Renfro would know about her. Maybe she's listed in my personnel file as a close relative to contact, but I wonder how they would have found out…"

"Hold on!" Adrianna shoved a raised palm into the front of the car. "Max left a text message. He said to call him as soon as possible. He discovered a person on the Islands who has a Renfro contact. Maybe that contact is the mysterious Tom Collins character."

They pulled into the condo parking lot. "I'll try calling him now before I go in. I warn you, though, it's hard to get through to St. John sometimes," she said, and waited for the ring tones to be answered. Sure enough, the signal was lost after several seconds before it got through to Max's phone.

They stayed seated in the car while Adrianna tried again, but they were disappointed. Adrianna tucked the phone into a pocket and told them she wanted to go up to her condo, get something to eat, and relax while she tried to call. She explained it sometimes took her an hour of trying before she could get through.

"Meanwhile," she said, "I need to call Mr. Montorlee, and I may have to leave him a message as well, since it's almost 6:00 on Saturday night. He has a personal life, I hope."

Beth and Meg walked Adrianna to her condo door. They told her they wanted to be sure she was in there with the door locked before they felt safe to leave. Beth didn't say she wanted to make sure no one was in the apartment waiting for Adrianna, but she felt better after they went in and looked around. Everything was normal. Psycho Cat yawned, jumped off the back of the sofa, and ambled over to rub around Adrianna's legs until she picked him up and petted him. He jumped out of her arms and do-si-doed around Beth and Meg before jumping back onto the sofa. Adrianna promised to call both of them as soon as she heard from Max, and Beth left feeling somewhat less uneasy.

Owing to the foresight of her understanding husband, Beth's Saturday evening was homey, comfortable, and almost peaceful. Arnie had been grocery shopping and found some halibut on sale which he planned to grill outside since the weather was so nice. While he washed, tore, and cut vegetables for a green salad and she prepared broccoli for steaming and wild rice for cooking, Beth relayed her experience at the funeral home.

As usual, Arnie kept interrupting her story with questions and comments. At first, it irritated Beth when she had to rephrase her recollections, but she had to admit the restatement helped her focus on precise details. She thought hard to describe how the men looked when they came out of the funeral home into the parking lot, and Arnie made her put into words why she panicked. She had to admit it confused her when Herb went to his car and Pete returned to the building. But since one of these men visited Abby the night she died, Beth figured she had good reason to be scared.

Out on the patio, Beth sipped a glass of their favorite Riesling and nibbled vegetable sticks with hummus while Arnie grilled the halibut. They both scanned the back of the lot with their eyes every so often. Beth noticed her husband's anxiety and put on a forced calm for his sake.

"So, do you think Herb Reynolds could be working with this Pete O'Neill fellow to steal from his own company?" she asked Arnie when he came to the table to grab some of the munchies.

"It's possible," Arnie said. "Herb must be having money problems. We believe he hasn't been able to pay his retired partner. He might have included Pete in a scheme to scam the company and his sub-contractors, since he knows Pete needs money for his women and to pay his child support. As head of the accounting department, Pete O'Neill would be in a position to create false vendors and authorize false payments. Renfro's insurance company will reimburse the company for most of the stolen funds. Abby could have been killed because she figured out what was up and threatened to tell."

"That's how I've been piecing it together, but there are problems. First, how did the two men know so much about Meredith? And if Abby was the source of that information and part of the scheme, why was she eliminated—so the two of them would have to split only two ways and not have to pay her? Would it be worth murder?

"Second, who is the Virgin Islands connection? Is it Max? Did they get his contact information from Meredith because they thought he might be part of the scheme in return for the money he wanted so much? Who would give them that idea? Abby? But if Max really agreed to put Adrianna under suspicion by helping to get her out of town when the audit was coming, is he such a good actor he could pretend to care so much about her when we were there?"

"What if Max was being used, too?" asked Arnie. "He might have been contacted by Abby, or by Meredith. Maybe, in order to implicate him in the scheme, someone told him Adrianna wanted to visit. It seemed to be general knowledge, except by her parents, that Adrianna and Max still had a thing going. If he got her down there, the police would tend to believe he was hiding Adrianna and the money. If both Max and Adrianna were convicted, the thieves would be free and clear. Abby could have been involved—she knew about Max—or, like you said, she could have merely gotten in the way."

"There are too many questions. I'm getting a headache, and not from the wine," Beth groaned, "Let's eat and then watch a video. We can stop it in case Adrianna calls."

Dinner was delicious, and the movie was a silly comedy. In the midst of her involuntary giggles at the antics of the "pet detective" on the screen, Beth had the fleeting wish her mystery involved a missing animal rather than a police investigation of theft and murder.

She was grateful the phone call from Adrianna came during a less humorous part of the movie. It sobered her to think, as she reached for the phone, how Adrianna was alone, probably frightened and fighting to stay positive, while here she sat laughing at a movie. However, the voice Beth heard sounded excited rather than depressed.

"Aunt Beth," Adrianna said, "I'm sorry it took so long to get back to you. Max didn't call back until this evening, and I now just finished talking to him. He said he talked to all of the guys at the construction site and then went to a couple of places in Cruz Bay. You remember that main town on St. John, don't you? Anyway, he went to a couple of bars there to talk to some people who know about the condo construction on the Island. Cruz Bay is so small that everyone knows everyone.

"So he found a former crew chief who worked with T.M. Blakely's firm for several years. This guy said Mr. Blakely has a relative— maybe a cousin or a sister—who's married to someone who works at Renfro. He didn't remember the woman's name. But he said he was thinking about moving to the States before he got the job he has now, and Mr. Blakely told him the relative might be a contact for him at Renfro Construction."

"Wow! So T.M. Blakely himself may be the Virgin Islands connection," Beth said.

"Well, yes," Adrianna said, "or his Kansas City relative may know other people on the Islands and made one of them part of the embezzlement deal. Mr. Blakely was so good to us. I have trouble believing he could be a criminal. Max is going to ask around some more and try to find out the name of this sister or cousin. But I told him to be really careful the wrong person doesn't get wind of his nosing around. I'm going to do some Internet searching to see if I can find out about the Blakely family. Mr. Blakely seems to be an important person on St. Thomas, and maybe there is a biographical sketch about him."

"Good idea. We might need police help with this, too. They probably have tons of resources for finding out about people. Did you have a chance to talk to your lawyer?"

"Yes, he finally returned my call about an hour ago. I haven't yet called him about Mr. Blakely's relative because I was so excited to tell you first. Anyway, I hope to get a name from Max before I call my lawyer to tell him about this. But I did inform him about the threat to Mom by the mysterious man with the mustache. You know, Tom Collins? And I told him about our scare at the funeral home. He sounded skeptical about Mr. Reynolds and Pete O'Neill really being after us this afternoon right in front of the funeral home. But he said he'll check with the police again to make sure they have put extra protection around this building. He'll also tell them about Mom's situation and about the possible witnesses at Abby's apartment building on the night of her murder. Oh, and he said not to be surprised if the police question you and Meg again to find out how you got your information about the witnesses."

Adrianna paused. "Sorry you have to go through this."

"Well, I expected it. There's nothing for you to be sorry about. We'll deal with the questioning. The police need to know what we know, and our promise to our source is our problem, not yours."

"When I talk to my lawyer again, I'm going to suggest you and Meg might need protection, too. I mean, I don't know how much was overheard this afternoon or if the wrong people overheard, or…"

Beth hesitated. She'd had the same thought, but she wanted to put on a brave front for Adrianna's sake.

"Don't worry about me. I've got Arnie. Take care of yourself," Beth said.

If a day can be judged by the amount of information one has gained, this day had been a good one. Now, if they were able to use the information to find the bad guys, this day could be called outstanding. Beth, who had begun to feel unequal to the challenge, felt her spirits lift, despite the unknown risk.

Chapter 38—Discovering the K.C. Connection

"Everything must be taken into account.

If the fact will not fit the theory---let the theory go."

- Agatha Christie, *The Mysterious Affair at Styles*

After the scare at the funeral home, the next morning Beth felt light and airy, as though the good feeling from the night before remained to give buoyancy to her outlook. She and Arnie walked for almost an hour on the Trolley Track Trail, cleaned up, and had French toast, fruit, and coffee at the kitchen table. From there, they could look out on the backyard through the bay window they had added to the breakfast room.

In the yard, squirrels were racing each other around and up the big maple tree. The little wire-haired terrier next door chased a rabbit across his yard until the rabbit skittered between the fence slats. The dog, standing with his front paws against the fence, yapped incessantly, causing several birds to fly off to the tops of the trees where they perched and scolded at the dog. After the rabbit disappeared into a hedge, the little dog lost interest and wandered off to find another adventure.

Beth found herself rooting for the bunny, and it hit her she was rooting for Adrianna's escape from injustice, too. Shaking off her feelings of impotence on both fronts, she stayed busy with household chores and laundry she had not had time to do since they came back from St. Thomas while she waited for a phone call from Adrianna or

Meg with information from the Virgin Islands, something which might give her another piece of the puzzle. Arnie, home today to support Beth, rather than off at the golf course, cleaned the kitchen and, unable to resist the call of sparkling sunshine and seventy degree temperature, took his yard tools into the front yard to prune some bushes.

Early in the afternoon, Detective Carl Rinquire contacted Beth and announced he would be at her house in an hour or so to ask her some questions. Beth told him she was surprised he'd be working on weekend afternoon, but she would be glad to answer his questions.

She called Meg right after her conversation with the detective. "Did you hear from Detective Rinquire today?"

"Yes," Meg said. "He's supposed to be here any minute to interview me again. I guess he found out about our photos and our suspicions. Maybe Joey told him. Or do you think Richard Montorlee told him after talking to Adrianna? Anyway, I won't break my promises to Abby's neighbors, Lisa and Trent. I'll tell him everything we found out and give him the photos to copy, but I won't reveal our sources unless Lisa agrees to it."

"I understand," Beth said. "Detective Rinquire is coming here, too, later. I'll keep your promise. For now, we'll let them try to figure it out. Joey knows. Maybe he'll tell the police about the young witness."

"I wonder if it's worth mentioning how the two men in the photos followed us into the parking lot after the wake yesterday."

"Maybe, but we don't really know for sure whether they were following us. By the way, have you heard if Max found out more about T.M. Blakely's relative, yet?"

"No. Adrianna tried to explain to me who this Blakely fellow is. I'll let Adrianna tell her lawyer or you about that. I'm afraid I'd get it all confused," Meg said.

As soon as she clicked her phone off, Beth decided she needed more information before she talked to Detective Rinquire. Right now she had questions and theories rather than answers. The police could help, but, as things stood, it was possible they wouldn't believe her or could spin all of this to further implicate Adrianna. After all, here were Adrianna's relatives with some mysterious unrevealed witnesses who thought they saw one of two Renfro men in Abby's building. To increase the skeptical nature of the information, at least one, and probably both, men would have little reason to rob the source of their bread and butter, let alone kill one of the employees. Should she tell the police they knew of a mysterious relative of T.M. Blakely's who happened to be married to someone who worked at Renfro? This wasn't very compelling evidence.

Beth pulled on her walking shoes and went outside to explain to Arnie she was going to find out how Adrianna was doing. Around the corner of the house she spotted the hoe lying in the yard, its metal edge up.

"Ha," she said to her husband who was busy cutting back a tangle of vines growing through the bushes, "It's a good thing I saw that hoe. I could have stepped on it and knocked myself out with the handle." Must be a good omen—she usually would have missed seeing the tool and hurt herself. Beth started to feel proud, until she neglected to stay alert and fell flat after tripping over the trimmer's power cord. Arnie helped her up with a grin and a shake of his head. She looked embarrassed, gave him a quick kiss, turned down his offer to walk with her, and set out for the condo. She figured she should have time to get there, talk to Adrianna, and jog back home before Detective Rinquire arrived—if she could stay on her feet.

Seven minutes after she left her front door, Beth rang the doorbell of Adrianna's apartment. She refrained from asking her step-niece how she was doing when she came to the door. How would a person be expected to be doing under such circumstances?

Adrianna welcomed her with an almost clinging hug before she said, "Aunt Beth, I've been sitting here all morning, thinking. All of my life I've tried to be in control—of my actions, my emotions, my appearance, my education, my choice of friends…. Maybe it was because my mother was out of control, or maybe it was because I felt if I couldn't control my parents' actions, at least I could control my own. Now, all of a sudden, I'm not in control. I can't even count on going back to my job next week, let alone prove my innocence. It's scary."

Beth took Adrianna's arm and led her distraught step-niece to an armchair. Adrianna sat down, looking limp as a wet dishrag, and watched her aunt, her eyes wide and shiny with emotion. Beth took a seat in the matching chair on the other side of a lamp table. Adrianna looked down at her folded hands, and a plump tear overflowed and dropped onto her cheek. "I think somehow I contributed to Abby's death by phoning her that-that night," she said.

"Oh, honey," Beth said, as she pulled her chair around to face Adrianna and took Adrianna's hands in hers, "you were *not* the cause of any of this. You have been harmed, too! I shouldn't have taken you to the service and subjected you to those curious and accusing looks from the people you know."

Beth had never felt herself to be adequate to the job of comforting or advising people. She remembered her own daughter's big teen heartbreaks and disappointments. Back then, she had listened in understanding until it felt as if her own heart was being squeezed tight. But she never felt her responses were especially helpful or consoling.

However, Adrianna was more mature than Beth's teenaged daughter had been, and she quickly blinked back her tears and hastened to proclaim her aunt's faultlessness. "No, it was the right thing to do. I needed to say good-bye to Abby. You know, when I was at the wake, I didn't mind the snide looks so much. I kept thinking about the good times Abby and I had—the lunchtime talks, shopping trips, pouring our hearts out to each other about relationships. I want to find out why she was murdered and by whom. It would almost be easier if it were some kind of drugged-out creepy burglary-gone-wrong than a murder by someone I might know."

"Part of the reason I came," Beth said, "is because I need to know what you've learned about T.M. Blakely's Renfro-connected relative. Knowing that association might give us a clue about who was able to facilitate the transfer of money to St. Thomas and then withdraw it from the banks. I know the police are looking into it, but they aren't convinced it wasn't you who arranged all of this, and I don't think they'll tell me the particulars of the investigation. Has Max called with more information, and have you found anything online about the Blakely family?"

"I haven't heard from Max yet, but there was a little blurb on the Web about T.M. Blakely's immediate family. I didn't find anything about his extended family. The article was written over two years ago when Blakely's construction company was celebrating its twentieth year. There was a picture showing the Blakely family—Mr. Blakely, his current wife, a son, a daughter-in-law, a step-son, and a daughter. The picture was a couple of years old, but the article said the two sons live and work in the United States and only the daughter still lives on the Islands. She looked quite a bit younger than her brothers; so she may still live at home. I'm surprised Mr. Blakely didn't mention his family when we were talking."

"It didn't mention a son who came back to the Islands after college and worked for the company?"

"No. It said the step-son is an attorney with his birth father on the East Coast, and the son is an I.T. specialist for some company. I have the article bookmarked and can look up the name of the firm if you want."

"No, that's okay. This information doesn't coincide with the story Blakely told us about his son," Beth said, wrinkling her brow. "I wonder..."

Adrianna's cell phone rang and vibrated around on the dining table, and she rushed over to answer it. Psycho Cat, disturbed by the sound, came ambling out of the bedroom, stretched his front legs out, yawned, and sat between the two women, watching with his big yellow eyes.

"Hi, Max, I've been waiting for your call."

Beth observed Adrianna's whole body straighten and her face brighten as she turned and pointed an index finger toward the phone with a big grin on her face.

"My Aunt Beth is here right now," she said into the phone. "Max says hi," she said aside. Beth smiled and nodded.

Psycho Cat roamed over toward Adrianna, but when no attention was forthcoming, he came over to rub his side against Beth's legs and get a nice rub around the ears as Beth listened to Adrianna's side of the conversation.

"Uh-huh… Really? I'm not sure… I always call her Mrs. Reynolds, but I think Herb Reynolds' wife is Nora, not Norma… Meg will know for sure… She did? You're kidding… He gave no clue all the times you talked?"

Finally, Adrianna went into the kitchen to finish her conversation, but Beth could hear her say, "Thanks, baby. You're my hero. I need to tell Aunt Beth all this right now because she has to get home to talk to a police detective pretty soon. I'll call you back in a few minutes." And then faintly, "Love you, too."

Adrianna hurried back into the living room and reseated herself in the chair facing Beth. Psycho Cat bolted out of her way and perched on the back of the sofa, watching. Almost breathless and wild-eyed as if the whole case was suddenly solved, Adrianna told Beth what Max had learned since last evening.

"T.M. Blakely's sister is married to someone who works at Renfro Construction. This guy told Max her name is either Nora or Norma, and I think it might be Herb Reynolds' wife, Nora.

"Max talked to a subcontractor who builds foundations. He told Max that Mr. Blakely's sister—call her Nora—visited the Virgin Islands in January while Blakely was considering a location for his condo development. She was with them when Blakely and the subcontractor were discussing how the buildings might sit and how the foundations would be built on the land. It was the same location which was later purchased and is now the construction site on St. John where Max works.

"The subcontractor also mentioned the fact that Nora's husband, at least he thought it was her husband, was there but stayed in the background and offered no input into the discussion. He remembered the sister's name was Nora or Norma, and the man's name was a common nickname like Tom for Thomas or Rob for Robert. Max said his contact remembered the sister was a mature but attractive brunette with dazzling green eyes, but he couldn't describe the man very well...brownish hair, medium build, that sort of thing. The foundation builder told Max there seemed to be a 'strange vibe' going on between Blakely and this fellow who was there with his sister. Max said there had been no definition of 'strange vibe.'

"Also, Max found out T.M. Blakely's business was doing poorly the last year or two. There had been very little new construction on the small islands, and his business off the islands had dried up. Then, this past winter, he suddenly came up with the money to begin the development of his current condo project on his own.

"Now, what do you think of all that, Aunt Beth?"

Chapter 39—Confusing Reports

"When you find that people are not telling you the truth---look out!"

- Agatha Christie, *The Mysterious Affair at Styles*

Beth burst through her front door less than thirty minutes after she had left. Detective Rinquire hadn't yet arrived. Arnie was no longer in the front yard, and her yell brought no reply from inside, but Beth found him outside the back door cleaning his gardening tools.

"You're not going to believe what I found out!" she exclaimed when he looked up. "I've got to check it out for sure, but I think Herb Reynolds' wife is T.M. Blakely's sister."

Arnie stood with the rake in one hand and the garden hose in the other. It took him a few seconds to process the information before he responded. "So that could mean Herb Reynolds robbed his own company and sent the money to his brother-in-law to hide in a St. Thomas account? Or his wife collaborated with someone else at Renfro to embezzle the money and send it to her brother in St. Thomas, or…"

"I know, I know. It doesn't give us all of the answers. But there's more. T.M. Blakely must have lied to us about his son who was supposedly killed in a motorcycle accident while working at Blakely Construction. Adrianna found an article about the family, and it did not mention a son working with him or a son who died, only a son and a step-son who both have non-construction jobs in the United States. Also, T.M. hasn't had money coming in for a couple of years but suddenly found the money to build his condo project this past winter. He surely has a loan for a big part of the project, but I think he would need a good deal of collateral to get started."

Arnie nodded. "You're going to give all of this information to the detective, right?"

"Right! The police department has the resources to check out all of this information and put it together. At last maybe the police will start suspecting someone other than Adrianna."

Beth first got out the telephone book, and then she searched the online White Pages in hopes she'd find "Reynolds, Herbert and Nora" listed, but she had no such luck. As she tidied the living room and waited for Meg to call to say Detective Rinquire was on his way, she kept rolling over in her mind all of the possible scenarios for this case.

When Meg called to say Detective Rinquire had left her house and was on his way over, Beth verified that Nora was, in fact, the name of Herb Reynolds' wife. Meg could not think of anyone working for Renfro or any of the employees' wives named Norma, nor of another Nora. Beth explained how she had learned Nora Reynolds was the sister of T.M. Blakely, the owner of the company for which Max worked on St. John Island. Meg grasped the significance of the connection, but she still had trouble believing her long-time friend Herb Reynolds was the thief, let alone a murderer, even after their scare the day before at the Funeral Home and now this news.

"Well, this connection certainly implicates him," Beth said, "but I'm not taking anyone off my list of suspects yet. There is some kind of collaboration. It could be Herb Reynolds and his wife and maybe her brother on the Virgin Islands, but what about the Tom Collins character? Does he sound like Herb Reynolds to you? It's hard to picture."

"It's all too much for me," Meg said. "I don't want to try to figure out the puzzle; I just want it to be over for Adrianna. After what happened yesterday, I've been a bundle of nerves. Paul keeps telling me to let the police solve this, but I can't help thinking Adrianna needs someone with her. She's being a little too independent—wanting to stay alone—but my guess would be it has to do with a need for privacy to talk to Max."

"Listen," Beth said, "I assure you I will tell Detective Rinquire all I know and all my theories and then let the police do their job. Um, that doesn't mean I won't keep working on it, too, of course."

Detective Carl Rinquire arrived at her door at precisely the time he had told Beth he'd be there. Arnie stood at the door with Beth when the detective rang the doorbell. They shook hands with the detective, asked him to have a seat in the living room, and offered iced tea or coffee, which the policeman refused in his staid but polite manner.

The questions he asked Beth were probably the exact ones he had asked Meg: Can you tell me any information you have suggesting Adrianna Knells and her mother Meredith Knells may be in danger from an unidentified man? How did you get this information? How did you and your sister find out one of these two men (he held up the photos) may have visited Abigail West at her apartment the evening of her murder?

Beth answered each question in detail, except for the identities of Abby's neighbors, Lisa and Trent, while Arnie listened with his arms crossed. Beth answered each question in detail, except for the identities of Abby's neighbors, Lisa and Trent, while Arnie listened with his arms crossed. She suggested Meredith might be able to identify one of these men in the photos if one of them had threatened her and volunteered more of what she had learned since she last spoke to the detective.

"Meredith told us the man had a mustache and a tattoo near his elbow, but the rest of her description could fit either of these men," Beth said.

"Hmm," Carl Rinquire said.

Maybe the detective could get more out of Meredith than she and Meg could. Beth's account of events and Meg's must have been essentially the same because the detective wrote down what she said and didn't argue or pursue the issues.

"Thank you Mrs. Stockwell. If you learn anything else, please let me know."

Beth leaned toward him from her seat on the edge of the sofa. "I have learned something important I need to tell you. While you were at my sister's house, Max Zeller called Adrianna from the Virgin Islands with some interesting news. Adrianna will let her lawyer know about it, but I'm telling you because this information may help you solve the crimes."

"Go on," urged the detective.

Beth reminded him about T.M. Blakely—what he did, how they had met him, how kind and accommodating he had been, and how he had helped them fly Adrianna home. She had given him this information at the police station, and Rinquire nodded and looked back at his notes as she spoke; so Beth made her recap brief.

"Well Max did some poking around and found out Blakely has a sister named Nora. She is Herb Reynolds' wife! Can you believe? It seems Nora Reynolds made a trip to Charlotte Amalie to visit her brother in January. Herb Reynolds may have been there, too. Also, I found out Blakely's construction firm has not done well the past two or three years, but now he's building a huge condo complex on St. John Island. He told us he is finally in the position of having the money and the time to build the condos."

Beth looked over toward Arnie for confirmation. He nodded. She looked back at Rinquire. "So where did he get the money, if his company hasn't built anything for at least two years?"

Beth stopped talking and sat with a self-satisfied smile, like a cat which has presented a dead mouse to her owner. However, Detective Rinquire seemed less than impressed.

"Yes," he said. "We're working on what the sibling relationship might have to do with the case. We determined that Nora Reynolds' brother, T.M. Blakely, lives in the Virgin Islands, and we are investigating whether Reynolds could have worked with Blakely to launder the money. We haven't found phone or electronic records to prove it yet. Airline records show Nora bought a plane ticket to St.

Thomas in January, but our investigation shows she goes there every year to visit her brother."

Beth's smile faded. "Did Herb Reynolds go with her?"

"I can't give you that information."

Beth studied for a minute. "Maybe she took another person along for the trip. I wonder if anyone else who works at Renfro purchased a ticket to the Virgin Islands during the same time period Nora Reynolds was there," she said.

She understood Detective Rinquire could tell her very little about the investigation beyond what he needed for her to know in order to get her to talk. The police already knew some facts she had only now learned. That was encouraging, because it meant the police were still investigating the case and looking at other suspects besides Adrianna. They didn't have enough evidence to accuse anyone else of the crimes, it seemed. Fitting Adrianna's Virgin Islands visit into the scheme of things could be their priority.

The detective asked a couple more questions about specific times and events related to T.M. Blakely and recorded Beth's answers in his notebook. Before he left, he asked Arnie a few questions, but the detective soon learned that what Arnie knew about this latest series of events was only second-hand from Beth.

That night, Meg and Paul came by on the way back from Adrianna's. "We took Adrianna some dinner--homemade soup and muffins," Meg said.

Paul and Arnie went into the kitchen for coffee.

"I'm afraid she won't eat right and will get sick. While we were there, Meredith called to tell Adrianna she had received another phone call from that mystery man Tom Collins. I guess it was even more threatening than before. Adrianna convinced her mom to stay at the condo with her tonight. Meredith agreed to spend the night with Adrianna as long as she can get to work tomorrow afternoon; she's going to drive that old car of hers down here. Knowing Adrianna, she'll probably give her mother the bed and sleep on the couch. Anyway, since the police are watching the condo building, which has twenty-four hour security, Adrianna thought Meredith would be safer there.

"I guess, for now, she's the answer to Adrianna not being left alone. Meredith will definitely give her daughter something to do besides thinking about her own situation. Adrianna will wait on her hand and foot."

Meg colored. "Sorry. That woman bothers me."

"Don't apologize," Beth said. "I get it.

"But it's interesting that Meredith received another threat now. Whoever thought he had successfully pinned the crime on Adrianna must be getting skittish. Tom Collins is dotting his I's and crossing his T's, trying to keep from being connected to Adrianna's visit to the Virgin Islands. Remember, he knew ahead of time Adrianna was returning home last Thursday. This guy is definitely in contact with someone on the Islands. The Virgin Islands person is probably getting worried, too."

"You know, the mystery man could even have called Meredith from there." Meg looked at the ceiling, as if more insights might fall from above. "Maybe this Tom Collins has been traveling back and forth. With cell phones, you can't tell where someone is calling from."

"That's right!" agreed Beth. "I'm going to let Detective Rinquire know about this latest threat. Maybe the police have a way of finding out where that phone call was made—maybe even by whom it was made."

A couple of hours later Beth received a call from Adrianna. Her step-niece spoke quietly, as if someone else might hear.

"Mom told me that about an hour ago a police detective stormed into her apartment and demanded to know exactly what the mystery caller said and how she responded. She told the detective she would be in danger if she revealed anything, but the policeman informed her she could be cited for withholding evidence unless she cooperated. They tried to track the call, but it was made from a public phone in Kansas; so there's no finding out who made it."

"It's my fault," Beth said. "I phoned Detective Rinquire to let him know about this latest threat to your mom. I'm sorry. I thought they would protect her, not treat her as a suspect."

"It's okay. You were trying to help. Mom is here now. I gave her a cold cloth for her eyes, and she's on my bed. This bully might know the police went to her place today, and he could plan to make another visit to her apartment, but I think she's safe here."

"Thanks for keeping me up-to-date," Beth said. "Is there anything you need for me to bring over?"

"Maybe a cup of calmness with a spoonful of patience," Adrianna said, deadpan.

Meredith had this uncanny ability to upset her daughter. In an effort to help, Beth asked if Adrianna and Meredith would go out to eat in Brookside with them this evening, but Adrianna declined, saying they were fine and felt safer at home. Beth told Adrianna to call with any updates and reminded her she and Arnie were only minutes away if needed.

When Arnie saw Beth pacing the house, placing another call to Meg, and then pacing some more, he talked her into going out to eat anyway. "It'll help you get your mind off this state of affairs for a time, if that's possible, and while we eat you can tell me everything that's going through your mind. Think about it. If we eat at a Brookside restaurant, you'll be closer to the condo than you are now."

Beth put on a colorful swirly skirt she liked to wear, a sweater, and some comfortable flats. They walked to Carmen's Café, a favorite Italian restaurant with a Latin flair. On this Sunday evening, the restaurant was romantic and soft with candlelight, white tablecloths, mirrored walls reflecting colorful paintings, and a well-stocked bar. She had two different tapas and the tasty house salad. The atmosphere, the food, a glass of tangy red wine, and Arnie's calm manner of listening to her rambling thoughts helped Beth relax. However, the results of weekend sleuthing did not put an end to her nightmares, which continued to disrupt her sleep.

Chapter 40—Distressing News

"The game is afoot."

Arthur Conan Doyle, Adventure of the Abbey Grange

Most events in people's lives are entirely forgettable. If it were otherwise, we would be mired in memories by age ten. It would be difficult to bear another eventful day. Mundane experience may not be memorable, but it's predictable and tranquil. This Monday began calmly enough, but it was destined to become a day Beth would never forget.

It being a Monday morning, the weekday world awoke to resume its daily routines. Arnie jogged on the Trolley Track Trail before getting ready for work. As he left for his office, he admonished Beth for the hundredth time to be patient and wait for the police to complete the investigation.

Meg called Beth to tell her she was on her way to school and Paul was already at his business office. "My school principal volunteered to take my classes at a moment's notice in case I need to leave. As I told Adrianna last evening, I'm relying on one of you to call immediately if anything new happens. My phone will be in my pocket all day."

Beth wasn't sure what Meg was expecting to happen, but she had an unnerving sense of expectancy herself today. She went to her computer to update the rental property bank balance register she had recently neglected. It was the first week of May, she had already received rent checks, and she had not yet recorded the money spent for expenses in April. Data entry was not her favorite activity, but Beth felt organized when she completed this bookkeeping task. By the time she had checked her e-mail and responded to an enquiry about one of her properties, it was after 10:00 a.m., and Beth decided to take her walk on the Trolley Track Trail.

Winter in Kansas City can be harsh or dreary, and summer can feel like a steam bath. However, mild, sunny spring and fall weather in this mid-western city gave Beth ample reason for loving her hometown. Everyone, it seemed, not confined to an indoor job, walked a dog, took a hike with a friend, or pushed a stroller on the trail today. Each one of them smiled a pleasant greeting as Beth huffed past at her power-walk speed, her arms pumping back and forth. She met a neighbor lady with her dog and paused long enough to comment on the weather and pet the shaggy white mutt, which was the apple of its elderly owner's eye. The lyrics to *April in Paris* came to mind. She decided springtime in Kansas City deserved a song.

Arnie had gone back to work after eating his quick lunch at home with her, and Beth chose to sort the mail outside on the patio table. She lapsed into a meditative mode as she sipped iced tea and watched a couple of squirrels play around the big oak tree. One of them ran almost vertically down the trunk, across the yard, and up a fence post where it sat looking around and sniffing the air. The squirrel's playmate took a spiral route down the tree trunk, paused every once in a while to observe and sniff, and then plunged a short way across the grass where it found a leftover acorn to nibble. In a flash, the first squirrel scampered down the fence, crossed the yard, and chased its friend around and up the tree trunk. Beth lost track of them in the thick young foliage which festooned the branches of the huge tree with springtime green.

She almost jumped out of her chair when her phone rang. It was Adrianna. She was in tears. "Oh Aunt Beth, I don't know what to do!"

Beth let the mail fall to the table and did jump, this time, to her feet. She hit the table with her legs, and the tea spilled on the papers. She grabbed them out of the liquid with uncontrolled agitation as she spoke. "What is it, Adrianna? Shall I get Arnie, or your dad, or the police, or...?"

"No, no, there's nothing anyone here can do. But I had to call and tell someone. Smitty—you remember Smitty from meeting him on St. John? He called to tell me Max fell off a rock ledge this morning and tumbled down the steep ridge on one side of the condo development. He's been taken to a clinic. Smitty said Max is alright because he was able to catch hold of some bushes on the way down—although he may have broken an arm and has lots of scrapes and bruises—but Smitty's not so sure someone didn't push or trip him. I haven't been able to talk to Max, but I left a message on his cell phone. I'm so scared for him. He's been asking questions around the construction site related to the money laundering, and now I think someone is trying to warn him off or even kill him."

"Okay, Adrianna, I'll be right over and we'll talk about what to do. Is your mother still there?"

"No, she left to go to her apartment and get ready for work this afternoon." Adrianna said this matter-of-factly, but Beth could hear a slight sense of relief in the intonation.

"Call your lawyer and tell him what happened. Leave a message if you can't talk to him," instructed Beth. "I'll be there in five minutes."

Beth decided it would be faster to run over to the condo building on the path than to mess with driving around on the roads, waiting for traffic, finding a place to park, and walking to the front door. When she arrived, somewhat out of breath, a different door man— Chuck wouldn't be in until later—called up to the apartment to make sure it was okay for her to go up. Beth was surprised but not displeased. Her step-niece didn't need unannounced visitors.

Adrianna was busy talking on her phone when Beth arrived at her door. She held up a "just a moment, please" finger and motioned to a chair.

"Okay. I'll let you know if I hear anything more," Adrianna said into the phone, "I haven't talked to him, only to a friend of his. You might wait a couple of hours to call him since he's in the medical facility. I'm sure he's going to be fine; I just wanted you to know about the accident."

"Sorry," she said as she put her phone on the table. "After I left the message for Richard Montorlee, I decided to call Max's mother and let her know what happened. She's a widow and lives in Nebraska where Max grew up. She has no money besides her widow's pension, and from Max's account, his brother and two sisters don't sound as if they are in any position to help her financially. I don't think she'll be flying down to visit Max if he gets laid up, but she sounded concerned."

"Do you know the lady?" Beth asked.

"Not really," Adrianna said. "Max hasn't lived in Nebraska since he was 18 and joined the military, and he doesn't visit very often. We drove up to Omaha once, before Max left to work on St. Thomas, and I met his family members at a picnic during that short visit, but I didn't get to talk to his mother much at all. Just now, I didn't tell her about my current situation, and I doubt if Max has. I don't want her to worry about something more happening to him when she can't do anything about it."

"It's probably best," said Beth. "I think you're doing enough worrying for his whole family. Adrianna, I think we need to call Detective Rinquire with this new development right away, or let your lawyer do it. Maybe the detective can coordinate with the St. John police to try to find out whether Max's 'accident' was set up—and to ask them to protect him, too."

"I agree," said Adrianna.

After she left the message for her attorney, Adrianna sat down, leaned forward with her elbows on the table and her chin in her hands, and focused on Beth finding Rinquire's cell number. Psycho Cat padded over to put his front paws on her lap and beg for a scratch, but, perhaps for the first time ever, she paid him no heed.

The cat slunk under the table and approached Beth, who gave him a dismissive pat as she waited for the connection. With a disappointed meow, Psycho Cat shook himself, dog-like, and loped into the bedroom and back as if being chased by something big. With a short yip of dissatisfaction, he jumped onto the arm of a chair and glared at them. A tiny smile of understanding on her face, Adrianna, his ever-doting mistress strode over to the easy chair and took the big cat into her lap.

Beth was obliged to leave a message for Detective Rinquire. She gave a brief description of what happened to Max Zeller and said she hoped there would be a coordinated investigation into how maybe an intentional push down a cliff might relate to the Renfro embezzlement and murder.

As she ended the call, Beth replayed her words in her mind. *Hmm, I could have sounded a little pushy there. The police are doing all they can. I definitely have trouble staying out of their business when my family is at stake.*

After she finished second guessing herself about the voice mail, Beth sat, feeling meek, thinking about Adrianna's, Meg's, and her own safety. If, indeed, Max had been shoved off a building site and could have been killed for asking questions about people who might be mixed up in the embezzlement, then what might happen to the three of them for getting too close to not only the theft, but also the murder investigation?

"Adrianna, has anyone followed you, or have you noticed anyone lurking around watching you the last few days?" Beth asked.

"No I haven't seen anyone. Why? Have you been followed and watched?"

"Yes, I'm pretty sure I have, and I'm worried that you, Meg, and I might find ourselves in Max's shoes if we aren't very, very careful."

"Oh, Aunt Beth, why don't you stay here until the police find this Tom Collins, or arrest Herb or Pete, or at least find out how Max was hurt? Meg can come, too. My mother isn't coming back. She spent the whole time she was here complaining about her lack of privacy and the long drive it would be to go to work this evening. She told me she thought about it and doesn't think Tom Collins will harm her because she swore she'd never testify against him. I couldn't convince her to stay. Sad to say, she might be missing the drugs and booze she always has around her place. She's going home tonight after work. I don't think anyone is going to hurt her, though. She's been seduced into staying mum, and she doesn't seem to have any more information than she's already told. Something would have happened to her already if it was going to."

"Well, if your mother won't be here, I can stay. But I don't know if Arnie and Paul will agree with—"

"We'll tell them. It's safe here. The police are watching the building, and Chuck and the other security guards are always at the doors monitoring people coming in. All the doormen have been told not to let anyone up to my apartment without my say-so."

Chapter 41—Holing Up

"One little Indian left all alone; he went out and hanged himself, and then there were none."

— Agatha Christie, *And Then There Were None*

A couple hours of phone calls and text messages, lots of explanation, some arguments, and a bit of backpedaling made for an exhausting afternoon. It ended with the family agreeing Beth would stay with Adrianna. Meg and Paul decided on an alternative; they would go to a hotel for a few days, have access to their house when they needed it, and be able to continue their work schedules without bothering anyone.

After she and Paul declined, Meg had appeared at Beth's house and had begged her sister to accept Adrianna's invitation. "You'll be safer there than at home, and Adrianna will have somebody to keep her from sitting around fretting all day."

It took longer for Arnie to support the arrangement. He came around after Meg presented him with her emotional and frightening account of the scare at the funeral home and told him in extreme hyperbole how grateful she'd be for Adrianna to have company.

"Okay, I agree Beth should stay with Adrianna," Arnie said. "But I'm staying at the house. I've got to go to work each day, like you and Paul. No cowardly break-and-enter guy can drive me away. I'll sleep with my phone and a baseball bat."

Beth rolled her eyes. Arnie thought everything could be solved with a baseball bat. He'd grown up playing baseball, was a star player in his high school, and either watched or carefully reviewed the statistics of every Royals' game. The recent opening day at Kaufmann Stadium still had him energized. It embarrassed her to know her husband's tendency to think of a bat as a first line of defense had rubbed off on her.

"Well, maybe I'll order a security system to be installed at the house tomorrow," she told him. "We've been talking about it anyway. I'd feel much better about you sleeping here alone that way—safer than you defending yourself with a baseball bat."

"Yes dear," Arnie said. His expression didn't convey agreement, but Beth was satisfied.

"I'll stay in touch, and—and you can have dinner with us. Okay? I'm hoping this won't last long. Maybe Max's accident was really just that, and maybe the police will solve this case, and…"

The whole afternoon, with her family in a frenzy and fear for her own safety and that of her family members playing havoc with her stomach acid levels, Beth found her overriding emotion to be rage. How could this villain, or this network of scuzzy criminals, do this to her own law-abiding, hard-working, society-contributing relatives? What they needed, in order to prove Adrianna's innocence and to insure their safety, were confessions and arrests.

At one point, after Beth returned to the condo to discuss sleeping arrangements and such, she sat on the sofa to try her call again and this time got Detective Carl Rinquire on the phone. "We're all really scared since Max Zeller had his so-called accident in the Virgin Islands. I need some assurance. Are the police there working to solve the case, and are they looking into the possibility that Max might be targeted? Are police officers here still patrolling close to the East-Gate Condos in case Adrianna needs help fast?"

"Yes, yes, and yes," Detective Rinquire said. "I spoke directly to the Chief of Police on St. Thomas, and he assured me they are doing all they can. As for the patrols near your niece's residence, they are watching for suspicious activity and can be there immediately in the event anyone is able to get by the security at the building. Miss Knells has the schedule and cell phone number of each officer who patrols the area. Also, a 911 call will bring someone at once."

"It's true," Adrianna confirmed when Beth asked. "I have them on my phone's speed dial and can have one of them up here immediately."

Not five minutes after Beth talked to the detective, Adrianna received a call from Max. She gave Beth a "sorry, I want this to be private" look and retreated to the bedroom. Beth busied herself preparing a list of items she'd need to bring from home to stay with Adrianna for an unforeseen amount of time. She knew Arnie could get to her whatever she forgot, but life as she knew it couldn't go on without her special herb tea before bedtime, the book she was reading, her soft slippers, and her laptop for working on bills and receipts, now could it?

When Adrianna came back into the living room, her relieved-looking smile graced the room. "Max says he has a broken arm," she said, "but it sounds as if that's his only serious injury, and he's already been sent home. I hate to say it, but I'm glad the arm will keep Max from working at the building site, because there are way too many opportunities on a construction job for someone to make another *accident* happen."

There was no mention of when Max might be able to return to Kansas City. Unfortunately, he was still not above suspicion and remained under police surveillance related to the Renfro embezzlement. The money was still missing. Beth hoped, for Adrianna's sake, Max would be found innocent of any involvement.

"I'm so glad Max is going to be okay and is going to be away from the job for a while," Beth said. "I wonder, though, if he shouldn't also stop asking so many questions for the time being. He needs to let the police do the investigating."

She felt her face get hot. Wasn't this what Arnie and Paul and Detective Rinquire had told her time and again? And now look.

"I told him that," Adrianna said, "but listen to what else he found out this afternoon. One of his buddies from the construction job went over to his and Smitty's apartment to see how he was doing. This guy saw Max fall and was one of the first to rush to the rescue. Anyway, Max's buddy told about seeing a worker he didn't know stick a steal beam right behind Max when he was backing up to direct a crane. It was the beam Max tripped over which made him fall down the bluff. The worker disappeared when Max fell, but there was no reason for the beam to be there. It didn't look like an accident."

"Wow," Beth said, "I hope Max's buddy is willing to identify that worker who put the beam down."

"Max thinks he will if he can; but the guy with the beam wasn't one of their regulars. That's not all. Max told his buddy all about the embezzlement and the murder and how I'm the main suspect. He told how he's been trying to find out who might be laundering the money in the Virgin Islands and who might have connections with Renfro Construction. Oh, and about Mr. Blakely's sister and her visit there in January." Adrianna stopped to take a deep breath and gave Beth a wide-eyed look. Beth waited for her to go on.

"Anyway, Max's friend has worked for the company for a long time. He saw Nora Reynolds at the construction site in January and knows for sure she was with someone other than her husband. He's met the Reynolds before when they were visiting. Her companion looked a little like Mr. Reynolds, he told Max, but was younger and had dark reddish hair. Aunt Beth, it had to be Pete O'Neill."

Now it was Beth's turn to look wide-eyed. "W-well, would Herb Reynolds have any reason to send Pete O'Neill to the Virgin Islands to look at construction sites?"

"I can't think of any good reason at all—especially not with Mrs. Reynolds."

"So, let's think about this. Herb Reynolds seems to be separated from his wife, Nora. Is there any possibility Pete O'Neill would have an affair with his boss's wife? Seems like rather risky business to me if a person wants to keep his job."

"Right now I could believe he'd have an affair with the company custodian, Jeremy, if there was anything in it for him."

"Well then," Beth said, with a frown and a pause, "If this womanizer, Pete O'Neill, uses women to his own ends, he could have been the older man dating Abby, the man who came to her apartment the night she was killed. He could have found out about Max from probing Abby for information about you and could have known about Nora's brother's construction business in the Virgin Islands from talking to Herb and Nora at company functions. It could have been part of his larger scheme to get rich. What would he care if he lost his job from a company he was planning to rob. By using Nora and getting Max to incriminate you--"

"No." Adrianna stopped the train of thought. "Max wasn't in on any scheme."

"Okay," Beth said. "When Arnie and I were on St. Thomas, we were told someone had been looking for Max several weeks before we asked about him. Could O'Neill be working with Nora's brother, T.M. Blakely? Maybe Blakely sent someone around to look for Max in order to hire him? They may have wanted to influence Max to invite you to the Virgin Islands at the right time to have you be suspected of hiding out. Mr. T.M. Blakely talks a good story. He could have cozied up to Max like a father figure—a mentor. Maybe Max was used as a pawn, too."

"We've got to tell the police!" Adrianna said.

"I don't know." Beth paused to think about it. "All I have is a theory. A lot of maybes. I'm hoping the police are all over this. It seems as if every time I've presented some new facts to Detective Rinquire, he already knew them. The only new fact we've learned for sure is that Nora wasn't with Herb at the St. John condo construction site in January. Let's lay low for a little while in case this mad man is out there waiting for us, Okay sweetie?"

On his way home from work, Arnie stopped by the condo building to collect Beth and take her home to pack for her stay. Chuck stopped him at the front door. Beth cringed when she heard

Adrianna take the call from Chuck, making sure it was okay to send Arnie up. She knew Arnie wasn't going to react well to such a precaution.

"Chuck has met me dozens of times," Arnie said when Beth opened the condo door for him. "He acted as if he needed to check my I.D. or something when I told him I was coming up here."

"He's merely doing his job," Beth said. "Adrianna asked the security people to not let anyone come up without approval from Adrianna. Heck, he'll probably call before letting me come back."

"Hey, that's true," Adrianna said. "I'd better go down to the lobby with you and let Chuck know he can let you come back without calling ahead. Otherwise, you'll be standing there waiting every time you come and go for the next couple of days."

"Thanks, dear. Good plan. How about Arnie, too?"

"Oh, sure. I meant both of you."

Chapter 42—Making a Move

"I wish I could write as mysterious as a cat."

- Edgar Allan Poe

That evening, despite Arnie's misgivings, Beth drove her own car the short distance to the condo building. She wanted to have transportation available during the day if needed, and she didn't want to bother Arnie at work. After she pulled into the visitors' parking lot at the side of the condo building, she noticed a hard-to-miss red Porsche convertible enter the lot right after. It was the same car which had turned in behind her from a side street near her house and had followed her all the way to the building. The driver parked at the other end of the lot. Beth admired the car for a minute; someone living here must have a well-heeled relative or friend. Then she didn't think any more about it as she gathered her things from the back seat, hefted the straps of all her bags onto a shoulder to free her hands to close and lock the car, and took off toward the condo building entrance with her heavy load of belongings.

Perhaps she packed a little too much? Beth shifted a couple of straps from one shoulder to the other while waiting for Chuck to open the front door for her. He grinned and bowed to her with a hand open toward the elevator when she stopped at the desk out of habit and opened her mouth to tell him where she was headed.

"Honored visitor," Chuck said. "I'm sure Adrianna needs your helpful presence right now."

"Thanks, Chuck. You're the best. We're trusting this roommate thing is very temporary, and I hope Adrianna won't regret letting me stay with her."

"You'll be a great guest, Mrs. Stockwell," Chuck said. "Can I help you get that load into the elevator?"

"I've got it, thanks."

"Well, let me know if I can be of any assistance."

"Will do, sir." She smiled and waved her free hand as she stepped into the elevator car.

Beth felt the strain on her shoulders and the sore spot where the computer case had banged against her thigh on the walk from the parking lot. She was feeling perturbed and ready to dig her own key out of her purse after waiting at the condo door for several minutes before Adrianna finally opened it a crack. A stricken look, a thumb pointing back into the room, and a slight shake of Adrianna's head completely missed their target. Beth's intent for getting inside and unburdening herself of her bags overcame her powers of observation. She practically pushed Adrianna out of the way to shove her bags through the door and lean over to drop them on the floor of the entry.

"Sorry, dear," she said. "I couldn't hold this stuff a second longer. I got carried away and brought everything but the living room sofa."

Adrianna didn't speak, didn't move. Beth straightened up and turned to her with incomprehension. She caught the look of fear on her niece's face. "What's wrong? Has something happened?"

In a slow arc, Beth's head followed Adrianna's eyes to the left and behind her. On the way, her eyes lit on Psycho Cat standing, his hackles raised and his ears back, in the doorway leading toward the bedroom hallway. She noticed Adrianna's phone lying on the sofa. It took a complete turn of her body before she spotted him—Pete O'Neill—standing with his arms crossed and one side of his mouth turned up enough to show some teeth. Was it a smirk or a sneer? It didn't matter. Beth shrank back and grabbed Adrianna's arm.

"Close the door, Adrianna," Pete O'Neill said. "This is your landlady, right? And your step-aunt—not a blood relative, just a biddy who likes to stick her nose where it doesn't belong."

Neither woman spoke. Beth experienced the sudden fast heartbeat and impossibility of movement which clarifies the description *her blood ran cold*. Pete O'Neill sauntered to the door to lock it behind her. Beth took hold of Adrianna's arm when the man came close to her. She released her hold with a slow caress when the young lady didn't move a muscle. Adrianna was in no condition to be her support.

A low growl escaped from Psycho Cat. He flattened his ears and switched his tail. Then the feline began to yowl with an almost bark-like sound.

"Shut that cat up—now," Pete said with a menacing look on his face.

Adrianna went to her Sylvester Cat, stooped down beside him and soothed him with shushing sounds. The sounds served to calm Beth as well. She regained enough of her senses to glance around the room and begin to consider means of escape. Pete O'Neill remained between her and the door. Her phone was buried inside a pocket of her purse, which lay on the floor by the door where she had plopped it, directly beside where Pete now stood. A hopeful thought hit her— perhaps they weren't in danger. Possibly he only intended to warn them, as he, it was now obvious, had threatened Meredith Knells while disguised as Tom Collins. Maybe that was all.

Beth's senses came alive. Her hands felt clammy. She heard the faint rumble of Eva Standish's television through the wall on one side of the room. Through the window she watched the traffic on the street far below—maybe a patrolman was cruising by unaware of who had snuck into the building. Did the police know Peter O'Neill drove the red Porsche convertible which was parked in the side lot? It was in a space far at the back, farthest from the street. It would be too much to hope...

Her attention returned to the room. She hadn't moved more than two feet since she'd entered, still standing close to Pete near the door.

In sudden dismay, she noticed the smell of liquor on his breath. His eyes were unfocused. A drunken person driven by emotion would be the worst kind with whom they could try to reason. He was standing there watching Adrianna pet the cat with an expression which seemed to be slowly becoming a leer. Beth strove for words which might distract him and deflect the threat.

"We call the kitty Psycho Cat, but he has never hurt anyone. I'm sorry. I didn't know Adrianna would have company. I should have called before I came up. Chuck probably called to let you know Mr. O'Neill was coming, right Adrianna?"

Adrianna stood up beside the cat, her eyes on the floor, her expression bedraggled. She shook her head back and forth for several seconds. "I thought it was you at the door and opened it without checking," she said in a whisper.

Pete O'Neill's laugh sounded as sick as this situation he had precipitated. "Oh, so that's the deal? That loser door-man is supposed to call and tell you who's coming to see you? It's a good thing I checked out this building earlier. I delivered that bouquet, left it by the door, and discovered the stairs in the process. It was easy to walk into the garage behind a car and run up the stairway before you could make it down the sidewalk and through the lobby, dear fumbling Fake Aunt Beth. I want to talk to both of you, and you might not have given me the opportunity otherwise."

Beth closed her eyes for a moment before she opened them in a frowning squint. Why had she been so self-absorbed with her luggage? Why hadn't she heeded her own caution and told Chuck about the car which had followed her into the parking lot? All of this small talk seemed to be taking an eternity, even though it had been a matter of only a few minutes since she'd entered the door. The longer they could keep this man bantering with them, the more chance she'd be able to get to her phone or Adrianna's or think of some other way to alert someone about his presence.

It was Adrianna who, sounding in control, offered the next opportunity to stall. "By the way, thank you again for the flowers, Pete. So what is it you want to talk to us about?"

"It could have been us, you know," Pete growled. "We could have done it so much better, gotten rich and disappeared from this rotten town together before anyone suspected anything. Your mom. Now there's a woman who has some sense, knows how to play the game. Abby—she was easy, but she couldn't hack it in the end. She was going to tell you everything. She blew her chance."

He took a step toward Adrianna—still not far enough from the door for Beth who desperately tried to estimate how much time it would take to reach the door, unlock it, turn the doorknob, open the door, and run down the hall for help.

"I didn't want to hurt you, Adrianna," Pete mumbled. "I never would have thought to blame it on you if it hadn't been for the luck of having your boyfriend in the right place at the right time. We used him to give you a reason to take off when I needed a scapegoat. You can thank your departed friend Abby for that bit of information about your heartthrob Maxie—and be grateful to Mommy Dearest for helping us to find him."

Chapter 43—Moving On

"Every murderer is probably somebody's old friend."

- Agatha Christie, *The Mysterious Affair at Styles*

"**W**ell, Pete," Adrianna said, "How do you know I wouldn't have helped you with your scheme? You never asked me. Are you sure I wouldn't come with you now, if you asked? It's not too late. We can still get away with the money."

Pete O'Neill's eyes grew wide. His expression became skeptical, edging toward hopeful. "I thought... I mean, what about your boyfriend, that dumb grunt who fell for all Blakely's bullshit and who's now going to get himself killed for his prying. Don't you want to be around to cry over him at his funeral?"

"Oh, I went down to see him for a tropical island vacation. That's all. It's beautiful, you know, and I had never been anywhere like that. It would have been soooo much nicer if I'd been there with you. I always liked you, Pete. It seemed wrong to date you when you were my boss, and then after I left the department you were with someone else."

He seemed to wobble a little; then Pete O'Neill walked in slow motion toward Adrianna, looking confused and almost misty-eyed. As soon as she thought it safe, Beth took her chance and took two steps toward the door. She turned the lock and clasped the doorknob, but she wasn't fast enough. O'Neill caught the click and her movement, swung back around, and pushed her roughly to the floor. Beth fell on her backside with a thud, her head barely missing the metal leg of a decorative entry table.

Adrianna flew at him yelling, "Leave her alone, you beast. It's me you want." She drove her fist into his shoulder blade and turned to help Beth.

The countenance again changed on Pete O'Neill's face, this time to rage. A great actor would have trouble changing expressions to display the range of emotions this man had communicated in such a short period of time. He yelped like an injured animal, grabbed Adrianna around the neck to drag her close to him with his left arm, and pulled a gun out of his trouser pocket with his right hand. He waved the gun toward Beth, now sitting up with her mouth open in disbelief and terror, and then placed the barrel against Adrianna's head. Psycho cat yowled loud enough to be heard on the tenth story of the building and then hissed. Pete pointed the gun in the cat's direction.

"Shhh, Sylvester it's okay," Adrianna said in a choked voice. The cat sat back on his haunches, and his growl turned to a low rumble in the back of his throat.

"I was ready to give you two a chance," Pete O'Neill said, then leveled the gun back against Adrianna's head and hissed in her ear. "If you had listened to my plan, we could have made a sweet deal. I would have been out of your life, and you would have been in the clear; we could have blamed the embezzlement and Abby's death on that blond whore now working in the accounting department. But I can see you two aren't going to be reasonable; so I'll have to go with Plan B."

"Now wait," Beth said. "We'll be reasonable. It was my fault. I don't know you very well, not well enough to understand you came with a plan, and Adrianna was scared when I fell. Let's talk, okay?"

"I don't think so. A beast can't talk—can he, Adrianna? Do you think you can calm me like you did that brainless cat over there?"

There was more pronounced hissing from the doorway. Pete snorted in derision.

He pulled Adrianna closer to the door and addressed his remarks to Beth. "This can't be pinned on me. The police haven't arrested me. There's no proof. Nothing links me to the crime. But Adrianna, now that's a different story. She's going to the police with me right now to tell them how she gave some of the money to her mother and sent the rest to the Virgin Islands. Her mother will back me up, if she wants to live and know her daughter will stay alive. And you, Auntie, will keep your mouth shut for the same reasons."

"You're wrong about you not being a suspect," Beth said. "This afternoon we learned that the man who tried to kill Max at the construction site on St. John was caught, and he revealed your Virgin Islands accomplice was the person who hired him. Your accomplice talked. He named you as the thief and murderer." Beth believed the little lie might work since Pete had mentioned Max's accident earlier. Maybe Pete would decide they couldn't help him, dead or alive, and would run away.

Pete looked indignant and unbelieving for a moment until his face became even more menacing and malicious than before, if that was possible. His grip on Adrianna's neck tightened enough to make her squeak.

"Blakely? That idiot!" he said to himself as much as to the women. "I don't care if he is a big shot on that island; he's a horse's ass. He's as deep into this shit as I am. He probably made a deal with his police buddies down there to get better treatment if he named me. Damn him. I'm going through all this because of his sister."

His tone changed. "It was for her," he said. "I wouldn't have done any of this if it wasn't for her." He looked at Beth beseechingly as if he could charm her into understanding. She displayed no sympathy.

He said, "Yeah, Nora. She fell for me big time. I went to St. Thomas with her and met her brother, the big shot T.M. Blakely. He needed the money for his construction deal. He's the one to blame."

"Should we blame them for Abby's death, too? And do you blame Blakely for you seducing his sister Nora Reynolds and using her? Is it his fault you tried to pin this on me? Did he cause me not to sleep with you? I pity the women who have." Adrianna said.

Beth winced.

"You high and mighty bitch. At least Abby didn't think she was better than me. She was willing to help, and gladly took money," he said, "Until she turned soft and threatened to tell you everything. You…"

Pete O'Neill raised his arm and again pressed the gun, which he had let drop to his side, tightly against Adrianna's head. He snarled into Adrianna's ear, "I used your scarf to kill Abby—I recognized it as one you used to wear to work so often. It was as though you and I did it together. I pulled it tighter while she struggled, felt her go limp, and then let her fall to the floor." He paused. "It was regrettable, but after it was done, she was nothing to me. Not a threat—not another stupid woman who wanted to betray me. Just a corpse. I killed her because she wouldn't cooperate, and I could kill again, unless *you* cooperate."

Pete pulled her toward the door, which seemed to open of its own accord. Standing on the threshold was Chuck, holding a huge metal wrench and looking ready to swing it. He didn't get the chance. Adrianna faced Chuck in the doorway, and Pete waved the gun he held to her head.

"Get out of my way. Adrianna's coming with me. I won't hesitate to kill her," Pete said. "I've killed once. What're they going to do, electrocute me twice?" He smirked as if he'd made a joke. "Don't worry, though, I'll let the girlie go if you give me time to get to the car and get out of here."

Chuck lowered the wrench. Beth pushed herself off the floor and found she was standing close enough to grab her niece. With a nervous twist, Pete turned toward her and pointed the gun at her face.

"I should kill you first. If you hadn't come up here snooping around in the first place, Adrianna would still be in the Virgin

Islands, and everything would have gone as planned." They all heard Pete releasing the safety on his gun.

Adrianna pushed against Pete's arm and let out a strangled scream. "No!"

Pete gripped her harder around the neck, making her choke, and Psycho Cat came to life. In two powerful leaps, the crazed feline, living up to his name, was through the living room and onto Pete's shoulder. He had no front claws, but he could do some damage with his hind claws, which now raked across the man's upper arm as the cat's head knocked into Pete's jaw and the razor-sharp feline teeth clamped onto his ear.

Emitting a ghastly curse, Pete released his grip from around Adrianna's neck to fling the cat away. He dropped his gun in the process. Beth could see part of his upper arm where the furry hero had done a good job of shredding the shirt from shoulder to elbow. Claw scratches coursed through a stylized tattoo.

Chuck kicked the revolver out of Pete's reach and grabbed one of his arms. At that instant, the reflection of revolving red lights, the brief bleep of a siren, and the screech of skidding tires turned everyone's attention toward the condo's wall of windows, which overlooked the street. With the strength of a trapped animal, Pete broke free from Chuck's grasp and fled toward the stairwell, Chuck on his heels. Pete flew through the door and slammed it hard into Chuck, who fell back stunned for a moment, giving Pete a head start down the stairs.

Psycho Cat yowled and ran to hide while the two women ran to the window. Adrianna grabbed her phone on the way, punched the first panic number she'd programmed into her phone, and explained the situation. From their sixth floor vantage, Beth could see four uniformed policemen jump out of two vehicles and advance toward the condo building's door, drawing their pistols as they went. It was impossible to see the entrance from her vantage point, but when, almost immediately, two of the cops started running toward the door and two others took off around the building, Beth realized Pete wouldn't get far if he ran outside toward his car in the parking lot.

Beth stood at the windowpane holding her breath, her hands clasped around her face, Adrianna beside her. Adrianna cranked opened two of the casement windows. Both leaned through and strained their necks to see more. Everything became quiet, and Beth supposed Pete could easily return to Adrianna's apartment to regain his hostage. She turned around, saw the door standing wide open, and, without a second thought, ran to close it. The door opened into the room, and as she approached she had to go past the opening to get to the knob. She peeked cautiously into the hallway, and her eye found the gun lying ten feet or so down the hall, away from the stairwell door.

Beth's heart beat harder than she thought she could survive, but she decided she had to get the gun before Pete could have access to it. She sprinted out, and, like sliding past third base and on into home plate, she grabbed the gun and charged back inside where she locked and bolted the door; then she stood with her back against it until she could breathe. Beth held the revolver by the barrel with two fingers and showed it to Adrianna.

"I—I don't know how to use one of these," Beth said, "but darn if I won't give it my best shot if that mad man gets back in here."

Adrianna approached with her hand out. "Hooray, Aunt Beth, I can't believe you did that. And you didn't trip or fall! But—um— maybe you'd better hand me the gun—carefully please. I'm not a great shot, but I have been to a shooting range before." She took the gun, locked the safety, and gave the door a grim look. "How about a glass of water?" she said with a forced smile. "You look as if you're about to faint."

Chapter 44—Closing the Case

"Eliminate all other factors, and the one which remains must be the truth."

- Sherlock Holmes -*The Sign of Four*

A loud knock at the now closed condo door caused Beth to jump up from her seat at the table and Adrianna to drop the filled water glass into the sink. The two women looked at each other, wide-eyed. Adrianna reached for the gun she had placed on the kitchen counter. A second knock was accompanied by a loud announcement.

"Kansas City Police, open please."

Adrianna had the presence of mind to put the gun down before she opened the door. There stood Chuck and a uniformed police officer. Chuck wore a large grin.

"This is Adrianna Knells," Chuck said, "and Beth Stockwell is her landlady. Ladies, this is Officer Droite. He has some good news."

"The suspect is in our custody, " the officer said. "I need to verify a few things, and we'll take him away. Detective Carl Rinquire is on his way to write up your statements."

"Thank goodness," Beth said. Adrianna breathed out a huge sigh and put an arm around her aunt.

The police officer made sure both ladies were unhurt before he began his questioning. Beth was in turmoil with leftover emotion and adrenalin surges. Revulsion, amazement, fear, shock, joy—she had experienced all within the last thirty minutes. Now she had to answer the officer's queries, as if being interrogated again? But she had questions of her own. She looked at Chuck. "How did you..."

"Hold on," Chuck said. "I'll tell you about the chase and my truly fine tackle after you tell the officer what happened up here."

As it turned out, Adrianna did most of the telling. She sounded angry. Beth merely nodded or added a few descriptors along the way. Apparently, on the way up in the elevator, Chuck had already given the police officer a summary of what he had seen. Those testimonies, Adrianna's emergency call, and Pete O'Neill's attempt to escape were enough for the police to be able to hold the perpetrator until charges could be filed.

Adrianna started to fill the police officer in on Pete's confession to them of robbery and murder, but the officer stopped her. "Save all that for Detective Rinquire," he said. "He'll be along shortly."

The officer took off, talking on his walkie-talkie all the way down the hall. Chuck remained outside the door, and Beth asked him in.

"Thanks, but I need to get back to the front desk. There's no one else around to fill in while I celebrate taking down the bad guy. I'm glad you gals are both safe. My plan to surprise that dude and get him out of here before he became violent didn't exactly go as planned. It's a good thing you have a trained attack cat."

Adrianna grinned, turned, and called out. "Sylvester, where are you?" Psycho Cat didn't appear; so she went to peek behind the sofa and then came back to the door. "His Royal Catliness is licking his paws and can't be disturbed right now. A really annoyed-looking flick of his ears told me I should leave him alone. Really, Sylvester is the sweetest cat around, usually. Now, though, he's also my hero. And so are you, Chuck. If you hadn't tackled Pete, he might have come back up here, or he might have escaped. Your courage, not to mention your football skills, made you a life-saver."

"How did you know to come to the apartment ready to fight an intruder?" Beth asked Chuck. "Pete O'Neill was already here when I came through the lobby. You can't have known he had been able to sneak in."

"You owe a big thanks to your neighbor, Eva Standish," Chuck said. "She called me to say she'd been looking out her windows when she saw a man follow you from the parking lot. The man, she told me, disappeared into the garage while you came through the front entry. Then she started hearing women's squeals, loud cat cries, and a man's voice over here, and thought I should check on it. After all our precautions to prevent anyone from getting into the building and harming Adrianna, I wasn't about to let something happen to you two. I called 911 and rushed up the stairs. Then, of course, the thug almost got away. Until—ta da—I caught up, pulled him down, and pinned his hands behind his back right at bottom of the steps leading to the first floor. When I stood him up and pushed him into the lobby, the police were there to take over."

Beth and Adrianna were about to pour out their thanks when Eva Standish cracked open her door to peek out and then stepped into the hall, "What's going on? This used to be a quiet, respectable building. My nerves can't take this. I hope it's all over."

They all suppressed nervous giggles.

"Everyone here is quite respectable," Beth said, "and it should be a lot quieter now that you've done such a good job of alerting Chuck to our trouble."

"Thank you so much, Eva," Adrianna said.

"Well, I saw—that is—I am glad you ladies are both safe," Eva said in her high crackly voice but with the usual whine dialed down this time, and when she stepped back into her condo with a small huff, a tiny smile played about her lips.

Chapter 45—Relating

"Meanwhile, news has been leaked to the press that the Hero of Drummond Street will be pictured on the cover of a national magazine, nude."

- Lilian Jackson Braun, *The Cat Who Had 14 Tales*

As if he'd made a touchdown, Chuck all but strutted across the hallway. Beth saw him start to race down the stairs before the stairwell door closed.

Beth and Adrianna fussed over each other, making sure there were no serious injuries, and then picked up their phones to call their relatives with the news of Pete O'Neill's arrest. Arnie, Paul, and Meg all said they were heading for their cars as soon as they heard the news, and they reached the condo building in record times. Chuck, catching them in the lobby, would have bent their ears with the entire story, but they all begged to go up to the apartment.

"Meg must have grabbed the phone from Poppa on the way to the car. She started plying me with questions," Adrianna told Beth while she strode over to answer the door.

Detective Carl Rinquire showed up only a few minutes after the family. At least the presence of all saved Adrianna from explaining the evening's turmoil twice. It was getting late, Beth was still shaking, and she could see Adrianna looking as if she'd like to pile into her cozy bed and sleep for a couple of days. The family stood around and listened to the interview, eyes wide, while Beth and Adrianna recounted the facts to Detective Rinquire. However, as the interview went on, Beth could see Meg barely concealing her impatience. She was sure Meg gritted her teeth while she waited to sit Adrianna down and make over her. It wasn't long until the detective put away his pen.

"Thank you," he said. "I've got what I need for now. You may be asked for further statements later."

"May I ask a question?" Adrianna asked.

"Sure."

"Well, Peter O'Neill admitted to us he took the money and killed Abby, but who's to say he won't say we're lying and recant his admission?"

"I wouldn't worry about that," Detective Rinquire said, "As soon as your security guard handed him over to the police, O'Neill started spilling his guts, not only about his own involvement but also about his co-conspirator on the Virgin Islands. He seemed to think the guy had already implicated him, and he wanted to make a deal."

"Uh, I guess I might have given him that impression," Beth said.

The detective looked at her with interest. "Good going."

Adrianna still had a frown on her face. "Since Pete admitted now for sure T.M. Blakely was his accomplice, will the police arrest Blakely and let Max come home?"

"The F.B.I. took Mr. Blakely in for questioning today. Pete O'Neill's confession to you and consequently to our police officers will help the case against Blakely, but a search of his financial records produced much of the evidence they needed. That guy has many friends among the law enforcement people on the Islands who didn't want to suspect him of wrong-doing, or were maybe covering up for him. I think he fooled a lot of people."

Adrianna looked sideways at Beth and Arnie. Arnie's grin of acknowledgement was lop-sided. Beth rolled her eyes and shook her head in disbelief at her own gullibility.

"What about Max?" Adrianna asked again.

"Max's part in the scheme is still being investigated," Rinquire admitted, "but after his so-called accident, I think he'll be cleared fairly quickly. Right now, he's still recuperating after his nasty fall. If my sources are correct, he's a tough guy to have survived with only a broken arm, bruises, and lacerations. However, I believe they want to keep an eye on him for a while because of the lump on his head."

Adrianna stepped back so abruptly that her step-mother, standing close behind, almost fell over backward. "Max didn't tell me about any lump on his head! Oh, this is entirely my fault. I should have objected, or—or refused when Blakely insisted Max stay there after I left."

Beth, and probably everyone else, started thinking how to assure Adrianna she wasn't responsible, but it was the big, blustery Detective Rinquire who said, in his deep voice, "You're not to blame for any of this, Miss Knells. Heck, you're a victim. Being framed for theft and murder can be almost as life threatening as being pushed off a cliff."

He left for the station house with the killer's gun in a plastic bag, his notes, and a few crime scene photos—of the red marks on Adrianna's neck and the tousled rug where Beth fell. Beth thought about it but didn't lower her pants to show him the bruise on her gluteus maximus. She noticed he wrote in his notebook while walking down the hall. It crossed her mind they might be seeing him again several times before all the T's were crossed in this case.

Upon the detective's departure, the atmosphere in the room changed like sunshine breaking through after a thunder storm. Smiles and hugs and quiet cheers erupted. Meg took over in her nurturing way. After careful checking of first Adrianna and then Beth for physical damage, she accepted orders for sodas, water, or wine and busied herself in the kitchen, sticking her head through the door every few seconds to hear what was being said or to pop in another question.

Psycho Cat appeared from behind the sofa and minced around purring from one friendly person's leg to another while Beth and Adrianna kept interrupting each other to tell the saga of his heroic deed. Finally, after the kitty had received his fair share of head and ear rubs, he wandered off to take a highly deserved cat nap.

Epilog

"Meow" means "woof" in cat."

— George Carlin

Two weeks later, Beth and Arnie hosted a celebration barbeque on their patio. Invitees included Meg, Paul, Herb Reynolds, who brought along his son Chad with his young family, Joey Zitelli, Chuck the doorman and his family, Adrianna, and Max Zeller with his friend Smitty, recently arrived from the Virgin Islands. Detective Rinquire, Richard Montorlee, Eva Standish, and Sylvester the Cat politely declined. The story of Psycho Cat's heroism had been picked up by a reporter for the *Kansas City Star* newspaper, and a local TV news program had featured a short segment and a video of the cat glowering at the camera from the back of Adrianna's sofa. The besieged feline hero deserved being excused for not attending the barbeque.

The youngsters played, the adults raised toasts to the heroes of the day, and Adrianna was given so many hugs of commiseration for the trouble she'd been through she finally held her hand out in front like a traffic cop stopping traffic.

"Thanks, everyone, for your kind words," she said. "I'm not the only one here who had some hard knocks." She took Max's hand. "I'd rather we concentrate on thanking the folks who helped me get through this ordeal and who helped catch the criminals. I raise my glass to all of you here and also to the people who couldn't be here tonight—and to my outstanding cat."

"Here, here." A happy buzz of stories and compliments, questions and exclamations, filled the patio for a few minutes until Chuck, towering above most of the group, held up his arm and cleared his throat for attention.

"Well, I appreciate all the praise for my part in the capture, but I'm also grateful—grateful for having been able to help two fine ladies and also grateful to have had this opportunity to prove something to myself. Because of it, I finally decided what I'll do with my life." He put his arm around his wife. "With the little lady's backing, this week I applied for the police academy. I'll be able to keep my job part time at the building until I'm through the training period."

During the revived chatter, Beth noticed Joey excuse himself from the group of men who had surrounded Chuck and were probing him about the police academy. He sidled over to Adrianna. Beth overheard part of their exchange.

"Adrianna, I want you to know I'm sorry," Joey said, "I never understood until now what all this did to you. Abby wouldn't talk to me about the theft, and after she was gone and the police mentioned you, I was too messed up to consider anyone but myself and what the murderer did to my life. I didn't think about you being arrested and in danger and forced to hide out. Forgive me. You were Abby's best friend before she was seduced and used by that creep. You should have been there at the funeral with me to mourn the Abby West we both once knew. I forgave her immediately when she came back to me. I hope you can forgive her, too."

Adrianna nodded and smiled. "I already have. She died because she wanted to tell me the truth. In the end, she turned out to be a friend to me and the decent person you wanted her to be."

Meg and Herb, who had been chatting at the hors d'œuvres table, brought a plate of samples around.

"Try some of Herb's inspired hummus," Meg said. "He makes his own. And he makes pesto, too. You won't believe... She paused as if she just then noticed the serious faces.

Beth hurried to her sister's side and dipped a celery stick into the hummus. "Mmm, good. Let's take some to the guys."

"No. It's okay," Joey said. "We were talking about the false accusations against Adrianna, and about Abby. I can do that now without falling apart." He frowned as if he were figuring out a chess move or a Sudoku puzzle. "What I can't understand, is how those crooks managed to get you down to St. John at exactly the time the company had its audit and found the embezzlement. It couldn't have been a coincidence that you asked for and were granted a long vacation at exactly the right time." He looked over at Herb Reynolds and then back at Adrianna as if trying to connect the dots.

"Max and I had been in contact since he went to the islands, and when he asked me to visit I told him I would be able to get some vacation time after my big project was finished," Adrianna said. "It happened the project was completely paid up, and all the paperwork, which usually hangs things up, was done in time for the audit."

"Max probably told T.M. Blakely he would need some time off when Adrianna's construction project was finished," Herb said. O'Neill could have pushed the billing and receiving of her project through so it would be done before the audit. That made it a perfect time for Adrianna to be gone, when the embezzlement was bound to be discovered."

"I'm sure you're right," Adrianna said. "Max said Blakely took him under his wing, listened to him talk about me, and urged him to invite me to the Virgin Islands. I didn't think about it at the time, but I guess that's why they got Max's contact information from my mother and located Max and Smitty. It was to offer them the jobs at Blakely Construction. Pete O'Neill, calling himself Tom Collins, visited my mom, and Max got his new job at about the same time the money was being transferred to the fake accounts. Smitty didn't have anything to do with it. Max said he recommended Smitty for the job when it was offered to him."

"There's no end to the duplicity!" Herb Reynolds said. "But I have one question. Did you actually believe I might have been guilty of these crimes?"

"T.M. Blakely is your brother-in-law," Adrianna said. "And we found out it could have been you who visited him with your wife and looked at his proposed building site in January. That would have given you the opportunity."

"And you scared us to death when you and Pete O'Neill chased us across the parking lot of the Funeral Home," Beth said.

"We know you have money issues," Meg said. "Isn't Renfro Construction being sued by Alex Frommer for back payments of his profit sharing proceeds? That would be motive."

"Well, it seems as if I'm not the only one guilty of having doubts about the wrong person," Herb Reynolds said. "In fact, Alex Frommer's claim that Renfro owes him money has been proven false by Renfro's lawyers, and the suit is being dropped."

With as sad a look as Beth could imagine, he said, "Adrianna, I'm sorry I believed for a second you could have robbed the company. Only a few weeks ago, long after her trip in January, I found out Nora was having an affair with Pete O'Neill. It must have been during that trip or soon after that Pete cooked up the money scheme with Nora's brother. Pete should have been my prime suspect—if it weren't for all the evidence on your computer." Herb's eyes looked sad. "I sincerely hope Nora is not guilty of collaborating with Pete O'Neill and her brother in the embezzlement.

"As for your mistaken idea that we chased you into the parking lot at the funeral home," he said, "I'm sorry you were frightened. The truth is I stopped Pete in the chapel to confront him about his brazen appearance there with our new bookkeeper right after his affair with Nora had ended. I pointed out to him I knew he had tried to have an affair with every young woman in our offices. I must have gestured toward you ladies when mentioning Adrianna, which, I guess, made you believe I meant you harm. It was bad timing. You left just as I insisted we finish our discussion outside of the building. I gave Pete his two weeks' notice when we got outside, and he went back inside to find the blond bookkeeper. Again, I'm sorry I played a part in your frightening experience."

Herb paused as the three women murmured their responses of belated relief. "The good news is I didn't have to wait the mandatory two weeks to get rid of that scum. The bad news is, now our accounting department is sparse." He looked at Adrianna. "Maybe you'll help me interview people for the accounting and payroll department? Together we can, I hope, pick someone who is skillful and has integrity. You're one of the few young women in the company who didn't fall for O'Neill's line."

"Thank you, Mr. Reynolds. I'll give interviewing a try. There can't be too many out there like Peter O'Neill."

"We'll take our time and find a good person," he said.

***

Months later, Beth and Meg were visiting Adrianna at the condo. While they walked down the hallway from the elevator, Meg looked Beth up and down.

"I haven't seen you stumble or fall down once since that murderer was captured," Meg said. "Did your mad rush to get the gun out of the hall scare you into paying attention to your steps?"

"Oh, you remember that story, huh?" Beth said. She thought about it. "I don't know; maybe it did." She was still considering the possibility she might be a cured klutz when she tripped over the threshold the minute Adrianna opened the door for them.

Adrianna had called them together this day, and she acted a little mysterious about it. Beth had Psycho Cat on her lap, giving him a much appreciated head and ear rub when Adrianna brought cookies into the living room and sat down.

"Meg," Adrianna said, giving her cat a regretful look, "would you consider keeping Sylvester if I move away for some time?"

"Well, I—that is—I don't think I can. I mean, if it was only a couple of days, but your dad is allergic to cats, you know, and…

248

Where—why—would you move away? And why wouldn't you take Psycho, I mean, Sylvester with you?"

"Herb Reynolds is pretty sure Renfro will be taking control of the condo project started on St. John. It's part of a reparations deal being worked out by the company and its insurance lawyers. He could sell it, but instead he gave me the option of moving there to manage the project. He wants Max to oversee the construction. It's a big chance for us to both prove our capabilities, and we wouldn't be there forever. It'd be really hard to take Sylvester along." Adrianna reached over to pet the cat. "He might have to stay in quarantine, and we'll have an apartment which might not allow pets."

Beth could see Meg struggling with doubt. "I'll keep Psycho Cat for you," she said. "We're not allergic, and I loved having him at my house for the short time you were missing, uh, I mean gone, er, on vacation."

***

At home Beth considered where she might buy a dog door so Psycho Cat could come and go from the litter box in the basement. So much had happened. One life had been lost and several damaged forever by bad people motivated by greed and poor self-image, but look at the accomplishments of the good people who surrounded her. With their help, she'd jump at a chance to help capture a villain again. She dropped the measuring tape she used to measure for the cat door and bumped her head on the edge of the kitchen counter when she leaned over to retrieve it.

Ouch!

On the other hand, maybe she had enough to do to keep from killing herself. Psycho Cat pawed toward her and rubbed around her legs. Beth rubbed her sore head and grinned at him.

###

Preview the second book in the "Psycho Cat and the Landlady Mysteries" series:

*FUR*TIVE INVESTIGATION

Chapter 1

Arizona RV Resort

The phone rang and vibrated on the picnic table next to Beth's elbow. She twitched, and her paintbrush slipped. "Damn!"

Beth slapped her free hand over her mouth and peered around like a kid fearful of chastisement for an inappropriate outburst. Neighbors were close in the RV Resort, many of the winter guests were of retirement ages, and numbers of them were outside on this sunny Saturday afternoon in Arizona. To Beth's relief, no one was gawking; maybe she didn't offend anyone with her expletive. Blundering. Stumbling. Normal for Beth. She shouldn't have gotten so upset over an easy-to-fix mistake on her clay pot, but the possibility that she might have spoiled her new, inspired creation exasperated her. She was trying so hard to be precise.

The caller ID read "Clay Stockwell." It was her son. "Hey, Clay," Beth said.

"Mom, are you sitting down?"

"I am," she said, wondering what was wrong.

Since he was in fifth grade, her son and she had used "Hey, Clay" and "'Lo, Mo" as their phone greetings. Clayton Stockwell was always called Clay, and he never forgot their special hello, not when he was with friends, not even during the four years he spent in the Marine Corps—although Beth had noticed the "'Lo, Mo" being spoken more quietly during those years—and not since he had been married—until now.

"What's up?" Beth asked. She set the glaze aside ignoring the slip-up on her handiwork.

"Psycho Cat found a skeleton in the attic!" Clay said.

Beth was momentarily too stunned to respond. Finally, she found her voice. "You mean, in the attic of the duplex?"

It was a silly question. Clay and his pretty wife, Janae, were living in one of the duplexes Beth's husband Arnie and she owned together. Beth managed the few properties under her name, Elizabeth Stockwell, but while they were in Arizona their son was managing and maintaining all their rental properties in lieu of rent. Clay and Janae were also pet-sitting the huge orange tiger-striped cat, Sylvester, nicknamed Psycho Cat, while they were wintering in Arizona. Beth knew the answer to the inane question she had asked about where the skeleton was found, but understanding that Clay found the body in the duplex attic didn't help her figure out the implications of this news. She followed up with, "Psycho Cat found a skeleton in the attic of the duplex?" Uh, another obvious remark—it was all she could think to say.

Beth's clear-thinking son must have realized his outburst of information had been a bit unsettling for her. He immediately reestablished his normal calm and came to her rescue in regards to his grisly late-breaking news.

"Since we've had him here with us, Psycho Cat has been jumping up onto those wide built-in storage shelves in the back of the master bedroom closet every time we opened the closet door. We thought he was merely being curious and exploring the place. Then Janae noticed the cat, sitting on the top shelf, pawing at the door in the ceiling which leads to the attic. I saw it one day, too. The cat walked around on the top shelf, reared up on his haunches, sniffed at the attic door, and pawed at different places, as if trying to push the attic cover open. Finally, just this morning, I decided to look myself and find out what was in there. I was expecting mice or some other rodents. Psycho Cat jumped into the attic when I opened the door and wouldn't come out; so I had to crawl up there to get him."

The word picture appeared to her like one of those satellite map images which pops up on a GPS and grows more and more detailed as one zooms in. How often she had cleaned and painted that closet after tenants moved out. Beth could visualize the two wide stair-step wooden shelves, one about three feet high, and the one behind it about five feet. They were built there to make space for the slant in the ceiling of the stairway below. Above the higher shelf was an opening to the attic, with a wooden door which she had never opened. She was never even curious to see what might be up there—just cobwebs and dust, she always thought. However, the duplex was built in 1952, long before she and her husband Arnie owned it. It wasn't surprising that someone stored something up there at one time. Then it hit her; this was one of Clay's little jokes. It was a Halloween skeleton they found. Beth snorted an involuntary chuckling splutter at the thought.

"What?" Clay said.

"Oh, I can just see that crazy curious cat escaping into the attic and then you pulling the door open and fitting your big shoulders into a cramped space."

She relaxed enough to hold her phone to her ear with her shoulder, pick up the paint brush, and eye the goof-up on the clay pot. When she turned her head slightly to better see the far side, the phone fell with a bounce and slid across the table. Beth clambered to grab it and shove it against her ear.

"Oops, sorry Clay. That was me dropping the phone on the table, not your skeleton rattling around in the attic."

With uncharacteristic impatience at his mom's attempt at humor, Clay hurried to tell her what happened after he climbed the short ladder connected to the attic door and crammed his six foot two, football player's body into the opening using a flashlight to see into the gloom and a whisk broom to brush aside the cobwebs. The only thing up there besides the cat in the corner, he told her, was an intricately carved wooden trunk, the kind people used to call a sea chest. It was hard to make it out in the dark, but the beam of the flashlight caught the metal latch. When he looked closely he saw there was a faint pathway across the wooden attic floor where the trunk had possibly been pushed away from the entrance into a corner under the roof joists. The trunk piqued his curiosity, but to get back there, Clay had to stoop over, and he had to kneel on the dusty flooring in order to pry open the chest.

"Mom, there are skeletal human remains in that trunk. The thing is bent at the knees, and the dried-out skin on it looks like leather, like it's partially mummified. Some rotted-looking pieces of clothing are still on the body, too, and some kind of white powder. It took me a few minutes to figure out what it was, because it had some plastic sheeting around it. I pulled the sheeting off the top and practically gagged. It was pretty hideous. As soon as I realized it was a body, I shut that lid, grabbed the cat, and got out of there as fast as I could. I regretted having touched the trunk and left my fingerprints after I found out what's there."

What? "Oh, Clay that's horrible."

All kinds of questions were racing through Beth's mind. Who, when, how, why? "Did you call the police?" she asked. "Is the trunk still up there? Is the body still in the trunk? How's Janae dealing with this? How are you doing...?" Beth would have asked more, but she ran out of breath.

"Janae was out doing some Saturday errands when I went up there. The police were here when she got home, and she's a little rattled. She wants the thing out of there and away from the house, but the police tell us that detectives have to come out and gather evidence before they can move anything. This matter isn't the most pressing case on their agenda, apparently, since any crime or missing person report about it may be years old. Janae is spooked, and we may be staying in a hotel room tonight, even though, I keep telling her, we've been sleeping here with the skeleton above us for more than four months now."

"Oh, I'm so sorry this happened," Beth said.

She was thinking trouble seemed to follow that Psycho Cat around, but she didn't say so. Beth and Arnie had adopted the cat from their niece after that very unpredictable feline jumped a murderer to save her life. The young lady was devastated to have to leave her heroic kitty behind when she married and moved away, but she was happy her aunt and uncle would care for him. Now it seemed as if Psycho Cat had discovered another nasty situation.

"Could you tell if the-the dead person is a male or a female?" Beth asked. "Or a child?" She shuddered.

"Not really," Clay said. "I've had a little experience with cadavers at the university, but this one has some powdery stuff on it and-and some partially decayed clothing. I believe there is hair, but I didn't examine it enough to be able to tell you the length or style. It's too large to be a young child, but it could be male or female. I didn't stand there and look at it for very long."

Clay and Beth talked for a while about when the detectives might show up and how long it could be before they'd be able to take the trunk out of the attic, and they speculated about how authorities would determine the age of the skeleton and how it got there. Beth assured Clay that Psycho Cat would do fine alone in the duplex if he and Janae left and spent the night elsewhere.

"Oh, Mom, the police are here," Clay said. "I need to go."

"Call me," Beth said before he could hang up, "The minute you know anything more." Then she sat for almost a minute, looking at her phone as if it could give an explanation for all this.

ABOUT THE AUTHOR

Joyce Ann Brown (http://joyceannbrown.com/) owns rental properties in Kansas City with her husband, but none of their tenants have so far been involved in theft, kidnapping, or murder. Her two cats, Moose and Chloe, are cuddly, not psycho. Besides being a landlady, Joyce has worked as a story teller, a library media specialist, a Realtor, and a freelance writer. Her writing has appeared in local and national publications and in the book *Cozy Food*. Her short stories have won numerous awards.

Catch a glimpse of Joyce Ann's writing about all cozy subjects on her blog at: http://retirementchoicescozymystery.wordpress.com/. Read about trails she walks in Kansas City at:

http://hikingkctrails.wordpress.com/.

Twice award-winning *Catastrophic Connections* is the first of her Psycho Cat and the Landlady Mysteries. *Furtive Investigation* will be the second book in the series.

A Word From the Author

Thank you for adding *CATastrophic Connections* to your library. Readers depend on readers to recommend good books, and authors depend on readers to generate positive word-of-mouth for their books. If you liked this cozy mystery, I hope you'll leave a review on Amazon, Goodreads, or your favorite retailer even if it's only a few words. It will make a big difference. I and other readers will be very thankful.

36342681R00151

Made in the USA
Lexington, KY
15 October 2014